"An engaging, multilayered story that finely balances action with introspection and the real with the mystical."
    - Kirkus Reviews

"A tangled tale of second chances, risky deals, and the curious kindness of strangers, *The Phoenix* ... is a fiendishly clever YA novel that crackles with Gothic energy."
    - Self-Publishing Reviews

"Magic, belief, and love intersect in the resolution."
    -Nancy Farrior, Blogger

"… a fun read for YA fans that want something that's atmospheric and not full-fledged complicated fantasy.
    -Tyler Mai, Goodreads

"There is a lot of honesty in this book when it comes to feelings of grief, loneliness and the struggles that the three children face."
    - April Goff, The Story Graph

"The Phoenix … is above all else a commentary on how easily children can fall between the cracks and be forgotten…"
    - Nancy Yager, Goodreads

"… a compelling debut that intertwines gritty realism with supernatural elements, delivering a poignant tale of resilience, trust, and transformation."
- Lauren Smith, NetGalley

"… a gripping tale of redemption, resilience, and rebirth … that inspires and captivates from start to finish."
- Tianna B., Instagram

The Phoenix

By Eric Van Allen

ISBN 979-8-218-59193-9
eBook ISBN 979-8-218-59177-9

This is a work of fiction. Names, characters, places and incidents are either the product of the author's imagination or are used fictitiously, and any resemblance to actual persons, living or dead, businesses, companies, events or locales is purely coincidental.

Printed and bound by Kindle Direct.

Lurking Lucy Press
Seattle, Washington

"For small creatures such as we, the vastness is bearable only through love."

-Carl Sagan

For my kids.

PART I

Three Things

I knew three things.

First, I had to be both the luckiest and unluckiest girl in my neighborhood or probably any neighborhood. I mean, I'd seen and heard things no way a kid should ever see and hear, had to do things a kid shouldn't ever have to do. And, no I do not mean my effing chores. I'd escaped from cops, escaped from pervs, run in front of cars, run in front of trucks, lived in some nasty filthy places and managed not to get sick and die. All that and I'd never once met Death face-to-face. So, yeah. My life was kind of cursed, but I'd also had a run of luck to sort of counteract it. I mean, I *was*, in fact, still breathing.

The next thing I knew is that everyone dies. Eventually. And, when they do, that's it. That's all folks. There's no coming back for another go at it. You only got the one try. If you screwed that up, tough luck. You didn't get a second try. No do-overs. It was pretty much game over with no one ups, no extra lives. My dad died, and he's still dead. I'll never see him again. My mom? Well, she's probably dead and the same was true for her. Adios, nice knowing you. Except, was it really? Nice, I mean.

On a related note, as sort of a corollary to the truth about dying, was that, when I died, it was entirely likely no one was gonna care enough to show up at my funeral. Maybe my little sister, but someone would have to, like, drive her to wherever they had the funeral. More likely, whoever was taking care of her wouldn't tell her about me dying or the funeral and just pretend the whole thing never happened. Until she was a teenager and decided to ask someone. If I even had a funeral, the only ones in attendance would be the guys with the backhoe digging the grave and the person or persons driving the vehicle carrying my casket. When it was all over, no one would remember me. My whole existence would be like so much cigarette smoke, gone in a second, no meaning to it, no memory of it that anyone kept close to their heart. No one to remember the name Callie Valentine.

The third thing I knew was that assholes exist and there's nothing you can do about it. Over the years, I had amended this fact to state that *everyone* is an asshole. That was my motto. Don't get me wrong, I was no angelic kid. I mean, I was probably at or near the top of the worst-asshole list. But hey, I had no problem with it. It served me well, for the most part.

Of those three great bits of wisdom, two were only half-true and one just wasn't true at all. How did I come to realize that a lot of my outlook on life was wicked twisted or just stupid wrong? The story, screwed up as it is, would probably explain a few things. But, to get through it you'd need a little patience and more than a little tolerance for stupidity. Then again, you might not care, you might just give up on it completely.

A lot of people already had.

Hunger Blindness

"I'm hungry."

Was I hungry? I wasn't sure.

"Callie." The voice belonged to my little sister, Jess. "Wake up."

Reddish-pink light glowed through my eyelids, triggering alarms telling me we should have been awake a long time ago. I jerked the sheet back and peeked through swollen eyes at the blurry shape I thought was my little sister.

"Wha-dime-is-it?" I groaned, hocking back snot and swallowing.

"Ten twenty-two," Jess said, looking at the digital clock on the cable box.

Shit, we were late for school. Throwing off the rest of the covers, I struggled to my feet, my heart pounding. We were so screwed. I staggered through a pile of dirty clothes, kicked an empty cereal box across the room, stepped on an empty plastic bottle of grape soda, fell backward and collapsed onto the mattress.

I grabbed up the bottle and had my arm cocked to throw it across the room when my brain engaged enough to realize school had been out for summer for over a week. Obviously, I had brain rot, probably the result of lack of sleep or some bacteria or bug in the carpet of our apartment that had crept into my nose and was eating its way through my head.

Half on, half off the lumpy bedding, my

body melted fully into the gray, sweat-stained mattress. After a minute or two, I sat up, my arms draped over my knees, and sniffed a few times, sucking up snot until I could smell the nasty apartment. Cigarettes and the faint hint of beer and urine, along with the scent of some fruity thing Mom sprayed on days ago all combined into one gassy mixture that reminded all of us exactly what kind of life we were living.

The darkened face of an anime character with spikey hair and a metal arm glared at me from a poster on the wall over our little TV. I couldn't see it clearly anymore because of my shitty eyesight, but from memory the character had a fierce, yet somehow friendly look. Water rushed through pipes in the walls around and below me. Doors closed, people mumbled in adjacent apartments, a baby cried.

"I'm still hungry," Jess repeated. "In case I wasn't clear a minute ago."

Jess sat cross-legged on the bed, her big blue eyes staring at me. I could easily sleep another two or three hours, but Jess was hungry. School being out used to be something we looked forward to. Unfortunately, no school meant no food. Every drop of milk was gone, we'd finished off the bread and eaten every Cheerio in the apartment including a few we found under the couch cushions.

Pushing myself up, I threaded my way

around the piles of clothes, dishes covered with the residue of ancient food, and long empty plastic soft drink bottles toward the bathroom. After doing my business, I tugged and twisted my way into a pair of old blue jeans and slipped on my second-hand, black Horseshoe Casino T-shirt and cross trainers with the soles torn loose at the front of both.

My younger brother, Thomas, lay stretched across the living room couch, dead to the world. Jess and I pulled him down onto the mattress where he lay as if he'd just fallen out of an airplane. I kicked him a couple of times accidentally-on-purpose.

Jess grinned evilly, then pounced on her brother.

"Get off me," he whined. "You're hurting my stomach."

"Uh," I started. "That might make it kinda hard for him to get up."

Jess slid off him and sat on the floor.

"Aww, he's a boy," she said. "He just needs a little extra attention."

Thomas rolled over on his stomach, his mouth less than an inch from the green scalloped carpet thick with old grease, the residue of ancient insecticide and whatever shit people had tracked in from outside.

"It's summer. There's no school," he moaned. "Plus, it's Saturday. Why do we have to get up?"

Okay, so he remembered school was out, but I felt kind of mad at him for knowing the day of the week.

"Get dressed," I said. "We're going to the store."

"Why don't you and Jess go?" he groaned.

"I'm not leaving anyone alone in this apartment."

Whenever we left the apartment, I had the feeling there was something or someone around each corner waiting for us. It didn't help that I couldn't see for shit, even with the pair of taped-up Frankenstein glasses I'd gotten when I was like in the sixth or seventh grade. I say Frankenstein because they were pieced together from parts of several pairs I'd had over the years. Only the lenses were the same, and they didn't help the way they used to or really at all.

Our every step down the concrete stairs produced a low rumble that announced our presence to anyone paying attention. It was late morning. Maybe all the pervs in the complex were still asleep, maybe they weren't.

An apartment door clicked shut behind us as we passed the second-floor landing. I'd only ever met the guy in that unit once and we didn't speak. We didn't have to. He let his eyes do the talking, his gaze finding every gap in my clothes, every hint of my skin. I assumed the

oval patch on his work clothes with the name
Pete was a clue to his identity. I didn't know
what he did for a living other than it involved
greasy overalls.

"Hurry up," I whispered, adjusting my
little kid glasses.

Jess came up behind me, grabbing me
around the waist. She'd gotten hyper clingy
lately. Thomas, as usual, seemed oblivious.
Ignoring shit was one of his superpowers. Jess
was an even better detector of evil creepy shit-
heads than I was. I just assumed everyone was
that sort of person. Jess was more discerning.
And she was afraid of Pete.

Jess was the product of a one-nighter
Mom had with some guy who picked her up in
a bar. At least, that's how Mom described it.
Lately, I'd wondered if that was how it actually
went down. Jess had never met her father. She
just knew she had a different dad from the rest
of us. The guy must have been a Leprechaun,
though, because my sister ended up with red
hair, light skin with freckles and blue eyes the
size of an anime character.

Morning was the best time to go
wandering around our neighborhood for the
simple fact most of the assholes were still
asleep. Also, cops didn't usually go cruising
around looking to hassle us in the mornings.
Even dogs weren't much awake yet.

I was a tall, skinny rail of a girl, even at

sixteen years old. Honestly, being boney-assed wasn't so bad. Hell, I wore a baseball cap half the time hoping people would think I was a guy. Apparently, I'd acquired enough femininity in my old age that guys in the neighborhood saw through my disguise fairly easily. Either that or gender didn't matter to them.

There probably wasn't a guy in the neighborhood who wouldn't drag me down some alley, behind some trash dumpster or into some grimy restroom if they could. A couple of them had tried, but I was smarter than most of those dumbasses, I was also faster and none of them could catch me. My main super-powers, running and hiding, came in handy sometimes.

In our crappy little neighborhood, there was always a bunch of idiots hanging out on the front porch of some house or gathered around a convenience store, all of them leering at me. Lately, there'd been this guy driving around in some old light blue hearse, window rolled down, probably staring at us, cigarette smoke wafting from the window. Corpse caddies always gave me the creeps. There was no telling what he kept in the back of that hearse. The guy probably had some sexual death fetish thing.

Thomas, who was twelve years old and seemingly never thought about girls, had decided I was crazy. "Not everyone is looking at you," he said.

"I'm tall and a girl. It's like I've got

flashing lights and sirens all over me."

"I think you're imagining things."

"Whatever, T."

Someone was always watching. Certain people really hated seeing kids without an adult. Busybody do-gooders who might call someone like the cops or social services. Shittier people might do the same just to mess with us.

Low clouds sailed overhead north toward Oklahoma, and the scent of wet dust and mowed grass was thick in the warm air. When the wind blew from the south, which it did most of the time, it brought the distinctive odor of the landfill a couple of miles from the apartment.

"It smells like a million urinal cakes," Thomas said.

"I wouldn't know," I replied.

"What's a urinal cake?" Jess asked.

"Not something to eat," I said.

We walked past a donut shop that smelled of cooking oil and baked goods. Smoke from a barbeque joint wafted across several blocks. Then there was a hole-in-the-wall Mexican restaurant that always smelled like grilled onions and peppers. Our neighborhood wreaked of something we didn't have. Food.

Thomas walked head down and would have walked into a car or a light pole if I wasn't there to shove him out of the way. You couldn't tell it much by looking, but my brother and I had the same dad. A Hispanic Marine our mom met and married out in California. Being part Hispanic, we both had brown hair and eyes, though Thomas's skin was a shade or two darker than mine and his hair wavier. Beyond having dark hair, we had nothing in common.

"I've heard of these community gardens," he said. "For that matter, some of the people in the neighborhoods around here have their own gardens."

"Yeah?" I said, my eyes squinting at both sides of the street. I don't know why I bothered to look. Even with my glasses, it was all a blurry mess.

He didn't respond, and I looked to see him smiling. Little weirdo — then it hit me what he was getting at.

"Are you suggesting we help ourselves?"

He explained. "In the Bible they refer to it as gleaning, collecting the leftovers in the fields after a harvest. It was apparently both allowed and expected. Perhaps we could manage a little surreptitious gleaning."

"Ser, sure, what?"

"Surreptitious. It just means without anybody seeing us."

"So, you're saying it's not stealing if no one sees us."

"That's not exactly what I ... If we lived back ancient times —."

"I don't care. Just look for a garden."

"Maybe if we prayed to God, we'd find some food," Jess said. "It couldn't hurt, right?"

"You can be our spokesperson," I said, grinning down at her. My sister's belief in the unlikely was partly what kept me from, I don't know, quitting, giving up. At least one of us believed in something. The last thing I wanted was to see her hope crushed.

But, wishing and hoping weren't going to put food in our stomachs. There was a Deluxe GrabNGo a couple of blocks from our apartment. We marched toward it, my brain empty as my stomach.

"There are methods of dumpster diving that can yield some fairly decent meals," Thomas said. "You look for items that are still wrapped in—"

"I got a better idea," I mumbled.

Seeing little beyond the moment was typical for me, but that got worse when I was starving. It was like some kind of hunger blindness.

"Oh, dear," Thomas said. "Now we need those prayers, Jess."

"On it."

"All you gotta do," I started, "is go in the GrabNGo there and ask for directions or something. I'll come in a few seconds later and, while you distract the clerk, I'll get us all a fried pie and maybe some milk. Jess, you go in with Thomas, look at the clerk and smile."

She tilted her head, showing me her big blue eyes and gentle smile. "Are you scared?"

"What? No." Damn, there was no getting anything past my little sister. "I just —."

"So, you intend to steal our breakfast then?" Thomas asked. His expression was so condescending, like he was so damn superior.

"If you wanna put it that way. Yeah, that's the general idea."

Drawn by movement to my left, I jerked around that way in time to see a huge blackbird, streaking toward my head. Beak wide open, toes and claws extended, it looked ready to tear my eyes out. I ducked, its feet dragging over my hair. I hadn't done anything to mess with that bird but, like so many people, it found my presence offensive for some reason.

Across the street parked at the gas pump at the GrabNGo was the light blue hearse I'd seen lurking around the neighborhood. Leaning against it, cigarette in his hand, was the guy I'd nicknamed the Grim Reaper for obvious reasons. Tall, with less hair on his head than on his face. The color of his tux matched the shade of the hearse. It looked like a shadow in the passenger seat. Did the Reaper have a partner in all that creepy death shit?

Thomas swallowed hard, then shook his head. "I want no part of that."

I glared at him. "Thomas, you were the one who had the idea about gleaning, you know, sure, ser, share — ."

"Surreptitious," he corrected.

"Whatever. I'm just going to do a little sir-ep-ti-shus gleaning at the GrabNGo."

"Gleaning is one thing. Not stealing is one of the Ten Commandments, as in thou shalt not steal. I think it's number eight."

He was such a little smart ass. "I had no idea you were such a Bible scholar," I said, cocking my head to one side. "Look, Thomas, you don't help clean up. You don't help cook. As far as I see, you don't do much other than watch TV, sleep, eat, and ..." I looked down at Jess. "Poop." She grinned. "The least you could do is cooperate in getting us something to eat."

"We need to find another way of getting food," he said. "Doing it this way is wrong."

So much for Plan A. "Okay, I'm going in there and I'm gonna come out with food one way or the other. If I get caught, you guys are on your own because I'll go to jail, and you'll end up in foster care. Is that what you want?

His breathing was shallow, and he swallowed hard. "We can avoid that if you just don't break the law."

"Guys," Jess said. "You're scaring me."

The blackbirds squawked nonstop in the trees above us. Could they tell what was about to happen? Because I sure as hell couldn't. A siren wailed in the distance. Thomas grimaced, rubbing his stomach. "Please don't."

Ignoring him, I dashed into the six-lane road. A horn blared, Jess screamed, and Thomas yelled something.

I looked up in time to see a utility van barreling straight toward me.

Grand Theft Fried Pie

Everything was quiet a moment as if the universe was waiting to see what would happen.

What did happen was I darted onto the concrete island in the middle of the street. The van sped past the horn blaring, the driver screaming something unintelligible that ended with "bitch." I wasn't sure how close I'd come to being a grease spot in the road, but, as I may have mentioned, I was lucky.

Across the street, Jess was still screaming. Thomas was bent over, hands on his knees. Had he thrown up? Not much probably as his stomach was as empty as mine. For a second, I thought I saw someone or something dark standing next to my brother and sister. Whoever it was over there looked to have on a dark green uniform kind of like my dad's fancy dress Marine outfit. I blinked a couple times and decided what I'd seen was just a shadow cast by a street sign.

Blackbirds, like some dozens of them, now gathered on the power lines above, cawing loud and long. What was I even doing out there standing on display in the middle of Old Home Road. Jess screaming, horns honking, damn blackbirds laughing at me. So much for staying hidden.

Finally, the traffic cleared, and I sprinted

across to the tiny asphalt parking lot of the GrabNGo. I stood there on the sidewalk, my body quivering from anger, terror, hunger or some combination of all three. I glanced around at the light blue hearse still sitting at the gas pump.

Was it some sign? An omen? Was I destined to go for a ride in that hearse? Did that guy somehow know I was about to die and was following me around? Was he trying to beat the competition? And what was that dark thing sitting in the passenger seat? Had he run out of room in the back and just stuffed a corpse in the front?

Damn, I wished I could see better.

Focus, Callie. Stay on task. Get food.

The Reaper sucked on his cigarette, then blew out white smoke the wind carried off across the road and into the trees like a ghost on the run. I stood there still as a signpost, the Reaper's eyes locking on mine. After a good two seconds, I managed to blink my way free of his penetrating stare. *Damn perv.*

The sun disappeared behind thickening clouds, darkening everything like it was early evening. I ducked my head and strode to the door of the GrabNGo, fighting queasiness. I wished I'd worn a jacket or hat or anything to disguise myself. I pulled open the door; a cowbell attached at the top clanged freezing me halfway inside the store like a photo taken from security camera footage. The clerk, an older guy, eyed me, frowning.

"In or out," he said. "You're letting the cool air escape."

The word "escape" echoed in my head. Like a deer caught in headlights, my eyes fixed on those of the clerk for what seemed like several seconds. I'd been in there before and if the clerk paid any attention at all he would have recognized me. One advantage was he didn't know my name or where we lived. At least, I hoped he didn't.

It took all my willpower to force my eyes down to the floor tiles and head toward the restrooms. My plan, if you could call it that, was simple. Thomas and Jess were supposed to come in and distract the clerk while I stuffed my pockets. If the clerk ignored me, I could slip out with whatever I could hide in my clothes.

I shoved all doubts to the back of my mind because there was one thing I knew for sure. If I got clear of the store with the food, it was a done deal. Unless the guy behind the counter was an ex-Olympic sprinter, there was no way he was ever gonna catch me.

The store had three aisles and two rows of things for sale plus all the stuff along the walls. I moved to the aisle where the snacks were located. I checked the ceiling. Two mirrors, one in each corner at the back of the store. All the store clerk had to do was look up and he'd see I was up to no good.

I heard Thomas chatting with the clerk, asking for directions or something. Apparently, my brother had a change of heart, and we were partners in crime at last. Was that really what I wanted? Shaking off a twinge of guilt at this, I focused on my illegal gleaning. They say never go shopping when you're hungry. God was that ever true. I stood in the aisle stuffing fried pies down my pants, up my shirt, anywhere I could stash them.

A box cutter lie on top of some cases of beer. I looked around, then grabbed the weapon and shoved it in my back pocket. No amount of magic or religion was going to help us. The box cutter was a practical and useful tool. It could open things, boxes, arteries, whatever you needed it for.

Thomas finished his fake conversation sooner than I'd hoped, and he and Jess were headed for the door. My shirt and pants crackled as I ambled toward the cash register. I was just a few feet from the clerk when his eyes darted in my direction.

"You gonna pay for those?"

As if on cue, one of the pies escaped my shirt and smacked the floor.

I stared down at the pie while shuffling backward in the general direction of the door. Heat rose up my neck, my head felt like it was about to explode.

The clerk had some superpower of quickness and was out from behind the counter and striding toward me before I could turn around. Despite a mindless urge to run, I couldn't make my legs move.

"Hey, I'm talking to you!" the clerk shouted.

It felt like a dream, like I was trying to move underwater. I twisted around, staggered, and somehow got to where I was facing the way out. After what seemed like minutes, I reached the door and flung it open, the cowbell clanking against the glass.

As soon as I was outside, everything returned to normal speed. Freed from my paralysis, I sprinted full out across the parking lot, my hands working to hold the stolen pies inside my shirt. My brain numb, all I focused on was running.

The bell from the convenience store door rattled behind me. "Hey!" the clerk yelled. "Stop! I'm telling you, stop!"

I looked over my shoulder to see my brother and sister inexplicably standing by the ice machine near the end of the GrabNGo. Thomas was bent over like he'd been throwing up again. He wiped his mouth, then looked up frowning at me, as if he had no clue why I was running like that. Jess just waved.

"Run, you idiots," I shouted.

I looked behind me and saw, not the

clerk, but the Grim Reaper, cigarette dangling from his mouth. For some reason, my eyesight was always better looking behind me. The guy walked past the gas pumps a little, then coughed a few times. He probably couldn't move from one side of the parking lot to the other without passing out, let alone chase me down over the span of a few blocks.

I was a good block down the street before it occurred to me to check on Thomas and Jess. They hadn't even crossed the street yet. Meanwhile, the clerk and the Reaper stood around the gas pumps just talking. The clerk probably wouldn't leave his store unattended, and the Reaper was too old, too sick, and too slow to run after me. Thomas and Jess, on the other hand, were probably closer to the store than to me.

In truth, I was the idiot. If I hadn't told Thomas and Jess to run, no one would have known we were related or together in any way. We didn't even look alike. But since I yelled at them to run, anyone paying attention knew we were in it together. Yeah, I know. Stupid.

There was no choice at that point but to go back for them. It looked like Thomas had Jess by the hand, but I wasn't sure who was leading who.

The blackbirds, maybe hundreds of them at that point, flew from the electric lines on one side of the road into a group of trees on the other. Clearly, they were tracking me for their own entertainment. Jabbering and cawing, they were like the neighborhood hecklers. Did they never fuck up? Fly into windows?

I squinted back at the GrabNGo. The clerk was nowhere to be seen and the Reaper was sliding into his hearse.

Thick clouds covered the sun. The wind picked up, blowing dust and debris into my face again. The bird mob rose as one dark mass from the treetops, their black bodies swirling around in the gray sky a couple times before fleeing the gusty wind. Cowards. Then again, it must be nice to just fly away like that.

"Callie," Jess called.

I ran across the street, picked up Jess, and threw her over my shoulder, another pie dropping to the concrete in the process.

"I'm not a sack of potatoes," she said.

Thomas was still half a block away, struggling like he was wearing a backpack full of school textbooks. Further back, the old hearse's orange right-turn signal flashed.

I pulled Jess into the street, a semi-truck rumbling toward us. Safely on the other side of the road, I glanced back to see if Thomas had made it. The truck had passed, but Thomas still looked both ways like eighteen times before going across. His vision was perfect, but it was like he didn't believe his own eyes or something and had to keep checking to see if some vehicle had materialized out of thin air.

We made it back to the apartment in stages, me and Jess first, Thomas dragging up maybe a minute later. The wind died down as we stomped up the sandy stairs, not even trying to be quiet. Waking Pete and the other pervs was lower on the priority list at that point.

A few seconds later we were inside our dirty gray apartment, snapping the dead bolts in place. Pivoting, I pulled out all the remaining pies from my shirt and jean pockets, tossed them on the kitchen countertop, and stood there gesturing proudly at the food treasure on the table.

"See, T," I said. "It all worked out. I know what I'm doing."

A wind gust smacked the side of out apartment building. Thomas's cheeks were red as an apple from exertion or, as it turned out, anger. "That," he said, holding his finger in the air to make a point, "was one of the most insanely stupid things you've ever done. And I'll thank you to never involve me in that kind of idiocy again. Ever."

"You know," I said, hands on my hips. "I'm getting really tired of you bashing everything I do."

"I literally begged you to not do it but you did it anyway!"

"Guys," Jess said. "Chill."

Thomas swallowed hard, then continued:

"You only think of yourself!"

"You are so full of crap," I said, glaring at my brother.

"You didn't even think about us. You just ran off down the road."

Part of me knew he was right about that. I hadn't given either of them a second thought in escaping the GrabNGo. What was wrong with me? Was I just so blinded by hunger or fear that I ignored them. Or was it just the excitement? Still, what Thomas said enraged me. Did he think we were just gonna stroll back to the apartment as if I hadn't just stolen a bunch of stuff?

"You little shit," I growled. "I changed your diapers!"

His eyes were tearing up, his face contorting. "You're just a bully!"

"Guys!" Jess yelled.

"What!" Thomas and I erupted in unison.

Jess aimed her huge blue eyes at our apartment door. "Some-one's coming up the stairs." A moment later, someone knocked.

We stood dead still, a family portrait of terror, staring at the front door.

The Reaper at the Door

"Gee, I wonder who that is," Thomas said, composing himself.

I silently shushed him with a finger to my lips. It sounded like a single knuckle, no fist, no menacing pounding. Just tap, tap, tap, like whoever it was wanted to convince us they weren't dangerous. It had to be Mormons. Or, God help us, Jehovah's Witnesses. It couldn't be ... *him*.

There was no possible way the Grim Reaper saw us enter our apartment. The last I looked, the hearse hadn't even turned onto the street. If he'd somehow seen us run into the complex, he still wouldn't know for certain where we lived. I mean, even if he'd gone door-to-door all we had to do was not open up.

"We should just give them back," Thomas said. "Please, can we just — "

I shushed him again. Blood surged up my neck and pounded in my ears. I paced around the living room.

Shit, shit, shit.

I went to the door and gazed out the peep hole. There, staring back at me through the fisheye glass, was the dark, distorted face of the Grim Reaper. My heart sent little shockwaves through my skinny body with each pulse. If my heart stopped beating right then, would there be a moment of peace and quiet I could enjoy before I collapsed? No more wondering what was going to happen to us?

Leaning against the wall, I slid down to the floor. My stupid heart kept pumping for no apparent reason other than the fact I was alive. Was I really, though? "Damn," I whispered.

Jess knelt in front of me. "Child," she whispered, then grinned. Irritation at my little sister flared. Did she just not realize the shit mess we were in? Or, was she trying to calm me down? My little sister, the caretaker.

"Is it the police?" Thomas whisper-whined. My brother's expression shifted from worry to fear. "I didn't do anything," he mumbled, looking from side to side. "I didn't break the law. I'm not the bad guy." He looked up at me. "You're the bad guy."

In the corner of the entryway was a section of linoleum that wasn't yellowed or pulled back from the floor. It looked brand new, unstained by all the people who'd ever lived there. It was like a tiny miracle.

For that matter, so was the Reaper finding our apartment. How the hell did he do that? Unless, for some reason, he already knew. *Shit!* Had he been stalking us? For how long? Weeks, months maybe. *Damn.* Of course, he was stalking us. That's what he did. Followed people around until they croaked.

After a few moments of renewed terror paralysis, my anger kicked in and I mouthed a string of my favorite curse words. Pushing myself up from the floor, I pulled the box cutter from my back pocket. Slowly, I eased the button forward, extending the razor-sharp blade. Thomas backed away, eyes wide.

"I don't think you need that," Jess said.

Was that how you were supposed to hold a blade? Out like that, or concealed? I stood in the entryway, my hand shaking, the razor blade inside the cutter rattling against its metal frame. Even my guts vibrated, and I had trouble catching my breath.

"Hide those pies," I hissed.

Thomas just stood there looking at me, frozen. I clenched my teeth, went to the kitchen table to collect all the pies, and tossed them in one of the cabinets.

More tapping on the door. "He doesn't sound very scary," Jess said.

"What are we going to do?" Thomas whined.

I gave up trying to keep my brother and sister quiet. It was like they had no under-standing of stealth. No clue how to hide. Maybe my ability to be unseen and unheard was a superpower after all. I felt superior, but only for a moment.

Most bad guys didn't want to work very hard. They just wanted an "easy score." This guy had put in some effort to find us. There was only one way to make the guy go away.

My breathing ragged, I undid the deadbolts. I hid the box cutter behind my leg, gripping the handle hard enough my hand was numb. I opened the door just a crack, bracing my foot against the bottom of the door.

The Reaper was slightly taller than me, which put him a little over six feet tall. Hands on his hips, he was breathing hard either from the climb up the stairs or too many cigarettes. Probably both. His dark skin contrasted with his light blue tux. His head was bald, and he wore a trimmed mustache and goatee that were nearly white. His nose was slightly flat and a little wide, and he looked at me through brown eyes. He had an unusual scent, cigarette mixed with ... what was it? Some spice from a bakery, cinnamon maybe.

"I'm sorry," I said. "We'll give them back. Just please don't call the cops."

I hated that it sounded like I was begging. But how was I supposed to sound? Demanding? He looked at Thomas and Jess who were lined up behind me and grinned. Fucking creep.

"It would appear you children are in enough trouble already without me adding to your difficulties."

How exactly did he know that just by seeing inside our apartment? It didn't look all that bad, did it? The air was stale. Could he smell the urine odor the way I did?

He took a deep breath but ended up coughing again. From a distance, the Reaper had looked like any number of pervs I'd known. Up close though, he looked kind of distinguished. He'd probably been a good-looking guy when he was younger.

"Where is your mother, child?"

The way he pronounced the word "child" was almost musical. For some reason, images of sugar-covered pastries filled my mind. His voice, deep and a little nasal, seemed, I don't know, compelling. It was like I had no choice but to answer.

"At work," I lied.

He smiled faintly. Did he think it was funny? Or did he know something. Like our mom's actual whereabouts.

"I see," he said.

The breezeway outside our apartment darkened a moment, like maybe an extra dark cloud was passing overhead. A splotchy shadow moved from right to left near the ceiling above the reaper and came to rest a little further down the passage. It must have been some weirdness of the light because where it hovered wasn't where a shadow should or could be.

The door opened a little wider, and I felt Jess slide in next to me.

"If I may ask, how long has it been since you have eaten anything?"

Of all the guys I'd met in my life, none of them had a voice that resonated like the Grim Reaper. I guess that was kind of appropriate though, come to think of it. I mean, if the Reaper came for your soul, he or she would need an authoritative voice.

Jess started to talk. "We had some cereal yester—"

I let my hand brush over her mouth trying to silence her. That information was none of the guy's business, no matter how authoritative his voice might sound. My motto was to be polite up until you had no choice but to be an asshole. But we weren't quite to the asshole stage, at least not yet.

"We're fine," I said.

God if I could figure the guy's intentions, but I didn't like him sticking his nose into our lives. Even if I had just robbed a convenience store and the Reaper possibly held our future in his cold, boney grasp.

"Well ... good," he said. He cleared his throat. "So, uh, about those pies ..."

"Mister Reaper, sir, if I had the money to pay for them, I wouldn't have lifted them. Believe me." He frowned a moment, then tilted his head a little and grinned. What was he smiling about? God, he was so weird.

Thomas came up next to Jess, fried pies in hand, and pulled the door open a little further.

"Water that has run downstream shall not return," the Reaper said. "What is done is done. You may keep the pies. In fact, those particular pies have been paid for."

I stared at him. "What?"

"I paid for them." He raised an eyebrow and cocked his head a little. "And convinced the store manager not to call the police."

He'd marched all the way up here to tell us *that*? No one did that out of the goodness of their heart. Obviously there were strings attached to this alleged random act of kindness. I waited to hear what he was angling for, but the guy just stood there looking at me. I didn't like uncomfortable silences, so I said something that would hopefully hurry him on his way.

"Thank you."

He looked toward the parking lot, and I thought he was about to leave. Instead, he turned to face me again. Thunder rumbled in the distance.

"You know what?"

Here it came. I gripped the box cutter a little tighter. I could feel a sneer twisting my face. "What?"

"I could use a little help around my place."

And there it was. The guy was just another vulture wanting to take advantage of our situation. I pushed Jess behind me a little. Fucking people like him needed to leave us the hell alone!

"Maybe a few hours a week," he continued, oblivious to the blade I held ready to slice and dice him and that powder blue tux. "More than enough to buy a few fried pies, some milk, and perhaps some other things."

He said the word "milk" as if it were some kind of magical substance. Like, what's the word? ... ambrosia. Sweet, creamy, satisfying. I felt my belly relax, my chest loosening up enough to get a deep breath.

"Doing ... what?" I asked.

"As for your work responsibilities, we would have to work that out." His voice seemed somehow less authoritative and more matter-of-fact. "Probably maintenance items, taking out the trash, unloading deliveries."

Thomas coughed a couple times as if choking on the Reaper's words. "Deliveries?" he asked.

The Reaper grinned, the crow's feet at the corners of his eyes deepening. It was the kind of innocent smile I used to see on Mom's face. Carefree, sincere. Perhaps even ... honest.

No! Do not get sucked into another lie.

"You know, stocking the supply room."

What kind of supplies did they have at funeral homes. Embalming fluid? Of course, embalming fluid. Despite the ick factor, and honestly against my will, I felt a burst of excitement. I'd never had a real job before.

"It is up to you, my dear," he added. "Dear" repeated in my head like the last word in a song. Maybe he was just stalling, waiting for the cops to get there. But the offer sounded like a sweet deal, the money part for sure. Sometimes, okay most of the time, thinking everyone is out to hurt you is the smart, safe thing to do. And I wasn't positive he'd been stalking us. What if he had just caught a glimpse of us going into our apartment?

The rain had stopped. Should I take a chance? Just because I was wearing a Horseshoe Casino T-shirt didn't mean I was some kind of gambler. What were the odds the man was legit? Maybe better than I thought.

I looked down at Jess. She grinned, then nodded her head a little. She was just a little kid and tended to see the best in people. She didn't know any better. But honestly, at that moment I really wanted to believe there was someone out there who simply wanted to help us. Like a virus, the belief rapidly spread. Infected with dangerous hope, I slid the blade inside the box cutter and slipped it back into my pocket.

"Uh ... sure," I said. "I'd ... yeah, I could do that."

"All right, then."

He reached into his shirt pocket. I stiffened, then relaxed a little as he pulled a business card from his coat and handed it to me. He swallowed and grimaced a little, like he had a sore throat or something. He bowed slightly as he spoke.

"I am Delamorte, Victor Delamorte."

"Callie," I said, placing my hand to my chest. "This is Jess." My little sister lifted her arms as if to say "ta-da."

My brother breathed a tired sigh and waved. "Thomas."

Delamorte held out his hand, and I just stared at it. Touching people was not something I did unless it was with my fist. In my head, the word "milk" repeated, so musical, so sweet. A strange desire grew warm in my chest. When was the last time I'd shaken anyone's hand? I couldn't even remember.

I reached out anticipating his touch as cold and clammy. You know, the very grip of death. Surprisingly, his palm was dry, his grasp firm and warm. At least he wasn't wearing an oily jumpsuit. I knew for a fact those guys were always shitbags. He let go of his grip after a moment, leaving my hand hovering in midair. I felt empty, letdown like I'd lost something important. Had he claimed part of me? Taken part of my soul?

The dark splotch further down the breezeway faded, the corridor returned to its normal color. Whatever cloud that hid the sun must have moved elsewhere and the entire passage brightened.

"I will look for you Monday. Perhaps

mid-afternoon, around three. In the meantime, maybe I could find you some real breakfast."

My mouth was open to say no, but Jess interrupted.

"McDonald's? Could we go to McDonald's?"

"Jess, no. We got food here."

"I am a gourmet chef," Delamorte said. "In another life I was *cuisinier* to kings and queens of France. I could prepare you a breakfast feast fit for them. I make a delightful hollandaise."

His voice sounded lighter, even a little playful. He spread his arms a little wider and even bowed slightly. It looked and sounded like he was inviting us to a banquet. I had no idea what the holland thing was or what he did for royalty. For all I knew at the time, he might have been chief ass wiper.

"We just met you," I said. "I appreciate your being nice to us, especially not calling the cops and all, but —"

"Why not, Callie?" Jess said, tugging on my hand. She licked her lips and rubbed her belly. "Feed me, Seymour, feed me now."

Delamorte frowned, looking around us inside the apartment. "Who might Seymour be?"

I twisted my mouth around to hide the grin that threatened. If it was just me, I might have taken him up on the offer. But I was responsible for my brother and sister and needed to keep them safe. Then again, hadn't I just involved them in theft? I'd put them at risk for the very thing I was trying to avoid. Foster care. God, what had I been thinking? It was so much easier looking back at what I'd done than ahead at what I needed to do or should do. The right answers were always so obvious *after* taking the exam.

My stomach betrayed me, growling nearly loud enough to echo off the walls of the third-floor breezeway. I wanted to trust this guy almost as much as I wanted something to fill my empty belly. Almost.

"No, thank you."

"Very well," he said. "I will look for you Monday afternoon then."

Delamorte bowed again and left. I closed the apartment door, snapping all the locks in place as fast as I could.

What had just happened? I blinked a few times, as if trying to wake from a dream. We all looked at each other, then Thomas dumped the fried pies he'd been holding onto the kitchen table where we pounced on them. Thomas hesitated, angling his head a little. His conscience apparently cleared by the knowledge we were no longer thieves, my brother opened one and took a tiny bit of it.

"See," I said. "You really weren't a thief."

"I was *never* the thief. And that," he said,

nibbling on the pie, "was an unlikely outcome."

Honestly, I had to agree. We'd — or at least I had — been caught stealing. And yet, there we sat eating the fruits of my thievery. Truly there was no justice in the world. At that moment though, I was kinda glad. Sometimes justice was damn overrated.

Thomas left most of his fried pie on the table. "I'm not that hungry," he said. Was it something to worry about that he didn't seem to be starving like the rest of us? I stuck the pie in the fridge in case he wanted more later.

Still chewing on a fried peach pie, I went out onto the veranda overlooking the parking lot in time to see Delamorte ambling toward the powder blue hearse. Next to him was what I thought was a woman maybe a foot shorter than him in a long, dark dress. At least, I thought it was a dress. Had she been there the whole time? Hiding just outside the door? An image flashed in my mind of the dark not-shadow in the doorway across from our apartment. It was hard to see with my crappy eyesight, but it looked like she'd hooked her arm around Delamorte's. Was she, like, his girlfriend?

There are some people you can look at and know they don't belong. Delamorte and the dark woman? No effing way they belonged in that neighborhood. In fact, I couldn't imagine any place that they *would* belong. Unless maybe some past historical era like a couple hundred years ago.

Looking back, it would have been so easy to avoid seeing Delamorte again. All I had to do was just not show up for work. Jesus, how that would have changed things.

The Delamorte Family Funeral Home

Thomas got on the computer at the public library and found directions to Delamorte's place. It was like a half-hour walk, but mostly past vacant lots and a few boarded up houses, so we didn't have to worry too much about drunk, high, or pervy guys. We crossed a bridge over the Trinity River and past a forest preserve.

I'd thought seriously about not going. It was just so damn weird. Ultimately I decided dusting the caskets of the dearly departed beat lying around our hot, stinking apartment. My brother and sister apparently agreed since they had no complaints about making the trip on foot through the early June heat, which was surprising in Thomas's case. Normally he whined and complained about anything involving physical activity.

The Delamorte Family Funeral Home was a two-story wood-frame building with a wrap-around porch conveniently located on Evergreen Road. Convenient because right across the street was the largest cemetery in the county, also called Evergreen.

If I hadn't already known it was a business, I would have thought it was just an old house out in the country. There were no other buildings anywhere in sight. And it was other worldly quiet. No roar from the interstate highway, no sirens. Just a warm breeze chilling the sweat on our backs.

The funeral home was surrounded by low shrubs, some dried-up crisp and brown, others green but overgrown. The building was painted a drab green with dark blue trim that somehow made the brown look brighter. A long driveway led around to the back where I could see the rear end of the powder blue Cadillac hearse.

A couple of blackbirds cawed, then took off from the corner of the funeral home roof and headed toward the cemetery. God, those birds liked following us around. Were we just good entertainment? Or were they, in that case, trying to warn us of something? Maybe reminding us it wasn't too late to just fly away, escape while we still could. Thomas noticed them, too. "Crows are very intelligent," he noted. "And they have great memory. Scientific studies have shown they also can hold a grudge for up to seventeen years."

Nearly as long as I'd been alive. Was that why they were always yacking at me? Were they somehow angry I'd been born? Honestly, there were times I felt the same way.

The wood sagged under our weight as we clomped onto a front porch painted the same dull green as the building itself. I raised my hand to knock, then gripped the doorknob.

"You shouldn't just go in like that,"

Thomas said. "It's like breaking in." I shrugged. The place was a business, not someone's house. No little bell greeted us like at the GrabNGo, only silence and cool, dry air. Thomas twisted his mouth around, then pushed the door closed behind. Inside, the three of us stood in the entryway still as corpses.

In contrast to our dark apartment, the funeral home was lit up inside enough to see all the way to the end of the hallway. Still, though, the place felt odd. No music played, no voices echoed, everything was quiet as a snow-covered graveyard in the dead of winter. Entering the funeral home wasn't creepy as much as it felt like we'd passed into the afterlife.

None of us said anything. I was barely even breathing, apparently afraid of disturbing ... what? The dead? I swallowed and moved further down the wood-paneled hallway, my cross trainers sinking deep into the thick, cushy carpet. There didn't seem to be another living soul in the place. Then again, what did I expect?

The deeper we went into the funeral home, the more it felt like the refrigerated section of the grocery store. Jess squeezed up against me, and I put my arm around her at least partly to stay warm myself.

My nose twitched at the scent of something floral mixed with lemon. It beat the hell out of the stale stink of our apartment. On the left was a room with several caskets of different colors and sizes. Across from that was a room with a glass door and huge windows. Inside was a desk and computer at one end and a couch and soft chairs at the other.

Where was damn Delamorte? Did he forget we were coming?

We passed a grandfather clock taller than I was, its pendulum silently swishing side to side. Below the clock face was a glass plate, behind it something dark swirled. I blinked a couple of times trying to see it better. Must have been a reflection or something.

We wandered into a barely lit chapel with several rows of what looked like church pews. Planters full of plastic greenery lined the walls just below the ceiling along either side of the room. A mysterious pale green glow from some source in the planters lit the room like dusk. With the exception of one, every corner of the room was a dim gray. The exceptional corner seemed unnaturally black, like a hole existed there that might suck you into some void of Hell.

We moved slowly down the center aisle toward a gray metal casket, its polished chrome edges gleaming even in the low light. The top half of the metal box was flipped open revealing a dark profile. Flower arrangements sat on either side of the casket, filling the room with the sweet smell of roses, lilies, and carnations.

It seemed so weird, the blend of death

with sweetness and beauty. Was that to make people feel better? Was it to remind them life still goes on even when someone dies? Or was it just a distraction? Like putting perfume on a garbage dumpster.

"I was not certain you would come."

My head jerked around to where a tall silhouette stood in the doorway. I stepped back into Thomas who'd crept up into the small of my back. As a group, we stumbled backward and sideways into one of the pews.

"Dammit, T. Give me some space."

The voice of the silhouette continued: "I am delighted you made it, though."

Still clumped together, the three of us inched toward what I really hoped was Delamorte. Once in the hallway, I caught the scent of cinnamon and cigarettes. Delamorte had smelled like that when he'd somewhat miraculously appeared at the door of our apartment.

He motioned us to follow. We moved along behind his lanky frame, his scent blending with that of the flowers in the chapel behind us. He silently strolled toward a wedge of extra bright light stabbing into the hallway.

Sensing something behind us, I looked over my shoulder in time to see a dark swirling something disappear into one of the rooms back up the hall. Was it a person or just the light playing tricks with my head? Whatever it was moved with an unnatural, jerky quickness that sent goose bumps up my back. It was probably just someone who worked there ... wandering around ... in the shadows ... in a building full of dead people.

Delamorte stood at the source of the light, beckoning us to join him as he disappeared into the light. What was in there? I felt like a little kid in a Halloween haunted house wondering what was around the next corner waiting to scare the bejesus out of me. Thomas and Jess must have felt the same way because they both pressed close to me like extra body appendages.

I imagined stacks of dead bodies in the room where Delamorte had disappeared. Did he need help moving them around? Still bunched up together, the three of us made it to the wedge of light. Pivoting, we beheld ... a huge black stove. And a microwave oven, a sink, a refrigerator, and a small table surrounded by four chairs. Damn, it was just a regular kitchen.

"This is our break room," Delamorte said. "It is also my favorite place in the entire building, *ma cuisine*."

Honestly, the room looked kind of ... ordinary. Except for the stove. Black and heavy with no digital clock or buttons, the thing looked like it was a hundred years old. It had, like, six burners and an oven that seemed to be right out of Hansel and Gretel. You know, the one the kids shoved the witch into after she threatened to roast them alive. Or was it the other way around?

Pots and pans hung from hooks overhead. Jars of beans, nuts, dried fruit slices, and racks and racks of herbs lined the countertops. A thick cutting board and a set of knives jammed into a wood block sat near the sink. Maybe it was the power of suggestion, but I could smell food. Had Delamorte cooked recently? What did the guy call himself? Some kind of chef?

The bright overhead light glared off Delamorte's bald head and made his goatee seem extra white. If he'd had an earring and a broadsword, the guy would have looked like a pirate.

"You go to school?" I asked. "I mean, to learn how to ... do whatever it is you do here?" He shook his head. "An associate took me on as an apprentice some years ago and allowed me to live upstairs. He passed unexpectedly, and I took over the business and the house."

Unexpectedly. For some reason that word bothered me. Had it been a heart attack? Stroke? Or, a more sinister cause of death.

"Anyone else work here?" I asked.

"Someone comes over once a month or so to make sure my finances are in good order." That must have been what—who—I'd seen earlier. The bookkeeper. I also wondered about the woman I'd seen in the parking lot of our apartment. The one who'd linked her arm with Delamorte.

"And our beautician, Lucinda," Delamorte said.

"What's a beautician?" Jess asked.

"Someone who does hair and makeup," I said.

Delamorte nodded. Why they needed a beautician at a funeral home was beyond me. At least I could add another actual living person to explain the shadow thing I'd seen earlier.

Delamorte opened a brown paper bag on the counter by the sink and took out three plastic containers of food and three Styrofoam cups with lids. The smell of something gloriously delicious billowed over me, saliva pooling in my mouth.

"Are you children hungry?"

"That a trick question?" I asked.

He grinned a little, set everything on the table, and opened up the boxes to reveal a buttton of barbecue brisket, rolls, beans, and corn on the cob. Moving as a single six-armed creature, we attacked the food as if it might disappear any second.

"Good Lord," Delamorte declared. "I am reminded of the piranhas of the Amazon."

In the span of less than five minutes all that was left of the food were a few crumbs and a drop or two of meat juice. Thomas, for some reason, only had a bite or two. It was Jess and I that ate most of the feast. Jess reached over and wiped her plate with her finger and stuck it in her mouth. "Thank you," she said.

"Life requires sustenance," Delamorte said. "People do not work well on an empty stomach."

"What exactly do you do in the funeral business?" Thomas asked. He hadn't eaten much, but more than the nibble he'd had of the stolen fried pie.

Delamorte leaned against the kitchen sink. "When a person passes, we collect their remains and bring them here where they are prepared."

"Prepared ... for what?" Jess asked.

"To meet their loved ones," he said. "Depending on their final wishes, the deceased is placed in a burial container, some refer to it as a casket, then moved to the Slumber Room for public visitation."

"I never got that whole concept," I said. "It just seems kinda sick having a dead body on display."

"When grieving," Delamorte went on, "family and friends will often settle for a few final moments with their loved ones even if they do not appear quite the same."

"Yeah, they appear to be dead," I said.

Thomas spoke. "In some cultures,

families keep the bodies of their dead loved ones in their house or out in the yard for weeks, months, or even years."

"Like skeletons?" Jess asked, looking totally grossed out. "Just laying around?"

"From what I saw —"

"Where'd you see that?" I asked, grinning out of one side of my mouth. The story sounded like an idea for a horror movie.

"National Geographic on YouTube. Family members bring their dead loved ones something to eat and drink, and when they do get around to burying someone, they dig them up a year or so later to literally dust them off and change their clothes. It's accepted in their culture."

"Holy shhh —" I stopped, looking over at Jess, who smiled.

After we'd eaten, Delamorte put all of us to work. Thomas helped inventory supplies, and Jess tagged along after me. I vacuumed the hallway and the so-called Slumber Room where the quiet corpse of Mr. Raymond Thibodeaux kept me company.

"Do you feel anything?" Jess asked, staring at the face in the casket. "When you're dead?"

"I got no clue," I said. "I'm pretty sure no one's ever come back to say one way or the other."

I thought Jess would ask more, but she just stared at Mr. Thibodeaux. She was just a little kid, but I would admit wondering the same thing. What did it feel like to be dead? Did you have any awareness at all?

Running the vacuum cleaner seemed to suck up most of the creepiness of being in a room with a dead person. I mean, the noise of the vacuum was just so ... normal.

As I cleaned up remnants of the "floral tributes" littering the carpet around the casket, I got to thinking about how I'd never actually been to a funeral. The closest thing maybe was when my dad came home from Afghanistan. He was in a box draped with an American flag. That was really all I remembered about him dying. That and Mom staying in her room for hours at a time while then five-year-old me tried to take care of two-year-old Thomas. I'd learned to change diapers at an early age.

Convinced the Slumber Room was cleaner than it had ever been, I wrapped the electric cord around the vacuum and pushed it into the hallway. Voices came from one of the rooms toward the front of the building, so Jess and I headed in that direction.

Along the way, we came upon a closed door with a sign that stated: "No Admittance." Believing myself somehow immune to the sign due to being an employee, I took hold of the doorknob.

Delamorte's voice boomed from directly behind me. "That is the Preparation Room." It was like I'd stuck my finger in an electric socket. I mean, literally jumped a few inches off the floor. "It is off limits at all times. Hence the sign that says No Admittance."

"What's in there?"

"That is ..." he paused, like he wasn't quite sure how to phrase what he was trying to say. "That is where I do most of my work, and where Lucinda works her magic."

"You mean, that's where you do the embalmings and stuff?"

He nodded. Adults tended to do weird shit behind closed doors, dangerous shit, things that might hurt us. Add to that the fact that I did not like being told what to do and I was thinking that day would be our first and last in the Delamorte Family Funeral Home.

"You are welcome to vacuum the Showroom and the office."

The Showroom had several caskets on display. Fortunately, they were empty and the room, having a window, was much brighter. The carpet was nearly white, and the caskets were of different tints giving the room kind of a cartoony look. It almost seemed ... cheerful. Even a room full of caskets was preferable to our stinking, drab little apartment.

"Can I help?" Jess asked.

"Why certainly," Delamorte said. "Just a

moment." He went down the hall and disappeared into a room next to the kitchen. He returned with a cloth and some spray polish.

Once done vacuuming the Showroom, I left Jess to polish the caskets and went to clean the office. I glanced at the grandfather clock in the hall, looking for the dark swirling thing was still inside the glass. But, there was nothing but my own reflection staring back.

The first thing I noticed about the office was the blood red carpet. I'd never seen carpet that color other than in movies, usually where there'd been some murder-suicide mess that left everything, everywhere, blood-soaked.

Delamorte said he didn't want to take up all our "leisure" time with work. Right, like we had anything to do in our so-called leisure time other than laying around the apartment. He loaded us up in the powder blue hearse, eventually letting us out in the parking lot just below the staircase leading to our apartment.

As Delamorte drove off, I got the feeling someone was watching us. I blinked up at the window of our apartment trying to bring it into focus. Did I see the curtain move? Was Mom finally home? The thought made me queasy for all kinds of reasons.

Trudging up the stairs, my throat tightened. Something didn't feel right. Was Pete the Perv lurking in the stairwell? The cops?

Social services?

"I knew if I waited around long enough, you'd eventually show up."

There in the third-floor breezeway stood a tall, wide guy with dark hair to his shoulders and full beard. If he hadn't been so heavy, I'd have thought he was Jesus himself come to lecture us. I didn't recognize him as one of Mom's boyfriends. It seemed like I'd seen him before around the complex but didn't think he actually lived there. Maybe a maintenance guy or manager or something.

Fists on his hips, Fat Jesus blocked the way to our apartment. His T-shirt was too short, and a roll of fat spilled out over the waist of his shorts. Knock-kneed and wearing sandals, he held a pink piece of paper in one hand.

I wanted to run, but Jess was right next to me and Thomas shuffled up behind us oblivious to what was happening.

"I'm supposed to deliver this to the occupant in person face-to-face. I am in person, you are in person. We are each of us face-to-face."

His voice wasn't mean or loud, just businesslike. He handed the pink paper to me.

"Our mom's not home."

"You'll do."

I took the paper. He stepped around me, headed for the stairs. "Sorry," he said. "Just doin' my job. Best of luck to 'ya."

With that, he pounded down the concrete steps to the parking lot. The landing was still shaking from the force of his weight as I unfolded the pink paper. I only had to read the heading to understand what it was.

NOTICE OF EVICTION.

Aggravated Assault

I stared at the pink paper, then crumpled it up and stuffed it in my pocket. Cursed, I thought. We were obviously cursed beyond all recognition.

"What is that?" Thomas asked.

"Nothing, T."

"Was it from Mom?" Jess asked.

"No, don't worry about it. It was just someone selling something."

"It was weird the way he said 'in person' and 'face to face,'" Thomas said. "Sounds more like a delivery than a sales pitch."

"Never mind, Thomas. It's not important." I could feel my brother staring at me.

"Are you lying?" he asked. He was oblivious most of the time for a reason. Once something got into his head, he worried about it. And then he'd start throwing up. I thought for just moment about telling him exactly what the paper was just to see him squirm.

"Jesus, T. Just leave it alone."

* * *

During summers, the only place to escape the apartment, and our cursed lives, was the public library. Inside, the library smelled of fresh paint, wood, and books. Jess and Thomas would stay occupied for hours, her reading, him on a computer doing whatever he did. Me? Well, there was nothing I absolutely had to do at the library, no hazards to watch out for. No pervs, no drug dealers, no worries. The sign on the front door said Safe Place, and it was.

The library could pull hope from hiding places in my mind. For a little while I could imagine we had a future. Living in a clean place, a place that smelled like the library. Somewhere we had enough food, not worrying about ... anything. Certainly not how our lives were cursed. Being at the library was like visiting the mansion of a rich relative. I could feel there were possibilities, even if I had no clue what they were. I didn't get that feeling anywhere else. Not even at school.

The eviction notice said we had seventy-two hours to "vacate the premises." What exactly happened when you got evicted? Did they throw you out in the street? Would Fat Jesus call the cops? Social services? We got a pretty clear picture of the whole eviction concept when we got home from the library that day.

I'd overheard someone at the library mention there was a tornado watch for our area that afternoon. Outside, the air was heavy and felt electrified. The birds in the trees by the creek screeched shrill and loud as I tried to put the key in the lock on our apartment door. The thing wouldn't even fit. I slammed my shoulder into the door, the only result being I hurt my shoulder.

A fire truck siren whined in the distance. Someone cleared their throat behind me, and a raspy voice spoke. I turned, and there slouched Pete the Perv at the top of the stairs.

"You locked out?"

Dark haired with narrow eyes and a small mouth, he was dressed in those goddamn greasy overalls. A cigarette dangled between two fingers.

I pushed Jess behind me to where Thomas was already standing. I felt for the box cutter and found nothing but the shape of my own butt. I'd left my weapon of choice inside the apartment. Pete shuffled closer, extending his cigarette offering me a drag. My stomach and chest tightened, my breathing shallow and choppy.

"I don't smoke," I managed to say.

"Afraid I'll give ya germs?" he said. He wheezed out a laugh, coughed, and spat a mass of yellow phlegm on the landing that oozed into a crack in the concrete.

"I heard about your eviction notice," he said. "I ain't seen your mom around. You need somewhere to stay? 'Cause, you know, I got room in my place if you want to crash there." He smiled, exposing his tobacco-stained teeth. His words slurred like he was high or drunk. He was on our landing, invading our territory, something he'd never done before.

Thunder rumbled in the distance. It was getting darker. I moved to go around Pete, keeping Thomas and Jess behind me. The asshole lurched to block my path.

Son of a bitch!

I was taller than him by maybe a couple inches or so, but he outweighed me by probably more than fifty pounds. Maybe a hundred.

"You know, staying with me is gotta be better than living in them foster homes. I hear they're god-awful places."

A second siren wailed, twisting together with the first, creating a haunting sound like the tornado warning alarms that blared sometimes. My face felt hot and swollen. His breath accumulated in the windless corridor, surrounding us with a poison blanket of cigarettes and decay coming from somewhere deep down inside. I tried not to breathe in his shit but started to feel dizzy.

"They don't feed ya, make ya take drugs, shit like that. Most of them folks're just in it for the money."

He was baiting a hook, but only for his own amusement. He was big enough to take what he wanted. And I knew what the motherfucker wanted. He leaned in closer, bracing his arm against the siding of the building.

"Callie?" Thomas whined. "Let's go."

Not even Thomas could ignore the situation. I tried, moving to go around Pete again.

"Whoa," he said, stepping in front of me, close enough the stink of decay forced its way through my nose and down my throat. "Callie, huh. Cute. I always wondered what your name was. I'd pay ya, you know. Give ya an allowance and all. You could be like my housekeeper. It'd be like a business arrangement. I'll scratch your back," he said, his mouth twisting into a foul grin, "you scratch mine."

My vision narrowed, everything around me fading to a gray blur. Sounds, even the fire trucks, faded into vague rumble. It felt like I was watching grainy old-time movie footage of myself from somewhere up near the ceiling of the breezeway. Like I was there, but not there.

The me in the movie stepped back, bumping into Jess or Thomas. Me, she, we, kicked Pete as hard as we could right between the legs. He doubled over, cursing, his cigarette dropping to the concrete landing where it smoldered.

On the cloudy periphery of my vision, Thomas dragged Jess by the hand toward the stairwell.

"Run to the GrabNGo," someone yelled. I yelled. We yelled.

A voice in my head screamed *Run!* I should have just listened to the voice, but someone or something else seemed to be controlling my actions. The girl that was me in the grainy movie hopped over directly in front of where Pete stood bent over moaning. Stepping back, her, my, leg swinging forward, her, my, cross trainer impacting against Pete's face.

He yelled, lost his balance, and staggered. I adjusted my glasses and watched, waiting for him to topple over and fall down the stairs, his bones snapping on the way down. Instead, he teetered right at the edge of the stairs.

As he tried to steady his feet, the girl in the movie ran like an idiot and hit Pete square in the stomach with her shoulder. He stepped back to absorb the hit, but when he did there was nowhere to go but down.

As we fell, Pete twisted around so we both landed sideways on the concrete steps, the entire structure booming as we landed. My shoulder smashed the hardest, my glasses skittering off the landing and over the edge. Nothing physically hurt. At least, not enough to stop what was happening.

The impact jolted me enough I was back in my own body. Panicked, I rolled off him and pulled myself up using the railing. An apartment door squeaked open somewhere, and a dog barked.

A voice in my head screamed again *Run!*

I tried to go down the stairs, but Pete wrapped his arm around my calf. Legs rubbery, knees buckling, falling ... on him, my kneecap landing in the middle of his face. There was a dull crunch, and he bellowed in pain and rage. I'd gotten lucky and fallen directly on the asshole's nose.

Someone called from above: "Hey, what's goin' on?" Was it God? Jesus, it took him long enough to notice what the fuck was happening down below.

All I wanted to do was get away. Pete growled and grabbed me by the shirt, pulling me off balance. I caught myself so I didn't fall, my hand and a forearm landing on his face. Purely on reflex, I shoved my fingers into his eye sockets.

A high-pitched shriek rattled my eardrums. Pete let go of my leg, and I pushed myself up off him. Legs shaky, body and mind numb, I dragged myself down to the next floor. My foot slipped and I slid down the sharp concrete steps all the way to the landing, the entire stair structure rocking under me like I was in one of those bounce houses. I lay there a second, then grabbed the railing. Pulling myself up, I leaped several steps at a time until I made it to the concrete sidewalk.

Blackbirds had gathered on the eaves of the surrounding apartments, screeching, yelling. It didn't sound like they were laughing this time. Were they rooting for me? Or were they on Pete's side? I remembered the grudge thing. Yeah, they were definitely on Pete's side.

I took off running, everything in front of me a blur. Lightning flashed. I stumbled and fell, my hands and knees sliding on the asphalt, got up and ran again. After a few strides, I stopped, another rage bomb exploding in my chest. Balling up my fists, I turned and screamed. Gasping for air, I yelled again, hoarsely belting out every combination of swear words that came to mind. Finally, I put every ounce of what little energy I had left into one last, loud, drawn-out curse:

"Fuhcckkk youuuuu!"

I turned to run but plowed straight into Fat Jesus. Fortunately, his ample belly padding lessened the impact like car airbags. He grabbed my arms to keep me from bouncing off him and falling down again.

"Hey, what's goin' on up there?" he asked, releasing me. I never thought I'd be so glad to run into that guy.

"Dude tried to fuckin' assault me," I said, breathless. My voice quivered and I could feel the tears coming. If I said another word, I'd start crying and end up embarrassing myself.

"Hey, buddy," Fat Jesus called. "I don't allow shit like that goin' on here."

Pete hurled his own string of curses down at the parking lot. I ignored most of what he said, but one thing he shouted got my attention. "You gotta come back here sometime you little shit." He cleared his throat and spat. "You gotta get your stuff, and I'll be waiting here for you when you do."

Thunder roared, raindrops stabbed my skin like icicles.

"You know what else," Pete screamed. "I'm gonna let social services know about your little situation, so they'll be waiting for you, too. They'll find you wherever you go! I'll make sure of that."

Huge raindrops created little dust explosions upon impacting the street. Mindlessly, I spun and staggered toward the GrabNGo. A familiar long, powder blue vehicle cruised toward me along Old Home Road. I stopped, blinking my eyes to make sure it was real. Delamorte slowed and rolled down the window. "Are you all right, miss?"

"Yeah," I rasped. "Mostly, I think." I leaned over, hands on my knees trying to catch my breath.

"That does not appear to be the case."

"No, really. I feel better than ever." I hissed a rough laugh but began to shake. *Dammit.* My face contorted, tears clouding my eyesight.

"Get in."

Rain came hard and heavy. I wiped my face and hopped in the front seat. Inside, the hearse smelled of the familiar cigarettes and cinnamon. I took a few breaths, trying to get it together. I was not going to cry. I refused to cry. But holding back the tears was like trying to control a river with just my hands.

"Best to let all that out," Delamorte declared.

As soon as he spoke, I lost all choice in the matter. Shaking, sobbing, I was a quivering mass of emotion. I was just hoping I could get it all out before Jess and Thomas saw me. Delamorte seemed to understand that and drove slow like he was in a parade or something. We pulled into the GrabNGo parking lot. Jess ran up to my side of the hearse, nearly soaked from the rain. Thomas lagged behind as usual and was even more drenched.

"Callie!" Jess called.

I wiped my face off, opened the door, and tried to get out but my little sister was draped all over me before I could stand up. I grabbed onto her like a teddy bear and sobbed a couple of times.

"Are you all right?" she asked.

"I'm fine."

She pulled away from me. "Is that blood?"

"Where?"

"On your shirt." I fingered the sticky red substance.

"I don't think it's mine."

Delamorte gazed at us. "Get in before —"

We didn't let him finish, all three of us piling into the hearse. The windshield wipers worked frantically to clear the water from the windshield.

"What did you do?" Thomas said.

"I'm not sure." And I wasn't. Whatever happened was quickly exiting my brain.

"Yeah, right," he said. "You could have just run." My little brother wasn't talking out of concern for me. Saint Thomas thought himself the all-knowing determiner of appropriate behavior. I was too tired to take him up on it. I was just glad to be out of there. He leaned his head back and sighed. I couldn't tell if he was irritated or relieved.

It was strange how fast you could go from scared to angry and back to scared again. Staring down the street toward the apartment complex, I half expected to see Pete heading toward us through the sheets of rain. Had he seen me get in the hearse? Would he somehow be able to find me?

I'd never taken on an adult like that before. Not in a fight. There'd always been a way to run or hide from them. Pete didn't leave me much choice when he kept jumping in front of me the way he did. The damn idiot.

It was nearly dark, and Delamorte turned on the headlights. The rain eased a little. Once past our apartment complex a couple blocks, he spoke. "Is anyone hungry?"

The response from Thomas and Jess was loud and unanimously in favor of food. I, on the other hand, was still a little nauseous.

"My place is fairly close," Delamorte said, matter-of-factly.

My stomach tightened. "What would your wife think of you bringing home a bunch of kids?" I asked, staring straight ahead.

"I am a man without attachments."

Shit! Was the guy trying to do the same thing Pete did? Lure us into his house, just with more style.

Was there no end to the Callie Valentine curse?

Pancake Coma

There was a stoplight up ahead. Could I get the three of us out of the hearse before the light turned green? At the red light, I scanned the side of the road for a place to escape.

Breathe, Callie. Breathe.

My breath slowed, my heart calming enough I could think. Were we really in trouble? I'd just had a fight with a guy who, as far as I was concerned, wanted to make me his sex slave. Was going to Delamorte's for a little food really on the same level as that?

"Do you have any kids?" Jess asked, oblivious to our possible predicament.

"I have no children."

"Must get lonely," Jess added. Delamorte looked down at my little sister.

"Rarely, my dear."

I assumed everyone was an asshole, mainly because they were. Jess, on the other hand, had an ability to read people I didn't have. She seemed relaxed. If she didn't seem worried, maybe there wasn't so much to worry about. God, I was tired, a fucking mess inside and out. The light changed to green. We moved forward.

After a few minutes, the hearse turned onto Evergreen Road. Did Delamorte live close to the funeral home? After a minute, we turned into the funeral home driveway.

I glanced in the back thinking there was a body bag there I'd missed, a customer he needed to drop off. "Why are we stopping here?"

He grinned, gesturing at the funeral home. "As you can see, there is a second floor. Therein is my humble abode."

Jess looked at him. "You live in the funeral home?"

What kind of weird-ass shit was this? Then I remembered Delamorte telling us about the guy who'd let me live on the second floor and apprentice to be a mortician.

"At the very least, it saves on fuel expenses," he said. "I can just walk downstairs *et voila*, I am at work."

Living in the same place you worked made some sense. But if it were me, I'd have wanted to put some distance between me and the dearly departed.

There'd been no tornadoes, just cold rain. Could have been worse. To the east, lightning flashed nonstop as Orville Redenbacher in the microwave. The sun had been swept away by the storm and darkness crept toward us from all directions.

We clomped up to the back porch of the old building. Delamorte flipped on a yellow light next to the backdoor, then disappeared inside the dark funeral home. A moment later, a sliver of yellow light sliced into the pitch-black hallway and the sound of pots and pans banging around came from the kitchen.

Insects swarmed the porch light, bugs crawling up my shirt and into my hair. Thomas once again moved up behind me, Jess hugging my waist from the side. I could understand Jess's need to stay in physical contact. On the other hand, I was getting a little tired of being Thomas's damn security blanket, especially when all he did was criticize me for breathing.

The funeral home at night probably felt creepier because I was already rattled by the storm and the fight with Pete. Still, it was dark and there were dead people literally chilling in the refrigerated drawers just a few steps away. And was that weird beautician, Lucinda, lurking somewhere?

There were some switches on the wall near the door so I flipped one of them up. The wood-paneled hallway lit up all the way to the front of the house. In the kitchen, a black cast iron skillet rested on one of the burners on the stove, blue flames licking out from underneath.

"Listen carefully," Delamorte said. He tossed several sausages into the skillet where they sizzled and sent the smell of animal fat wafting throughout the kitchen and likely all the way into the Slumber Room. If my corpse friend, Mr. Raymond Thibodeaux, had any life left in him, he would have joined us shortly for dinner.

"Yum," Jess said.

"Breakfast?" Thomas said. "For dinner?"

Delamorte grinned and nodded his head. "What better time for your first meal of the day." What did he mean by that? Did he know we hadn't eaten yet that day?

We gathered around the little table by the window watching Delamorte move with more energy than he had when we'd been there working. "Make yourselves at home. You are my guests."

My body quivered and my hands were shaking. I guess from hunger and what had happened earlier. I rubbed the side of my neck where I'd fallen on the stairs back at our apartment. Delamorte must have noticed.

"In the cabinet over the dishwasher there is a jar of stuff that might help what ails you."

I looked at him, got up, opened the cabinet, and found a jar full of what appeared to be bacon grease. "What is this?"

"An old remedy."

"Yeah, but what's in it?"

I unscrewed the lid and sniffed the contents of the jar. Can something smell hot without being hot? I dipped two fingers into the pasty stuff but found it cool to the touch.

"Aloe mainly."

"Is this a ... bug wing?" I pulled out a lacey piece of debris and waved it around on my finger.

"Dragonfly wings, I believe. Ancient medicine. There are a few other ingredients in that mixture as well, at least some of which you likely would not wish to hear described."

A strange, tingling sensation worked its way through the two fingers I'd dipped in the creamy mixture. Numbness spread into the first two sets of knuckles. I stared at my hand, flexing my fingers to make sure they still worked. "The restroom is across the hall if you want to rub some of that on your shoulder. It is not for internal consumption though."

"What happens if you eat it?" Thomas asked.

"We have seen some cases of that here at the home," Delamorte said, staring off. "Sad thing, sad thing. People must learn to follow directions."

Thomas's mouth opened, then he turned to look at me, shaking his head slightly as if to say I was crazy if I put the stuff anywhere near me. On the other hand, Delamorte nodded and maybe winked at me. I couldn't exactly tell from that distance. Thomas's disapproval was enough to convince me to go across the hall and grease up my shoulder and neck. What was Thomas worried about? It wasn't him using the goop. Plus, what did he care about me?

Stepping out of the kitchen, something moved in the further down the hall toward the Preparation Room. Like a shadow or, honestly, a blur of black smoke. I sniffed the air for the scent of something burning, but all I could smell was sausages sizzling in the pan. I rubbed my eyes, hoping I was seeing things that weren't there. I thought of the swirling dark thing I'd seen behind the glass of the grandfather clock. Was something lurking down the hall? Honestly, I was getting tired of wondering about creepy shit in the house.

By the time I was sitting down around the little kitchen table, I'd forgotten about whatever I'd seen or not seen in the hall and was feeling no pain. Not in my shoulder, my neck, or part of my face. Basically, everywhere the cream touched my skin and several layers beneath felt numb. "That's some good stuff," I said, moving my neck from side-to-side searching for sore spots.

"Indeed, it is," Delamorte said. "I was apprentice to an apothecary in Constantinople some centuries back. It was he who taught me how to make that substance, and I have kept a jar of it around ever since."

Thomas frowned at me. My brain wasn't functioning enough to understand why. I shrugged at him.

Delamorte mixed up some flour, milk, and an egg or two, and ladled out thin round pools of batter onto a flat griddle he'd placed on another burner. Picking up the pan, he tossed the contents, flipping them over. Saliva flooded into my mouth and threatened to leak out onto my chin.

"Pardon me, do you have any hand sanitizer?" Thomas said.

"But of course," Delamorte said, strolling over and handing Thomas a squirt bottle of gel. Thomas grinned, then went to work cleaning his hands like he was preparing for surgery rather than eating. He could be such a germaphobe.

Jess admired the wallpaper in the kitchen depicting a cook engaged in various activities of food preparation. Dinner arrived on the table about ten minutes later, including what looked like a gravy bowl full of warm syrup. "That is genuine maple syrup imported from Vermont," Delamorte said.

I poured the syrup over everything, including the sausages. Looking around, Thomas and Jess had the same idea. Together, we stuffed our faces, grunting and moaning the whole time. Even Thomas ate more than he had in a while.

"We are thankful for this sustenance," Delamorte said. "And for the miracle of life and the company of friends." With that, he picked up a fork and stabbed it into a sausage.

At that moment, thankfulness was an attitude I could embrace. People talked about drinking alcohol for "medicinal purposes," but I swear maple syrup must be just as powerful as the hard stuff. I mean, one taste of that syrup and my brain went completely numb. I could have easily poured some in a cup and sipped it like orange juice.

Jess picked up her plate when she was done and literally licked it clean. Delamorte wet some paper towels and brought them over to us.

"That ... was magnificent," Thomas said, wiping his hands then his mouth with the wet paper.

"Better than fried pies?" Delamorte asked.

"Definitely," Thomas answered. A grin spread over his entire face. He could be a judgmental jerk, but it felt good seeing him that happy. At least he wasn't sick at his stomach.

We talked about what happened earlier.

"The gentleman is probably correct," Delamorte said. I wondered what gentleman he was talking about, then realized he meant piece-of-shit Pete. "At some point, you may wish to go back there to collect your belongings."

"I'm never going back there as long as that ass—" I glanced at Jess—"jerk is around."

"What's an assjerk?" Jess asked.

Thomas coughed and I was afraid he was about to spew his pancakes all over the table. Thomas cleared his throat enough to speak. "What about our things? My..." He didn't finish. I knew he was thinking about his books and that Lego spaceship he'd worked on since he was a preschooler. How he'd kept that thing for so long was a mystery.

"What about our library books?" Jess said.

"Yeah, we can't just leave them," Thomas said. "There'll be fines, and ... they might not let us go to the library or ... or use the computer." He looked horrified at the thought.

I sighed. "Guys, I don't think we can ever go back. I mean, that guy pretty much wants to kill me."

And there was Pete's threat about social services. Had he really called them? I was more worried about that possibility than getting our stuff from the apartment.

"Maybe you could, like, hold him off long enough so we could get our things," Thomas suggested.

"Oh. So, it's okay if I beat someone up as long as it benefits *you*?"

"I ... I ... That's not what I meant."

"Yeah, right."

"Ah," Thomas said. "We can't get in the apartment anyway. The key didn't work."

The look on his face cycled through hope, resignation, disappointment, and finally sadness. I didn't see that look on his face often. He usually kept his head in a book or a computer monitor to distract him from all the

shit in our lives . Delamorte set down his fork
and leaned his elbows on the edge of the table,
his fingers folded in front of him. Tilting his
head, he stared across at Thomas.

After all the food was gone, I offered to
help do the dishes. Delamorte had none of it.
"You are my guests and I aim to be a good
host."

As Delamorte washed the dishes, we
talked about what was going to happen next.
Thomas suggested we go to a shelter. I pointed
out that going to a shelter pretty much
automatically meant going into foster care.

"So?" he said. He obviously had no clue
what would happen in foster care. Either that or
he just didn't care. Did he want to be separated
from me, from us? Part of me wondered if he'd
prefer to be by himself all the time, just
withdraw into the Internet.

I'd seen a couple of homeless people
living in tents under the bridge near our
apartment. "We could camp out down by the
creek," I suggested.

Thomas, still looking dejected, rolled his
eyes. "Yeah, along with the skunks and
possums."

"Maybe we could sneak into my school
at night and sleep there," Jess said. Honestly, I
considered doing the same thing at the public
library but didn't say it out loud.

Jess got up and eased over to the sink.

"Can I dry?" she asked, looked up at Delamorte. My little sister loved to help. She blinked a couple of times, using the magic of her huge blue eyes on him. It was fun watching Jess work.

"Certainly," Delamorte said, his face softening.

After the dishes were washed, dried and put away, Delamorte addressed us. "I think you children should rest tonight and sort it out in the morning." Sounded good to me. But rest where? "You are most welcome to spend the night here." He lifted his chin, expecting a response.

I waited for what I assumed would be a wave of panic, but nothing happened. Maybe it was the way Delamorte used the word "welcome," like he was leading us unto the Gates of Heaven or something. It was a far cry from Pete's slurred "you can crash at my place" sleeze.

I licked syrup from the corners of my mouth. Drugged up with hotcakes, sugar, and dragonfly wing paste, the only part of my brain still working was the one telling my stomach to digest.

Thomas shrugged, his face still downcast. Jess raised her eyebrows and grinned. She seemed okay with the idea, and that was good enough for me.

We followed Delamorte toward the

spiral staircase catacorner from the kitchen. I glanced down the hall toward the Preparation Room, looking for the smoky shadow I'd seen earlier. But nothing was there.

A velvet cord stretched from one rail to the other, I guess to keep the families and friends of customers from wandering upstairs. I doubted it would have any effect on ghosts or spirits of the dead, if any of them wandered loose at night. I mean, they probably went wherever they wanted.

The staircase, wide enough the three of us could walk side by side, creaked under our weight as we slowly marched up. A long, dark hallway greeted us at the top. Delamorte flipped a light switch revealing several doors, all of them closed.

To my right, something moved. Just a shadow retreating from the light, but weirdly slow. Like a person slipping into the crack of the closed door at the end of the hall. I blinked a few times. It was the same kind of thing I'd seen downstairs. Was I hallucinating? God, I was tired.

In contrast to the plush carpet in the business part of the building below, the flooring upstairs was just bare-ass wood save for a layer of fine dust and grit. As far as I could tell, the upstairs had five rooms. Two along one side, one along the other, and one at each end. All the doors were shut, giving the upstairs a cramped feel that seemed to make it harder to breathe.

Delamorte led us to a door just across from and to the left of the staircase that opened to a bedroom full of, as far as I could tell, junk. Mainly papers, envelopes, and magazines. No *Playboys*, *Penthouses,* or any other sign of bare breasts and butts were in sight, but stacks of ancient *Billboards*. The room smelled dusty and stale like no one had lived in there for a while.

"Music lover?" I asked, holding up one of the *Billboards* close enough to read the title.

"The music of this modern era is unlike any other," Delamorte responded. "It is, as they say, accessible and quite compelling. Not all things must be a symphony."

What was compelling to *me* was the accessibility of the bed. Delamorte moved things around and gradually exposed a full-sized mattress complete with box springs, a metal frame, and actual headboard. In other words, it was a real bed. There were even a couple of side tables with lamps.

I helped him clear the rest of the junk away, and Jess and I got the bed ready to use. Thomas found a dusty book from somewhere in the room and made himself comfortable on the floor in the hallway as far as possible from any work.

"You and your little sister may use the bed," Delamorte said. He got a bunch of blankets and laid them out on the floor like a pallet. "Any objections to your brother sleeping on the floor."

"None whatsoever," I said.

"I suspected as much," Delamorte said.

Thomas leaned his head into the room. "What's going on?"

"You get the floor," I said.

He frowned, examining the surrounding floor. "Any bugs in here?"

"One cannot say for certain," Delamorte said.

"Great," Thomas said, screwing up his mouth. "Just great."

I stared at the bed. I was about two seconds from falling onto it and not getting up. From the doorway, Delamorte looked me up and down.

"We must get you out of those clothes."

What the actual fuck?

All in Good Time

The pancakes balled up hard in my belly, and I swallowed repeatedly to keep them there.

"What?" I rasped.

So much for falling into bed. Lacking my box cutter, I squared up, ready to physically fight my way past a guy for the second time that day. Delamorte noticed my change in posture. He looked at the ceiling, motioned his hand up and down in my direction, and sighed. "You simply cannot wear those clothes anywhere tomorrow, my dear. Unless you wish others to assume you require medical attention or have perpetrated some violent crime and are in need of apprehension by the authorities."

Thomas laughed from the hallway. I wished I could have seen him, his smile restored. Keeping one eye on Delamorte, I looked down at the blood stains on my shirt. Inhaling a deep breath, I blew it out slowly.

"I don't suppose I could use your bathtub," I asked. Delamorte cocked his head and frowned. "To wash our clothes."

"Of course, that would be fine. However, most use a washer and dryer for that sort of thing."

I opened my mouth, then shut it. It'd been so long since we had money to go to a laundromat, I'd forgotten that was how normal people washed their clothes.

"I would be pleased to take care of your laundry," he said.

It occurred to me we had nothing else to wear that night. Delamorte must have realized the same thing. "I believe I have some clothes you might wear in the meantime."

How was it he had clothes that would fit all three of us? Did he strip dead bodies? God, of course he did. Would all of us be okay with wearing something a person might have died in even if it was washed?

My brain was still numb from the food and exhaustion. I gave in, took the clothes Delamorte offered, and went to the bathroom across the hall to change. Pink tile covered the tub and shower area and the floor linoleum was cream colored with splotches of what looked like caramel. It kind of reminded me of the *dulce de leche* ice cream Mom used to bring home from the grocery store. Back when she was a real mom and we had money for ice cream.

I slipped into an oversized pair of jeans and a T-shirt. Once dressed, I climbed into a bed that felt solid like it had roots in the floor. Jess curled up next to me, Thomas taking his place on the pallet of blankets on the floor.

"I wish you a good night," Delamorte said from somewhere in the hall. His footsteps faded down the staircase. I shut the bedroom door and locked it.

Delamorte's place was nothing like our

apartment. No water rushing through pipes, muffled voices or babies crying. No sounds of the outside world penetrated the barrier surrounding us. Instead, other noises kept me from falling asleep as soon as my head hit the pillow. A creak here, a bump there.

Somehow, the ticking of the grandfather clock was audible all the way upstairs. A mechanical tone started up somewhere. I sat up on the edge of the bed and stared down at the floorboards. Was that the air conditioner? The washing machine maybe? The furnace where they cremated bodies? The conveyor belt transporting all the dead people down to Hell? Satan laughing?

One sound, a regular hum, rumbled through the bed. Focusing on that, my head felt heavy, like it was about to topple off my shoulders. I lay back, my limp body sinking deeper into the solid bed, my thoughts disintegrating into a welcome mindless nothing.

* * *

Sleeping somewhere different screwed up my internal alarm clock, and I was still dead asleep when Delamorte knocked softly on the door the next morning. Instantly awake, I threw off the covers, spun around, and tried to stand up. Forgetting where I was, I dropped what felt like ten feet onto the floor, my knees and hands impacting the hard wood with a dull thud.

"Are you all right in there?" The voice was Delamorte's.

"Yeah," I groaned.

"I have your clothes here and will leave them by the door."

"Yeah ... sure." I rubbed my knees.

Had Delamorte been just standing around in the hall waiting for us to wake up? I leaned against the bed. My shoulder throbbed, reminding me of the reason we'd spent the night in a funeral home. I needed to find that jar of dragonfly wing goop Delamorte gave me the night before.

"Breakfast is prepared when you are ready."

Delamorte's footsteps retreated from the door, the staircase creaking under his weight. I found our clothes outside the door folded neatly and smelling fresher than they had in weeks and probably months. Delamorte had also left the jar of dragonfly wing goop next to our clothes.

Jess was sitting up cross-legged in the bed, but Thomas was still asleep. I handed Jess her clothes and kicked Thomas a couple of times. He groaned and rolled over. I left his clothes next to his pallet and went to the bathroom to grease up my shoulder and get dressed.

At the top of the staircase, my eyes stared down the dark hallway. Delamorte didn't mention anyone else living there in the funeral home. Were the other rooms for storage maybe? Guestrooms? Was one of them where Delamorte kept his drug stash? Was there any weird sexual shit in there?

Renewed hunger shoved the questions from my head and sent me downstairs to the kitchen where scrambled eggs with cheese, cooked onions, and toast awaited in the kitchen. I wasn't much of a breakfast eater. A bowl of cereal would have been fine. Honestly, though, breakfast wasn't really a thing in the summer. I mean, most of the time we didn't get up until noon.

Thomas and Jess were already in the kitchen. We downed our breakfast, just not quite in such a frenzy as with the hotcakes and sausage the previous night. Thomas ate less, but still more than his usual nibble. And he didn't immediately head to the bathroom.

Delamorte suggested we make ourselves at home. Whatever that meant. I mean, come on. It may have been better smelling and a little safer than our old apartment, but it was a funeral home for God's sake. There was nothing to do.

"Can we get on your computer?" Thomas asked. I frowned at him. "What? I was just asking."

Delamorte got him and Jess set up on the office computer, then went to work in the

Preparation Room. I wasn't interested in the computer and went outside onto the back porch.

Thinking it would be good to get away from Thomas and Jess for a little while, I strode across the street to the cemetery where it was cooler and very quiet. It was a little foggy that first morning, kind of like a dream. The air smelled mainly of cut grass and damp concrete. Gray shadows of trees loomed in the fog like souls lost in the afterlife.

The cemetery itself was flat and covered with a butt-ton of headstones. At least there were no pervs there. Well, dead ones maybe, but unless they were zombies, I didn't have to worry about fighting any of them off. Did ghosts leer at you? I decided they had better things to do now they were dead.

I walked down a row of graves. It was mostly old folks rotting beneath my feet, with a few younger ones scattered here and there. Some of the markers said things about the person buried there, others just had the birth and death dates.

What would my own headstone look like? Would they write anything about me on it? Sister? Daughter? Or something else. Like "Poor idiot had no clue what the hell was happening." Could you even write curse words on headstones? Did they make you replace some of the letters with, like, asterisks or something? You know, like "F**k you, a**holes!" Would people remember my name longer if I swore at them from the grave? I filed the idea away in my head.

The cemetery was far enough away from any houses or businesses, I could forget I was even close to a city. In other words, it was like I'd been transported to a different world. From across the street, the funeral home looked like a dark castle. The kind they have in places like Scotland or England where they had foggy mist and mystery and lots of old, gloomy shit.

I felt like a ghost wandering around alone through all those grave markers. God, what was I even doing there? An ache formed in my chest, like the worse hunger pang ever. All I wanted was to see my brother and sister.

Marching, then jogging, toward the funeral home, I slipped in the back door in time to hear Jess and Thomas laugh from down in the office. I grinned and headed that way but stopped short. In the kitchen, Delamorte was talking with someone. Whoever it was in there with him had an unusual accent.

"You said you liked me in this form." Her—I decided it was a woman—voice was kind of deep for someone female.

"I appreciate your effort to maintain that form," Delamorte said, "but sometimes it produces more grief than joy."

"I would advise making up your mind

quickly. Now that you have guests, I'll be needing to maintain a consistent appearance lest they become confused or, worse, ask too many questions."

Delamorte sighed. "Stay the way you are then. It is more than palatable most of the time."

"Palatable. That's not what you used to think."

"I have wonderful memories of the person whose form you take, but grief persists."

What kind of conversation was I listening to?

"It was never my intention, Victor, to prolong your sadness."

"I realize this. Our life together was so full."

"Piracy rather lends itself to that."

Piracy? What the hell were they talking about? They were quiet a few moments, and I was about to go into the kitchen when the lady spoke again.

"When do you intend to tell them the rest?"

The rest? The rest of what?

"I would request you keep your voice down. They may not be aware of everything but their ears, I am certain, work perfectly well."

There was a pause, then: "Will you tell them what you have hidden in that room upstairs and its purpose."

Delamorte lowered his voice again: "As

for that device upstairs, when and if I inform them of its purpose or even of its existence, it will be because they absolutely need to know."

"Or, more likely, if *you* absolutely need them to know."

"I would not—"

"Ask them to be involved in that way? Shall we place a little wager on that?"

I'd heard enough. "What device?" I asked, pivoting into the kitchen to see an Asian-looking woman with long, shimmering silver hair sitting across from Delamorte at the kitchen table. Goosebumps ran up and down my spine for some reason. Small cups of something sat in front of each of them. The woman wore a sapphire-colored, long-sleeved dress that sort of glistened in the morning light streaming in from the kitchen window. Her outfit seemed a weird choice for a hot summer day. Was she somehow immune to the heat?

"Well, well," she said, looking me up and down with icy light blue eyes. "Look at the pair of ears that has been lurking out in the hallway. And for who knows how long."

The woman had high cheek bones, a rounded nose, and freakishly great posture. Other than looking a little like some kind of Asian Ice Queen, she was actually kind of attractive. Her pale blue eyes stared into mine. Didn't most Asian people have brown eyes? I suddenly felt trapped, vulnerable, like I'd stepped in front of a firing squad or something. I looked down at the floor, then off down the hall.

Delamorte sighed again, then gestured at the woman. "Let me introduce you to my associate, Lucinda."

In one smooth, single motion she was standing. I thought she might extend a hand, but she kept them folded in front of her. "Lucy," she said, nodding her head.

"Callie," I said, folding my arms and leaning against the doorframe. "What were you saying about the device upstairs?"

Delamorte rolled his eyes, wiped his mouth with a finger, then rose. He took the little cups from the table and placed them in the sink.

"I'll leave it with the two of you, then," Lucy said, but from behind me. She'd been standing directly in front of me only a second ago. I must have been so focused on Delamorte I didn't see her walk past me. Moving down the hall, she seemed to disappear every couple of steps only to reappear a little further down until she came to the Preparation Room. Must have been some trick of the light or maybe my crappy eyesight. She glanced at me a second, then went inside the Room of No Admittance.

Delamorte washed up the tiny cups. What had the two of them been talking about? The so-called device, and the thing about Lucy's *form*. Was that like a figure of speech? Maybe they were talking about her dress. Yeah, that had to be it.

"If you will excuse me, I have some business to attend to —"

"In the Preparation Room?" I interrupted. "With Lucy? She your girlfriend or something?" It was a fair question. He looked down and to the side, just enough to know he was still talking to me.

"All in good time."

The *Novus Stellar*

The funeral home air conditioning worked
great, and it got kind of chilly just sitting
around in the office or the kitchen. I'd just
stepped out onto the back porch to thaw out
when an ancient pickup pulled into the
driveway behind the funeral home. The back
was loaded with some cardboard boxes and a
couple of plastic trash bags.

A small-framed guy with stringy brown
hair got out of the truck. He wore a dark outer
coat, which was weird because it was hot out.

"Some of this belongs to y'all," the guy
said, grabbing one of the boxes.

"Huh?" I went down the back steps onto
the driveway. Opening up a box from the bed of
the truck, I began to recognize some of the
things as being from our old apartment. Library
books, for one.

Thomas and Jess came out to see what
was going on. Delamorte followed a moment
later. "Children, this is Mr. Gerard. He works
for me as needed."

The guy looked around at us, the corners
of his mouth turning up in a way that reminded
me a little bit of the Grinch.

"Kids," he said, saying in three syllables
what most said in one.

Mr. Gerard brought over a box and set it
down on the porch. As he did so, his coat

parted revealing a sidearm. It was one of those pearl handled old-style revolvers, and with his outfit he kind of looked like a gunfighter from the Old West.

Jess reached in the box and pulled out one of the library books. "Cool," she said.

"Did you get everything?" Thomas asked.

"Got everything wurf gettin'," Mr. Gerard said, then wiped his nose with his wrist. The guy had a speech impediment I hadn't noticed before. Or was he drunk? Maybe high on some shit? I sniffed in his general direction, but there was no scent of alcohol.

"Where's the TV?" I asked.

Mr. Gerard's pearl-handled revolver knocked against the side of the pickup as he reached for one of the plastic bags. "There weren't none to get. Y'all had one?"

"The TV was gone?" I asked.

"Didn't see none. Maybe the maintenance feller helped hisself. Or maybe the apartment manager. Y'all owe back rent?"

I pictured Fat Jesus and the eviction notice. "I have no idea," I said. "Doesn't look like you got our mattress either ... or the dresser."

"'Fraid that dresser was fallin' apart, not much use. Same for the couch. As for yer old mattress ... I could always go back and get it later. We can just take the one ya slept on last night and put it in storge."

Did he mean storage? "Uh, that won't be necessary." He could set that old mattress on fire for all I cared.

Mom had a dresser, and for a second I wondered why he hadn't gotten it. Then it hit me; there was nothing in the pickup from Mom's room.

"Wait, how'd you get in?" Thomas asked.

"Oh, the locks weren't no problem," Mr. Gerard said. What did that mean?

"You check every room?" I asked.

Mr. Gerard swallowed, his Adam's apple bobbing up and down. He glanced past me at Delamorte.

"There weren't but three rooms. It'd be hard to forget one of 'em. You, uh, questionin' my competence and capability young lady?"

"Uh, I ... no."

"Well, I'm glad to know that after I went to the trouble of collectin' all this. I can assure you I took everything ... salvageable."

Mr. Gerard, clearly irritated at first, seemed more nervous. Was he hiding something? As far as I was concerned, Mom had just taken off and not come back. Had Mr. Gerard seen her?

"You might consider thanking Mr. Gerard," Delamorte said.

Thomas and Jess said their thank-yous.

Mr. Gerard shoved a hand into one of his pants pockets and pulled out a roll of cherry Lifesaver candies. He pried three loose and stuck his hand in our direction.

"Help yourselfs," he said.

Thomas said, "No, thank you," and I sure wasn't about to put anything in my mouth that had been in that man's pants pocket. Jess had no problem with the source of the Lifesavers, grabbed all three and crammed them in her mouth before I could stop her.

"Tonk you," she said, her mouth full of cherry saliva. The Grinch grin formed on Mr. Gerard's face.

We got all our stuff unloaded and into the hallway.

"You run into anyone else?" I asked between trips out to the pickup truck. Delamorte, who'd been piddling in the kitchen, came near to listen.

Mr. Gerard answered." I presume you mean that mom a yours." He stood in the hallway staring at the wall. "Might be better this way," he said.

"What way?"

"Your mama bein' gone." He looked over at Delamorte. "My mama was a vicious ..." He stopped, literally biting his lip. "She was a lovely woman cursed with the face of a toad and the ways of a serpent. She'd lie in wait like a snake in the grass for the unsuspecting victim, usually one of us kids, then she'd slice us up. Not with a blade, mind you, but her words. Some people have a gift for that sort of thing."

Delamorte shook his head. "Sorry to hear that, Gerry."

Personally, I didn't give a shit about Mr. Gerard's toad-ugly mother, only my own.

"To answer your question," Mr. Gerard continued. "I did not see yer mom or any other livin' soul for that matter. I take that back. I did see this one feller with kinda greasy black hair smokin' a cigarette in a doorway when I was carryin' down some boxes. Had a black eye, little bloody 'round the edges where it shoulda been white."

"Seriously?" I asked. God, I wish I had a picture of Pete's face. I'd have cherished it all the way to the grave. I'd beaten the curse, at least for a day. My satisfaction faded quickly, replaced by anger, then fear. He'd threatened to call social services. Had he done it? Did he know where we lived?

"You the one responsible for the way he look?"

"Depends on who's asking," I said, allowing one corner of my mouth to turn up. I looked at Delamorte and saw he was grinning.

"Man, here's hopin' I never manage to cross ya," Mr. Gerard said.

Even if the cops tracked me down, I'd have a story to tell them. Then again, I doubt they'd have believed me, especially if they found out we had no parents. Well, we did have parents. They just weren't ... available. Permanently, in my dad's case. Honestly, I was still more concerned about social services than even the cops. Most people didn't care about us. Why couldn't social services do the same?

I helped lug some other items from Mr. Gerard's gray pickup truck, mostly boxes of tissues, paper towels, and a butt-ton of toilet paper. What was all the toilet paper for? Dead people had no need of it. Did their loved ones tend to take a shit at the funeral home? Was that somehow part of the grieving process?

"Gerry, if I may trouble you a moment." Delamorte and Mr. Gerard stepped into a room next to the kitchen with a sign stating Private, and closed the door. I was holding a huge box of toilet paper at the time, so I couldn't see inside the room. A moment later I heard a mechanical sound, like some machine starting up. What was behind that door?

I brought in the last of the boxes from the old pickup truck. I was just about to hit the first step on the way up to the porch and heard Delamorte and Mr. Gerard talking. Hoping to get a glimpse inside the Private room, I leapt up the steps, jerked open the door, and kind of fell inside dropping the box in the process. Delamorte had just closed the door by the time I got there.

"Such youthful energy," Delamorte said.

Mr. Gerard held a white envelope stuffed with something. Money maybe? As far as I was concerned, an envelope of cash usually meant something illegal was going down. Was Delamorte secretly selling drugs? Or buying them?

The three of us stood in the hallway just looking at each other. Mr. Gerard jerked his head up, glaring down the hallway. I turned to see Lucy standing maybe thirty feet away.

Mr. Gerard swallowed hard. "Lord Jesus." He backed up slowly, his beady eyes wide.

"You appear to have seen a ghost," Delamorte said.

"You know that woman's unnatural … an abomination."

"I thought you had grown used to having her around."

"Some … *things*, there's no gettin' used to."

Lucy pivoted until she and Mr. Gerard faced each other like gunfighters squaring off for a shootout. Mr. Gerard was the one who blinked. Stumbling, he managed to get turned around completely and nearly ran out the back door. Jogging to his old gray pickup, he jumped in and fired up the engine, pistons knocking. The guy literally burned rubber backing out of the driveway like he was leaving the scene of a

crime. What was it about Lucy that so obviously scared the shit out of him?

Delamorte removed the red velvet cord
hanging in front of the stairs, then looked at me
expectantly.

"Hey, you guys," I called. "Come help
me get our stuff upstairs."

Thomas, looking intrigued, got one of the
boxes of our things and took it upstairs. Jess and
I carried the plastic bags containing our clothes
as far as our bedroom door. Inside, Thomas and
Delamorte were eyeing a dresser that sat
against the opposite wall. How did Delamorte
get that thing up the stairs without me knowing
it? Had someone delivered it?

"Where'd you get the dresser?" I asked.
"Walmart?"

"Hardly, my dear," Delamorte said.
"Over the years I have acquired a few treasures.
I thought you might put this one to good use."

Treasures? Strange word choice for an old
piece of furniture. Then again, hadn't Lucy said
something about him being a pirate? Was the
dresser part of his loot? It was made of light-
brown wood and only as tall as my waist. The
front was curved like waves, each crest a
drawer with a fancy handle. Thomas ran his
hand over the top of the wood.

"This seems like an antique," Thomas
said. "How old is it?"

"Likely in the range of four centuries,"

Delamorte said.

"This thing is four hundred years old?" Thomas asked, clearly amazed.

"Probably not more than three hundred fifty-odd. Belonged to the Sun God himself, I believe."

I had no idea who the Sun God was. I don't think Thomas did either, but he'd never admit it.

"How did you get it?" Thomas asked.

"As I said, I have been a collector of treasures."

"Honestly, we don't have enough clothes to fit in a normal dresser let alone something fancy like this."

"Perhaps we could remedy that at some point."

I stared at him, hands on my hips. "Why you doin' this, Delamorte?"

"You may call me Vic," he said. I waited for him to answer my question.

"Why didn't you just call the cops after I stole those fried pies?"

"In old times, you might have lost your hand for such behavior."

"True," Thomas said. "They used to chop off the hands of thieves."

"Seriously?" I asked. "For a couple of effing fried pies."

Delamorte nodded. "Indeed, for less than that. There are a few instances where notifying law enforcement might be the correct course of action," he said. "And that was not one of them." I couldn't help but agree with the man. In my experience, the cops didn't want to trouble themselves with people's difficulties and a lot of times just ended up making things worse.

Delamorte scrunched up his mouth a little. There was more. He scratched his chin. "Plus, from a purely selfish point of view, it is rather nice for the living to outnumber the dead around here, especially at the end of the day."

It all sounded too good to be true. I suspected Delamorte was full of horseshit about his "treasure," but there was a butt-ton of mystery to the guy. All those closed, forbidden doors and private rooms? Hidden behind one of them, on the same floor as our bedroom, was the device Lucy had mentioned. Then there was Lucy herself, who was strange as hell and terrified Mr. Gerard.

And where was Mom? Should I search for her? If I found her, could we ever be a family again? Like years ago, when Mom was happy and carefree. I doubted it. That life was so long ago. Many hopes and dreams had died since then.

I'd had years to get her to rehab, and I'd failed. Not like I'd failed algebra. It was failing to help her live, failing to keep our family together. And there we were living in a funeral home as a result. It was somehow fitting.

Jess and I emptied out all the trash bags onto the bed and put our clothes in the newly acquired dresser or tossed them in the hall for washing. We dumped out one of the bags and Thomas's Lego spaceship came tumbling out crashing into the wood floor into like a zillion tiny pieces.

Thomas looked stunned at first, and I thought he was gonna yell at me, burst into tears, or throw up. Instead, he pushed his thick, dark hair back with both hands and went to work. He searched over every square inch of the floor, under the bed and in the closet, for the smaller pieces, and brought them over with the rest of the wreck-age. From there it was like watching one of those people solving a Rubik's Cube. You know, the ones that can do it in, like, just a few seconds. Honestly, he moved with more energy, more urgency, than I'd probably ever seen before. It was like he couldn't stand not having ship together.

Within a few moments he had the spaceship rebuilt. Of course, it wasn't the same as before, but he was always revising it anyway. In the end, I think he liked his new creation even better than the old one. It reflected his current way of thinking. When he finished, he placed the little spaceship on top of the dresser, stood back, and sighed in contentment.

"The *Novus Stellar* is restored to its

former glory," he said.

"What's that mean?" I asked. "*Novus Stellar*?"

"It's Latin and means new star."

I started to ask where he'd learned Latin but knew better. He could have picked up the words from anywhere. It seemed like he was born with a Wi-Fi chip in his brain.

"Someday," Thomas began, "maybe in my lifetime, humans will leave this world. I'd like to be one of them. We'll build a new world somewhere. A place better than this. A place that's clean and smells good and is safe for everyone. A place where sickness is rare and people live longer, and don't have to worry about ... anything."

A ray of sunlight shined through the window directly on the colorful ship. Seeing it rebuilt, I felt my body relax. For a moment, the world felt okay.

But would it last?

PART II

The Phoenix

About a week after we'd first arrived at the funeral home, a van arrived one morning to deliver a mass of floral tributes. I'd counted at least four "customers" arriving the past week and seven over the two weeks since we'd made the funeral home our semipermanent home. I mean, the place was kind of crawling with corpses. Oh, yeah, it was creepy, but also weirdly cool. And, there was food and a decent bed that didn't stink of old sweat.

Delamorte was in the middle of fixing waffles but stopped long enough to show the driver where to put the arrangements. The scent of lilies, carnations, and mums blended with the smell of Delamorte's cigarettes, cinnamon, grilled onions, and a hint of garlic. Despite all the dead people around, the aroma of the funeral home was full of life, at least in comparison to our old apartment.

As the delivery guy carted in the flowers, Delamorte sat us all down around the kitchen table for a late morning breakfast and a "talk."

"There are some things we need to work out."

My waffles clumped up about halfway down my throat on the way to my stomach. Would we hear some bullshit about "you scratch my back, I'll scratch yours?" Delamorte had shown no interest in that kind of arrangement. What if he'd had a change of heart? Would it be worth it? Should I be looking for a campsite under some overpass? What did he have in mind? Slave labor? Or something more ... personal.

"Like church, for one thing," he said. Well, that sure never entered my mind.

"Church?" Thomas said, looking horrified. He swallowed hard, maybe trying to keep his breakfast down.

"We will be attending church services every Sunday. I firmly believe it is important that young people receive a spiritual education."

"Spiritual education?" Thomas said. "I believe that is an example of an oxymoron. You know, Karl Marx said religion is the opiate of the masses."

"I recall this Mr. Marx." I had no clue at the time who Karl Marx was or what he'd said about anything. "Yes," Delamorte continued. "My position was that Mr. Marx, though passionate and idealistic, was naïve to the tendency people have to seek out their own individual good rather than that of the collective."

Thomas nodded. "Sounds like a valid point."

"In our only conversation, I told him that it might be different if humans were ants or bees or some other creature with a hive mentality." Thomas frowned. "He accused me of being a corrupt proletariat determined to keep the neck of the working man under my boot."

"Wait," Thomas began, "you're saying you actually spoke with Karl Marx?"

"Indeed. We both served in the Prussian Army briefly."

Thomas cocked his head in disbelief. "But, Karl Marx died like over a hundred years ago."

Delamorte raised his eyebrows. "Be that as it may, and all debates past or present notwithstanding, I think it is necessary to understand the importance of faith in one's life and to develop a spiritual perspective."

Thomas looked at me seemingly for support. I just shrugged at him. "Weren't you quoting the Ten Commandments to me a few weeks ago?" He twisted up his mouth even more, folded his arms, and sat back in his chair. It was as close to a tantrum as my brother could manage. I learned a long time ago the only person to put your faith in is yourself. That's just common sense. Everyone else will let you down or more likely try to take advantage of you.

"What church?" I asked.

"It is called the New Life Church of the Resurrection."

"What's resurrection?" Jess asked.

"It's when you're raised from the dead," Thomas said. "Something that happens in fairy tales ... like the Bible."

Delamorte grinned, his eyes twinkling, like he knew something my brother didn't. "There are more things in heaven and earth than you have dreamt of, my young friend."

If I had to be honest, church might not be so bad. For one thing, I liked the singing. Plus, some of the stories were, you know, damn interesting. Not the ones they teach you in Sunday school, but the ones you read right out of the Bible so you won't fall asleep during the sermon. The ones they don't want you to read.

Like the story where this lady drove a tent peg through some guy's head while he was sleeping. Or the time this one guy shoved a sword into the stomach of this certain king and his "bowels discharged" and the fat closed over the whole damn sword. God, there was no story like a good Bible story.

Dad was Catholic, I think. I had vague memories of going to mass a few times as a little kid, but I usually didn't last the whole time. I'd end up outside, my dad holding me, trying to calm me down. Mom wasn't much of a churchgoer without Dad around, but there were a few times we'd made it to Sunday service. Easter, Christmas. Mom liked to go around New Year's Day, one of those resolutions things, I guess. She was a resolutions sort of person, always saying things would be better next year.

The delivery guy stood in the kitchen doorway. "I need a signature." Delamorte rose from his seat, signed the guy's clipboard, and watched him return to his van.

A couple days before our appearance at church, Delamorte loaded us up in the hearse to go clothes shopping. Most of our clothes were old school uniforms with missing buttons, torn hems, and missing belt loops. Either that or we'd just grown out of them.

I was thinking we'd head to this huge mall over in Mesquite, a suburb east of downtown. They had lots of new clothing stores over there. Was that where we went? Nope. Instead, we went to the goddamn Goodwill.

"The funeral industry not pay much?" I asked.

"Money tends to go much further here," Delamorte said. "Many times I have found very nice outfits for ..." He trailed off.

"For?" I asked. Then it hit me. "For your *customers.*"

"Some are indigent and do not have the means to obtain nice clothes."

"At least we know where we stand," I said.

At the Goodwill, Jess found this white, lacy dress that could have been some little flower girl's dress for a wedding. It was a pretty dress, and I wondered why anyone would want to give it up unless there was some tragedy associated with it and people didn't want a reminder hanging in the closet.

Thomas got a couple pairs of dark dress pants, long and short sleeve button-down shirts, and even a pearly white clip-on tie. One of his long-sleeve shirts was purple, another one maroon. He was just glad he didn't have to wear a white shirt with a black tie. "I do *not* want to look like a Mormon," he said.

Delamorte wanted to buy me a dress. In that way, he was no different from any other guy. All of them, for some reason, wanted to see me in girly clothes. In a dress, it was like half of me disappeared. It was all about how "cute" I looked. No one gave a shit about what I felt or thought. I settled for a couple pairs of jeans and some button-down shirts I found in the men's section.

I decided if I was going to meet a bunch of new people, I probably needed to do something with my hair. It just touched my shoulders and had gotten a little longer and bushier than I preferred. Getting it styled just wasn't who I was. On the other hand, getting it cut seemed like a great idea. I mentioned the possibility of a haircut to Delamorte in the hearse on the way back to the funeral home.

"I believe Lucy could help you," he said.

"Lucy," I repeated. "The beautician ... at the funeral home."

Thomas jerked his head up, looked at Delamorte, and burst out laughing.

"Shut up, T. How'd you like to have your hair done by someone who played with dead people all day?"

"I would have you know that Lucy is very good at what she does," Delamorte said.

Lucy. The creepy person that wandered around the funeral home like a ghost, marking up the faces of corpses, doing God knows what else. The woman with the strange relationship with Delamorte. It didn't matter how good she was at what she did. She was still the hair stylist of the dead.

Then again, Lucy knew something about Delamorte's torture device or whatever it was hidden upstairs. If I could get her talking about it …

"Fine," I said. Thomas looked up at me, frowning, mouth open, shaking his head. "What? You think I'm not open to new experiences? We live in a funeral home for God's sake. Who else is gonna cut my hair."

"That is a little weird," Jess said.

"Not so weird as digging up your dead family and dusting them off, right T?"

"I suppose not," Thomas said. "I'm sure there are plenty of dead things in your hair that need cleaning out."

I wanted to tell him to go fuck himself, but Jess was sitting right next to me. "That'd make two of us then," I said. He ran a hand through his hair, glancing down at his finger-nails when he thought I wasn't looking.

Thomas's words got stuck in my head. What if I *did* have lice or something?

Lucy didn't have any customers to work with that day, dead ones that is. After she stopped by the Preparation Room to grab her black apron and some scissors, we headed down to the kitchen.

Her long silver hair flowed down the back of a close-fitting ruby red satiny dress with a slit up the side. The dress had kind of a collar at the top and these super short sleeves that revealed her thin, bare arms. The dress had these white birds — no, dragons — embroidered all over it.

"I like your dragons," I said.

"Thank you," she said. "Some are dragons. The big one in the middle is a Phoenix."

"A ... Phoenix?"

"You've never heard of a Phoenix?"

"I've heard of the city."

"Well, then, let me enlighten you." She stepped back from me, her thin arms falling to her sides. "Observe."

I blinked and squinted. Were the dragons moving? I looked up at her.

"Try to stay focused on the subject," she said, looking down at her own dress.

The dragons hovered over the Phoenix, spewing out streams of fire that set it blazing. The bird turned up its head, and I could literally hear screeching from all around me like I was in some theater watching a horror movie. I started to cover my ears, but the bird was quickly silenced, its body reduced to a gray pile. The dragons landed, then surrounded the remains of the Phoenix.

The dragons lifted their wings and began fanning the ashes until they rose up spiraling into a single column. In moments, the ash took the shape of a huge bird. As long plumes of feathers emerged from its body, it spread its wings and let loose a powerful ear-piercing scream that I was sure would wake all the dead in the funeral home as well as those in the cemetery across the street. The dragons bowed down to the enormous bird.

"Quite a tale, wouldn't you say?" My mouth hung open. I had no words. "Out of the ashes, something greater shall emerge."

Staring at the bird, I felt a strange combination of emotions. Fear, then grief and finally a joy that left me wanting to shout. I blinked a couple of times until I was able to take my eyes off the Phoenix spread across the front of Lucy's red dress.

"What kind of dress ... is that?"

"*Cheongsam*," she said, fast enough I didn't hear all the sounds clearly. "Traditional Chinese evening dress. If one must wear clothes, one might as well look good."

The way she spoke reminded me of Delamorte. I looked again at her dress, waiting for the intricate designs to move again. But they remained motionless on the rich red cloth. I'd hallucinated things before. Shadows mostly, but also my dead dad. Were the animated designs on Lucy's dress just another sign of being mentally screwed up?

Lucy had me sit in a chair she'd pulled from around the kitchen table. "I am having trouble remembering the last time I worked with a living person. At least, in this manner."

I wanted to keep staring at the Phoenix on her dress, but she moved around behind me so I couldn't see. She cracked her knuckles, then fluffed my hair with her hands. After a moment, I felt her fingers massaging my scalp. "Do you do that to the corpses?"

"This? No, there is no need."

My head cooled, like I'd stuck it in the freezer while searching for loose ice cubes. It felt kind of nice at first, then it started burning. "What are you doing?"

"Just taking care of a few strays."

"What?" Stray what? *Shit, were there actually lice?* Thomas could never find out. I'd never live it down.

"There, I got them all. Nothing survives my touch."

"What?" What did she mean? What did she do to my hair exactly?

"Not to worry. I can titrate the dose, as it were."

"Tight ... what?"

She ignored my question. What the hell was she talking about? I wished I had a mirror so I could see what was happening up there.

"What would you like today?"

At that moment, I couldn't think about anything but the Phoenix, Lucy's icy touch, and the lice corpses infesting my head. What was I supposed to say? I had no idea what I wanted. I mean, other than to be bug-free.

Lucy paused to put on her black apron. She guided me to the sink where I leaned forward on my elbows, my head under the faucet. The sink had one of those sprayer attachments, which Lucy used to wet my hair. I watched in horror as an entire village of little black dots littered the bottom of the sink. Damn, it was so embarrassing. I'd been walking around sharing my head with a gillion of those tiny little shits for God knows how long.

Lucy attacked the mop on my head with brush, yanking and jerking until the tangles straightened out.

"Do you ... ow!"

"My apologies, dear. I, myself, am

insensitive to pain, so I tend to neglect the fact that … others are rather slaves to their pain receptors."

What the hell was she talking about? Another jerk to my head rattled any further questions out of my brain. "Do you … wash … corpses' hair?" I managed to say, despite the assault taking place to my head.

"On occasion. It is necessary if they are to look good for their people. Dying can take a toll on one's hair, blood, sweat, that sort of thing. Death can be a fairly arduous process at times. Other times, not so much."

It seemed that everyone in the funeral home knew a shit-ton more about death than I did. But, did I need or want to know any more about dying? At some point, everyone stops moving, breathing, thinking. The whole concept seemed strange, even impossible. Surely, some part of a person continued after the body died. I'd seen no evidence of that, but it was hard to imagine a person completely ceasing to exist.

After washing and combing my hair, Lucy sat me down in one of the kitchen chairs, wrapped a white towel around my upper half, pinning it shut in the front. After a moment, clumps of my hair were dropping lifeless onto the kitchen tile.

Good riddance, to the lice, to the shitty place that gave them to me, to the whole fucking mess. I was finally free from that little dim, gray cave of an apartment, free from its stink, the oily grime covering every surface, the residue of countless other people.

I still had no idea what was going to happen to us at the funeral home. For a moment, though, I felt a few old worries come loose from their semipermanent places in my mind. No doubt, we were cursed bad luck. But, at that moment, I felt a little bit lucky. Like finding a twenty-dollar bill in the street lucky.

When she was done cutting and had dried my hair, Lucy offered me a hand mirror. The back of my neck felt chilled, as did my ears. They probably hadn't been that bare since I was a toddler.

"You look a bit like Mr. Barrie's Peter Pan, if you ask me. Rather like a pixie."

Well, that was probably the first time someone had used the word "pixie" to describe anything about me. Being a tall beanpole didn't exactly produce that kind of impression. As I examined my hair, Lucy's expressionless face appeared next to mine in the mirror. A chill ran down my back.

"Do you like it?"

I nodded. "Oh, yeah."

Lucy undid the towel from around my neck. "Perhaps we can add some finishing touches another time."

I stepped out of the kitchen and over to a mirror hanging in the hallway. A blood red blur passed behind me as I stared in the mirror. Was that Lucy? The way she moved was so damn weird, like some kind of magical creature. But, magical people didn't exist. Did they?

"Wow, Callie!" Jess said, coming up to me. She put both hands over her mouth and giggled. "Your eyes," she said. "They're so big."

I stared at myself in the mirror. Dammit, it was true. Having less hair made my eyes stand out, but it also made my mouth seem even more enormous than it normally looked. Crap! I'd been so preoccupied with my lack of hair I'd ignored what was left behind.

My face.

The New Life Church

It was Sunday, the day we were supposed to be carted off to church for our so-called "spiritual education." I leaned closer to the mirror over the bathroom sink upstairs, horror gripping me around the throat. My face looked effing humongous. I mean, it was carnival funhouse messed up. The excitement of my new haircut evaporated like a drop of rain on a hot summer sidewalk.

My forehead, the way it stuck out over my eyes like eaves on a house. And that bend on the bridge of my nose. Had I broken it somewhere along the way? Did one of Mom's boyfriends smack me in the face once and I just blocked it out? It was certainly possible.

Thomas once said some people were part Neanderthal. You know, their genes and all. Did I have an extra amount of caveman DNA? Honestly, that would actually explain a lot about my behavior. Like the number of fights I'd been in or how angry I seemed to be all the time. Were cavemen naturally angry? Or was it just because of all the crap they had to deal with back in the day. Then again, I was probably just brain damaged. I'd inhaled enough shit living with Mom for that to happen.

The worst thing about seeing my face exposed was I'd done it to myself. I'd told Lucy exactly what I wanted. It was like some monkey's paw wish. I'd gotten what I'd asked for but with some bizarro horror twist. God, what had I been thinking?

There was nothing I could do to change anything about the way my face looked. It was bad enough I was about to be dragged into a building full of smiling Jesus freaks, but I was going to have to walk in there looking like Frankenstein's monster.

Thomas passed by the bathroom door.

"How do I look?" I asked. "Do you think my mouth looks too big?"

"It's an objective fact you have a big mouth."

"Thanks, T. And fuck you, too."

For a split second, he looked shocked. He dropped his eyes to the floor and marched off down the stairs toward the kitchen. I fought off a twinge of something. Regret? Maybe he didn't deserve that last part. He was kind of mindless at times, but he was one of the few people I knew who wasn't really an asshole.

A minute later, Jess hopped up to the door. She spread the hem of her new dress out a little and swayed from side-to-side. "How do I look?"

"Like a princess," I said.

She beamed. "Which one? There's like a thousand."

"Is there one with curly red hair and blue eyes?"

"Yeah, but I'd need a green dress and a bow and arrow to look like her."

"I doubt they allow weapons in church," I said.

"Yeah, probably not." She started to go, but stopped. "I heard what you said to Thomas." Yeah, I definitely shouldn't have said that last part to my brother. "Why do you swear so much?"

I looked around the bathroom as if trying to find an answer to my sister's question. Why did I swear so much? It was usually due to some situation that sucked, but not always. Honestly, at that point in my swearing career it was probably a lot of it just habit.

"I don't know, Jess. Words just … come out sometimes."

She cocked her head at me, then hopped off downstairs leaving me to stare at myself in the mirror again and grimacing at all my flaws. In the mirror, a form materialized behind me. Wearing his dark Marine dress uniform, crew cut hair, hands folded in front of his shiny belt buckle. Stern looking at first, like in his photograph.

"Hey, Dad."

He'd appeared to me before from time to time. I'd come to accept his occasional visits. It was the best I could hope for in terms of having a dad. He seemed more real than usual that morning. He had more depth to him, like he was more than just a memory of a photograph.

"What do you think?" I asked.

I didn't expect a response. My imaginary dad never spoke. I wanted so much for him to actually be there. What would he think of the daughter he'd left behind? Would he have thought I was pretty? Or that I looked too much like a boy? What would we have said to each other?

His face took on a strange blank look. He stepped closer, which sent my heart flopping around in my chest. He normally stood still, well, as a photograph. Something was weird about this version of my dad.

"You look fine, my dear."

I didn't remember how my dad's voice sounded and had relied on my imagination to create that part of him. But his voice was not remotely like the one I'd manufactured for him. It was, however, familiar.

"Lucy?"

A smile flickered on his, or apparently her, face. The apparition blurred and vanished, reappearing a moment later in the hall just outside the bathroom door. It was still my dad but with Lucy's voice.

"Victor has not told you everything."

"What do you mean?"

"You should be prepared. What he has to say is not like anything you can easily imagine."

With that, my dad's form blurred, and

vanished into the shadows of the dark hallway. Had I imagined the whole thing? Maybe it was just my mind reminding me Delamorte had his secrets. Either that or I was just going batshit crazy. My money was on the latter.

I'd made it to the bottom of the stairs when the back door opened and in stepped Mr. Gerard carrying a cardboard box of God knows what. He looked up, saw me. "Oh," he said, then swallowed hard. Obviously shocked, he moved around me with the box and headed down to the Preparation Room.

"What?" I asked. "You never saw a girl with short hair." He ignored me.

In the kitchen, Lucy, dressed in a full-length emerald-colored dress, sat at the table sipping on a cup of something. Her long silver hair hung over one shoulder and was gathered in her lap like a sleeping cat. I glanced at her outfit for any sign of dragons, birds or any other wildlife with a story, but found nothing but shimmering green fabric. I could, however, feel Lucy's icy blue eyes gazing at me.

Thomas and Jess sat across from her eating some pastry thing. Delamorte leaned against the kitchen sink.

"You look very nice, my dear," Lucy said with a slight nod. "Especially that haircut."

She spoke as if she hadn't just appeared to me upstairs in the form of my dad, reinforcing my concerns about my mental state. No way was I going to say anything to anyone about it. That was probably a sure way to end up in the psych hospital.

"Would you like a profiterole?" Delamorte asked.

I stared at him. Was there, in fact, something he hadn't told us? What could it be? Something about himself? Us? Why would Lucy — if that's who was really talking to me upstairs — say anything to me about it? What was I supposed to do with that knowledge? Ask Delamorte? How would I even bring it up?

I noticed Jess had this look of ecstasy on her face, and Thomas was eating with his eyes closed, both seemingly savoring every bite. I didn't even know what a profiterole was. It didn't matter. My appetite was kind of crappy that morning, especially when I was about to put myself on display for a bunch of strangers.

Later that morning, Callie Valentine and her entourage made their first appearance at the New Life Church of the Resurrection. It was the first time I'd been to church in years and was a little rusty as to how to act. I just hoped I wouldn't do anything real obviously wrong, like pick my nose or fart. Swearing seemed more likely.

At church, they had a band on the stage in the main auditorium, which was a little different and kind of nice.

"So, what kind of church is this?" I asked Delamorte.

"Unitarian Universalist." Whatever the hell that was.

The band played mostly rock songs, none of which I recognized. Later, the band members returned to their seats with the rest of us, and we all sang together. No instruments, no choir, just the voices of other humans. There was no mention of Heaven or Hell in the songs, not once were the words God or Jesus uttered, nothing about sin or sinners. All or most of the words expressed appreciation for the beauty of the world, an encouragement to live in kindness, or both.

It was a lot different from other churches I'd been forced to go to. The ones with the helpless looking man with the beard in the painting over the baptistery. I swear, if Jesus ever looked that pathetic in real life no one would have followed him. God, what an emo.

The preacher was a woman, maybe my mom's age. She wore a loose button-down blouse and blue jeans. She had red, almost orange, hair. Mom's hair had been red before it turned completely white and she'd started dying it black. The pastor's hair was trimmed to her neckline and styled in a way that looked like she'd gotten up late, headed out the door, and wandered through a windstorm in the process of getting to church.

The pastor read a scripture or two from the Bible, recited some poems and song lyrics and something from a book with a title I couldn't pronounce. One thing she read from that book talked of happiness and distress being like winter and summer. As in, they were temporary. Along the same lines, she followed that up with a Bible quote about there being a season for everything.

The whole thing was like mixing religion and rock music, along with stuff I'd read in my high school English class. Despite my worries about being in the same room with a bunch of weird ass religious idiots, I actually kind of liked it. At least there was none of that "everyone is guilty and going to hell" bullshit. I already knew I was guilty of a lot of crap and didn't need anyone else reminding me about it.

Thomas sat a few feet away from me, head down, arms folded, drool-leaking-out-his-mouth unconscious. My brother could fall asleep anywhere. It was another one of his superpowers. At least he wasn't on the verge of throwing up. Jess, on the other hand, was wide awake, looking around at the people, smiling. Unlike myself, she actually enjoyed people and seemed to be soaking up the positive vibes from the service. Good! She craved that sort of thing and was getting filled up.

Based on what the pastor said, many of the good church people thought of God as a mystery or life spirit or something like that. Not some angry old guy throwing shade down on everyone from his throne in the sky. Knowing that, I felt less judged. And, I'd totally forgotten about my huge face.

After the service, the preacher came over and introduced herself. "I'm Melissa Priest, pastor here at the New Life congregation."

"Great name for a preacher," I said, trying to blink some focus into my eyesight.

"It does rather cover more than one base." She grinned. It was a sincere smile, like she was enjoying some humor with me. Her smile reminded me of my mom.

I once had a little wallet-size photograph of my mother smiling. I didn't know the occasion, but she looked so innocent and carefree. As if she was full of joy about life. Whenever I felt disgusted with her, I pulled that picture out of the only family album I had, the one in my head. It reminded me it was Mom, not just some shriveled shell of an addict. Thinking of it at that moment, I felt an ache in my chest. Grief, I supposed. Mom didn't deserve the things that happened to her.

The pastor's flaming orange-red hair was partially tucked behind ears that seemed slightly pointed. In that way, the pastor looked part Vulcan or fairy ... if those things were real. Up close, her red hair had streaks of gray suggesting she was maybe older than she looked.

"You have some of the most beautiful eyes I have ever seen," the pastor asked. "Are they from your mother or from your father?"

"My mother's eyes were blue," I said. "My father was Latino. His eyes were brown."

"I see," she said. "How are your parents, dear?" I knew she meant *where*. Why did people have to be so damn nosey? Who cared if we didn't have parents? What angle was the preacher lady going for? Was she planning to call social services? Shit, I didn't even think about that. Going to church was like inviting do-gooders to come mess with our lives. Delamorte probably never even considered that. Or maybe he did. Was the whole goddamn church thing a setup? All the good feelings I'd gotten from the service evaporated like my breath on a cold January morning.

"My father died when I was five." I didn't say anything about Mom. That was a place I definitely did not want to go. Delamorte was watching me carefully.

"Do you remember him?" the pastor asked. I was not expecting her to ask that. Most people would just say they were sorry for my loss.

"Some," I said. "Mostly just from a picture of him." And my repeated hallucinations of him, but I didn't say that either.

She nodded. "Is there anything I can do?"

"Not unless you can raise the dead," I snarked.

"I have mostly involved myself in burying the dead," she said. She glanced at Delamorte who'd been listening to the whole conversation. "That's generally where people need my assistance."

I glanced over at Thomas. He looked at the pastor, then down at the floor. He'd lost a dad just as much as I had. Jess fiddled with the food on her plate. She never even knew her dad.

The pastor continued: "I asked if you remembered your father because sometimes when we lose someone we love, it's like losing part of ourselves, like an arm or a leg. If you don't remember much about your father, perhaps you experience your grief a bit differently."

I never thought of it like that, especially with my dad dying when I was so young. I guess in my case it was more like growing up never knowing what it was like having an arm or a leg.

But what about Mom? She was gone, but I had no idea what happened to her. Was I a bad person for feeling more relieved than sad? Relieved to be out of a place that had no food and stunk like a porta potty in August.

I appreciated the pastor's words but

wondered if she was acting solely out of compassion. I imagined there might be people like that out there in the world, ones that actually cared. But there were too many people whose so-called compassion was just a mask. A way of hiding who they really were and what they wanted. Just a trick to con people.

As soon as we got home from New Life, I put on a T-shirt, blue jeans, and cross trainers. Jess similarly shed her dress in favor of a pair of shorts and a tank top. As she was changing, I noticed what looked like an old profiterole stashed in her dresser drawer. "You saving that profiterole for hard times?"

Without saying a word, Jess reached down, slid the drawer shut, turned and marched out of the room. *What the hell?* Was it anything to worry about? I wasn't sure.

The church service had been a welcome distraction, if nothing else. But, later that afternoon, Lucy's words came back to me. What secrets was Delamorte keeping from us.

I stood in the hallway staring at all the closed doors. Was there anything behind them I needed to know about. A meth lab? Honestly, the Preparation Room seemed a more likely candidate for a meth lab than the room upstairs. Did Delamorte have a pornography warehouse somewhere? Was he secretly a gun nut? And what was the device I overheard Lucy mention the other day?

Distracted by lice and Phoenixes, I'd forgotten to ask Lucy about what supposedly lay hidden just a few steps from our bedroom. So, I decided I needed to do a little surreptitious exploring around the funeral home. Yeah, I used Thomas words sometimes.

I wandered toward the end of the dark wood-paneled hall and placed my hand on the doorknob. I didn't expect it to be open, but it was unlocked. I took a breath and eased open the door.

Still gripping the doorknob, I squinted at the contents of the room. Best I could tell there was furniture, bookshelves, ornate frames, and some rugs rolled up against one wall. Sculptures, piles of books, a rack of old clothes, a dining table. The room was just a big closet full of old junk. My eyes scanned for anything that might be a "device," but there was no machinery or anything that looked mechanical.

What I did see off to the side sitting on two wooden sawhorses was a large oblong box. I went over to get a closer look. A little longer than I was tall, the container had a lid that was raised kind of like some of those silver covers on the hot food bins in my school cafeteria. The thing was entirely black and was shaped like a diamond but with the ends flattened.

The more I looked at it, the more the box

looked familiar. Then it hit me. It was a coffin. I mean, it had to be. Could it somehow be the device Lucy mentioned?

A voice behind me boomed. "This room is off limits."

Closed Doors

I literally jumped like three inches off the floor. I turned to face Delamorte who'd apparently snuck up behind me.

"What are you doing in here?" He spoke slowly, emphasizing each word.

After a couple seconds of stammering, I remembered why I had violated Delamorte's rule about not entering closed doors and was standing in that room.

"Wha ... what is that box?" I asked.

"It is of no concern to you."

"What's in there, your dead mother?" I have no idea why I asked that. It just sort of popped in my head and was out my mouth before I thought. Delamorte frowned at me. "Okay, is that the device thing Lucy was talking about?"

He rolled his eyes and sighed. "As I said, it is nothing of any concern to you." He moved closer. "Stay out of this room. Do I make myself clear?" His tone was close to angry. I'd not seen the man angry before and wondered why my seeing a bunch of old furniture would get him so upset.

"Sorry," I said, walking past him out into the hallway. "I was just looking around, getting my bearings." *Finding out if you had a meth lab or a porn library.*

"It is important you respect my wishes in

this regard."

"Well ... sure," I said. "I guess, whatever."

I slid past Delamorte, headed for the staircase. Adults and their stupid rules irritated the hell out of me. Then again, I thought—no, I knew—what lay behind certain doors could unleash nightmares almost beyond imagination.

Downstairs, I marched past the kitchen and headed out the back door to the big, warm outside. Standing on the porch, I stretched and scanned the area behind the funeral home. I could make out a rectangular patch of ground with withered vines clinging to several poles at one end and other dead vegetation scattered at random over the rest of the space.

I had many questions about our new home. What exactly did Delamorte do in the Preparation Room when the door was shut? Was that dark coffin thing in the Forbidden Room the mysterious "device" Lucy talked about? What was it for? And, finally, had there once been a garden behind the funeral home?

* * *

A couple days after I'd gone exploring the Forbidden Room at the end of the hall, I stood outside the Preparation Room. I could have just accepted what the No Admittance sign said and walked away but, as I may have mentioned, I had a thing about knowing what was behind closed doors. Mostly who was behind them and what they were doing.

Jess walked up behind me. "It says not to go in there."

"I'm just taking a peek."

Jess folded her arms and leaned against the wall. "You're gonna get in trouble."

"Don't you have a profiterole to eat or something?" Jess kept silent a moment, then walked off down the hall.

I grabbed the knob and eased open the door. My eyes scanned the room. Inside looked kinda like one of those autopsy rooms on TV shows. The ones with cold storage drawers, shiny silver tables, and bright lights. I looked around. There was a deep sink, some cabinets, cream-colored tile flooring, and, yeah, a shiny metal table.

The room smelled like my high school biology lab where we dissected frogs last year. There were vats of chemicals along one side of the room and a table covered with various instruments that reminded me of things I'd seen years ago in a dentist's office.

A blur of motion and a glint of light to my left drew my attention to that side of the room. Lucy sat on a stool leaning over the head of a body. The corpse lay in a long, gray drawer that extended into the room, one of many such compartments on that side of the room.

Lucy wore a black apron over a turquoise

dress that sparkled like it was covered with glitter. Silver with streaks of darkness, her hair trailed down her back nearly to the floor and seemed to shimmer in the same way as her dress. A bright lamp attached to her head lit up the features of the person she was leaning over. She moved a small brush over the face of the corpse as if painting a portrait. Her mouth hung open over the body before her, as if she'd been sucking the soul from the remains of the deceased.

In a flash, her head jerked up in my direction, the bright light glaring directly at me. Talk about a deer in headlights. I mean, my eyes felt like they were gonna pop out of my head. She looked at me a moment, then redirected her attention to the corpse.

"Does Mr. Delamorte know you are in here?" I stammered, hemmed and hawed. "You need to stay out of here, my dear." I mindlessly nodded, turned, and walked straight into Delamorte who had snuck up behind me.

"If I may trouble you a moment," he said. "We need to have a conversation."

"Told you," Jess said from across the hall. Had she told on me? Jess? She was always on my side. What was happening?

Delamorte lead me to the office and motioned for me to sit down in one of the cloth chairs in front of a loveseat. I glanced out the windows at the hallway thinking Lucy might be going to join us, but no one was there.

It felt like being summoned to the principal's office at school. Delamorte sat down across from me, crossed his legs, and folded his hands in his lap.

"I need to address a few issues that have arisen since your arrival. Upon the occasion of your first visit to this establishment, you nearly entered the Preparation Room. You were advised not to go in that room. That is, in fact, the meaning of the sign on the door. The one with the red letters on the black background stating No Admittance. Now, today, you ignored both the sign and my explicit instructions."

"I'm sorry, but I think I have a right to know what's going on behind all these closed doors."

"Also, recently there was your incursion into the room upstairs." I looked at different parts of the office, file cabinets, the cluttered desk, anywhere but directly at Delamorte. He continued: "That room, as I mentioned, is also off limits."

"Yeah, you've said that now, like eighteen times."

"I am concerned that you will not honor my wishes in this regard." Why was the guy harping on all this?

"The Preparation Room is off limits to you. That is not just my rule, but that of the

Funeral Service Commission. Even the dead have a right to privacy. Plus, there are chemicals in there that are hazardous to the living."

I forced myself to look him in the face.

"I do not like having conversations like this, but it seems necessary if your living arrangement here is to be successful."

Was he really going to make a major thing of it? "All I did was go in a room."

Delamorte held up his hand as if to tell me to be quiet. "I know you are used to living on your own without a parent in charge telling you what to do."

"So? I don't *need* anyone telling me what to do." Especially someone who was half-awake or high all the time. Turns out, I didn't need anyone like that at all. So what if Delamorte seemed to have his act together a little better than my mom or her boyfriends. I was fine all on my own.

He ran his fingers around the edge of his goatee. "You must have noticed that you are not living in the same circumstances as before. Your surroundings have changed."

Yeah, there are a lot more dead people.

He moved his hand around making deliberate circular motions. The guy could have been an orchestra director.

"I have made it clear there are limitations as to what you may and may not do. If you think about it, these limitations are not unreasonable or difficult to abide by."

"Those are just rooms," I said, the heat growing in my face. "There's nothing special about them."

He lifted his head to look at the ceiling briefly, then down at the floor. "I am not going to justify any further my telling you not to enter those places." I opened my mouth to speak, but he held up his hand again. "If speech be of silver, silence is gold." He stopped a moment, then continued: "I need to know that you will not put one foot inside those rooms for the simple reason I told you not to do it."

Thomas drifted by the door, glancing in at me as he passed. At the bottom of the glass window with a view to the hallway, I caught sight of a shock of red hair. Jess.

The conversation with Delamorte was really pissing me off. "You think you got magic? That you can just hold up your hand and I'll shut up? Well, that ain't the case."

He grasped his hands together in front of his chest, looked across the room a second, then whipped his head around toward me. "If you cannot do as I ask, I am afraid I cannot help you."

Jesus, his gaze was intense. Eyes like lasers burning into mine. "What's that supposed to mean?"

He cleared his throat, swallowed hard. "It means we will need to find you other living arrangements if you will not comply with my wishes."

"Uh, in case you haven't noticed, our apartment is gone and so is our mom. You're gonna kick us out now that we have nowhere else to go?

He unfolded his hands and leaned forward. "I am most certainly aware of those facts."

Yeah, but what did it matter to him. He had a permanent place to sleep and we didn't. Or was he just emphasizing that he had us where he wanted us. Was this finally the part he asked for something personal in return for his alleged kindness?

He cleared his throat and looked away across the room again. "Alternative living arrangements might not be so bad as you imagine. I ... I looked into it."

A buzzing wave of ice and heat swept over my head, down my back and into my stomach, launching acid into my throat. I swallowed it back down. Twice. Instantly, all my old worries returned. Was my luck about to run out?

He nodded, but still wasn't looking straight at me. "The homes are licensed and monitored, or at least so they say. You would have regular meals and a bed to sleep in." He looked at me again. What was that look? Was he ... was he ... sad? Or was he just faking it? Did he think I was an idiot? Why would he be sad? We weren't his family. We weren't important to him. I wasn't buying any of that shit.

"The advantage to you living here was that each of you could have continued to attend the same school and live in an area with which you are at least somewhat familiar."

Was? Could have? He said it like we weren't going to live there anymore. Like it was a done deal. I swallowed hard again.

"You're gonna call social services."

Scent of a Ghost

The shock of red hair at the base of the window outside the office retreated down out of view. Was my sister hiding? Served her right. She started this mess by being a little rat.

Delamorte closed his eyes and shook his head. "Believe me, that is the last thing I want to do. It is the conviction of my heart that you are better off living here. But the arrangement must work for all parties concerned. Do you understand?"

I stared at the floor, jaws clenched, fists tight.

"I need some sort of acknowledgment."

My teeth ground together; my breathing rough. It was all I could do to make my head move up and down once. I had just begun to believe Delamorte might be an okay guy. If he was willing to ship us off to foster care over something so trivial as going into a forbidden room or two, then he wasn't such a nice guy after all. That was just logic.

"I am glad that is settled then." I started to get up and go. "There is something else," he said, leaning back in his chair. "I think it would be good if you kept busy this summer and not wander around looking for things to do."

I looked him in the eye again. "What do you mean?"

"I think it a basic rule that if you mess

something up, you be the ones to clean it up. I am referring to your bathroom and bedroom."

If he'd said that to me before he threatened to call social services, I would have thought cleaning up was a fair enough expectation. But because he'd brought up foster care, it felt like he was trying to take advantage of us and order us around like we were his personal slaves. I mean, just because he fed us and gave us a place to sleep didn't give him the right to tell us what to do. Right?

After our conversation, which I thought was damn one-sided, Delamorte found some degreaser spray and Windex, along with several cloths I decided were old socks.

"We're doing what?" Thomas asked, frowning.

"Cleaning," I said. I tossed him an old sock. He examined it like it was a foreign object.

Jess strolled up from wherever she'd been laying low. "Cool," she said. "I love cleaning. At our old place it didn't really matter cause it was like—" She stuck two fingers in her mouth and made a gagging sound. I tried to scowl at her, but couldn't quite manage it. Why had she told on me? Was it because of my profiterole comment?

Thomas looked around like someone was going to give him the punchline in a joke. Did he think I was kidding? Realizing I wasn't, he examined the old sock.

"These clean?" he asked.

"As far as I know," Delamorte said, then sniffed one. "I would say enough for our purposes."

As irritated as I was about the events of that whole morning, cleaning wasn't so bad. Delamorte didn't have a damn TV and I'd been bored out of my mind. As justified as I felt about opening all the doors in the funeral home, I also thought maybe cleaning was a way to work my way back into Delamorte's good graces. Plus, I was actually pretty good at dusting and shining things.

I succeeded in not getting into any more trouble over the next few days. But chores weren't the only thing Delamorte had in mind for us. He was increasingly all up in our business and started telling us when it was time to go to bed. "You have been staying up too late. I was up one night and could hear you talking and laughing. It was nearly two in the morning."

This, of course, flew all over me. "In case you hadn't noticed, we don't have school in the summer. So there isn't any reason to go to bed early."

"Regular people do not stay up all hours of the night."

"If you didn't go to bed so early —"

"Eleven o'clock is late enough. I expect you to be in bed by that time with the lights out."

"You know what? Fuck this shit." I went to leave, but Delamorte interrupted.

"And that is another thing. Your language. I am aware that many swear. Indeed, I have heard swearing that would make your ears bleed. But, there is virtually always a more eloquent manner of expressing oneself."

"Whatever," I said, and basically stomped off. I'd talk the way I wanted. As far as staying up at night, I was the one who got everyone to bed and up in the morning long before Delamorte ever showed up on the scene. If that wasn't enough, the guy started telling us when to take a bath or shower. This didn't seem to bother anyone else, and looking back it wasn't an unreasonable request. Then again, I was sixteen years old and could make up my own mind when to bathe. Now that there was no school, I just didn't need to wash so much.

Who did Delamorte think he was? Our parent? God? How much was I willing to put up with to avoid foster care?

Jess avoided me the next few days. She pretended to be asleep when I went to bed and was always awake and downstairs by the time I woke up. I made it a point to check her drawer one morning. Not only was there the profiterole, but one of Delamorte's croissants and something that looked like a fried pie. What was she up to? Stockpiling food in case of the apocalypse?

I woke up one night a few days after my so-called conversation with Delamorte. A summer wind was blowing, the funeral home creaking and cracking. None of us had ever been in foster care. Maybe it wasn't that bad. Then I remembered a kid at school, the only one I'd known who'd been in the system. He said he hated it and never stopped wanting to go home. I asked how he got in foster care, and he told me his stepdad was a "paranoid ass tweaker."

"A what?" I'd asked.

"A tweaker, you know, a meth head."

He said his stepdad liked to talk about the government spying on everybody and was all the time accusing his mom of "screwing around." His stepdad would beat up his mom and sometimes would beat him up too if he got in the way. How bad was foster care that a kid would rather deal with that crap every day?

What if, when social services came to collect us, we didn't all go to the same place? What if they separated us? Sitting in bed, it started to feel like I'd swallowed a rock. There had to be some way to live on the streets or out in the country, somewhere social services wouldn't find us. I took a deep, shaky breath.

I thought we had some family out in California. I didn't know if they were grandparents, aunts and uncles, or some third cousin in a trailer park. Mom had no contact with any of them, at least not during my lifetime.

I sat up in bed, my heart pounding. After a moment I noticed another part of my body was also throbbing. I started to put my feet on the wood floor but stopped short, feeling strangely aware of the number of dead people that passed through the funeral home.

Did any of their spirits linger? Were there literally ghosts hanging around downstairs? If they heard me walking around up on the second floor, would they decide to drift up through the floorboards and bite at my ankles trying to drag me down with them?

Full of the courage that comes with needing to pee, I leaped into the middle of the floor hoping to surprise the ghost creatures by landing in the middle of the room instead of right next to the bed where they undoubtedly lay in wait.

A light shone from under Delamorte's bedroom door. He had some balls telling us to be in bed early when he was still up. I guess he went to his room early but didn't go to sleep right away.

I did my business on the toilet then stood in the hallway near Delamorte's bedroom. I heard soft music and low voices coming from his room. One belonged to Delamorte, the other sounded like the beautician, Lucy. Were they more than business acquaintances? I mean, she was in his bedroom late at night. I thought of all the shit I used to hear going on in Mom's bedroom late at night. The groaning and moaning, the thudding and rhythmic bumping.

I stood just outside Delamorte's door.

"It's a matter of months, maybe less." The voice was Lucy's. "And ... you know, I have an affinity for knowing these things."

There was a sigh, Delamorte's I assume. "I am most aware of your affinities and would admit the timing is poor."

There was some inaudible mumbling, then Lucy's voice spoke: "That Mr. Gerard is about as reliable as sand."

"He has his utility and has been with me for many years."

"Will you place your life in his hands?"

What were they talking about?

Lucy continued. "The girl is still your backup plan?"

"It is my sincere hope not to involve the children."

Backup plan for what? Was that what Delamorte hadn't told us? Some purpose he had for us? So, he intended to use us after all.

Their conversation took a backseat to the pungent odor tickling my nose and burning the back of my throat. The smell of a ghost from my past.

Weed.

An Empty Shell

The next morning I came downstairs to find my brother and sister sitting at the kitchen table with Delamorte. No Lucy, though. It was Sunday and I assumed she was off that day.

The kitchen smelled of toast, warm butter and something fruity and sweet. And really strong coffee. Delamorte held one of those tiny little cups sipping whatever the stuff was that dribbled out of the fancy, shiny machine with all the buttons and spouts and levers at the end of the kitchen countertop.

Thomas and Jess sat on either side of Delamorte eating some fat little pastries called beignets. Undoubtedly, I'd find one of those little fat pastries in Jess' dresser drawer later that day. Small jars scattered across the table offered different jams and jellies. Each jar had a tiny silver spoon stuck in it, and there was some seriously yellow butter on a rectangular glass plate that had its own lid. I couldn't remember if I'd ever had real butter. Growing up, we'd only eaten some pale mystery spread from a plastic tub. That shit seemed to last forever in the fridge.

"Can I have some milk?" Jess asked.

Delamorte immediately got up to get her some from the fridge. Real parents didn't do that crap. They'd tell you to get up and get it yourself. Delamorte was being totally unrealistic. Then it occurred to me maybe that was why Jess had told on me. To get special favors from Delamorte. She was still a little rat if that was true, but at least it was strategic. She was getting something out of it.

When Delamorte wasn't getting them stuff, it was like he enjoyed just watching my brother and sister eat. The man was really getting into the parent thing. Cooking, listening, driving us places, or just ... being there. I mean, it was hugely annoying knowing he was just trying to set us up to use for some purpose.

I wanted to say something about the weed I smelled the night before and I wanted to do it in front of my brother and sister. They needed to know Delamorte probably wasn't any better than our mom's druggie boyfriends.

"Hey guys," I said. "Guess what?"

Thomas and Jess looked up at me from the kitchen table, as did Delamorte. The morning sunlight from the window shone on the faces of my brother and sister, and for a moment they looked almost angelic. I stared at them, my mouth moving like a puppet's but with no words coming out. "Uh," I grunted.

God, they all looked so damn ... happy. Saying anything might destroy all that. I'd tried to shield my brother and sister from as much shit as possible, but they'd still had too much disappointment in their lives. Even if their contentment was based on ignorance, I didn't want to take that away from them. At least, not until I had to.

"Never mind," I said. I felt more queasy than hungry and decided to skip breakfast. "I'm gonna take a walk."

"When will you be home?" Delamorte asked.

I added that to the long list of things that irritated me, asking when I'd be back if I so much as stepped out onto the back porch. "Jesus, I'm just going across the street. You could probably see me if you looked out the front door."

Delamorte scrunched up his mouth. I sighed as loud as I could and aggressively rolled my eyes. "Maybe an hour." He nodded. Fuck him.

I wandered around the cemetery enjoying the semi-cool morning. It was mostly old people buried there, but every now and then I'd come across a kid or someone else strangely young to be lying under some stone marker.

A blackbird fluttered up and landed on a stone figure of a cherub a few feet away. Hopping a couple of times, it faced me and cawed. "Good morning," I said. It swiveled its head side-to-side in a jerky motion, its shiny eyes merely dark wells on either side of a beak bent slightly at the tip. It angled its head down as if looking at the head-stone where it sat. It marked the grave of a girl almost my exact same age. I squatted down close enough to read the inscription: "Taken too young."

No shit.

The blackbird cawed repeatedly. "Fuck off," I said. The bird flew off cackling. Bastard piece of shit. What did I ever do to it?

Back inside the funeral home, I looked for Thomas and Jess in the office. But they weren't there. I jogged up the staircase, pausing just as I got to the second floor. Peering into our room, I saw a pair of legs, Delamorte's, extending toward the end of the bed. He was on my side of the bed, no less.

Stepping into the room, I saw Jess sprawled across the end of the bed, head propped up on one arm. I started to freak out until I heard some familiar words. Those of Dr. Seuss from the book *Oh, the Places You'll Go.*

> ... I sat on our dirty mattress, my back propped against a patch of sweat-stained drywall. Our bedroom door was barricaded by our dresser and a pile of dirty clothes, a single dim bulb in a tiny shadeless lamp our only light.
>
> I held a picture book in my hands. Jess burrowed up next to me on one side, Thomas on the other, I read one book after another until they were asleep. If their eyes didn't close with me reading, I

would sing a lullaby our mom used to sing. I mostly hummed it because I couldn't remember all the words.

Once they were asleep, I slid down the wall until my head lay on the pillow. Staring at the popcorn ceiling, listening to what was happening in the bedroom next to us and hoping my brother and sister didn't wake up ...

I walked into our bedroom, calmly took hold of the book, and slid it from Delamorte's hands. Jess sat up and looked at him, then up at me with her big blue eyes. Delamorte's hands hovered in the air a moment as if still holding the book, then he folded them in his lap.

"That's *our* book," I said, my voice scratchy and rough.

"I asked Vic to read to me," Jess said. *Vic?*

Delamorte got up from the bed and moved past me into the hallway. He spoke, mostly over one shoulder. "I apologize if I stepped on any toes." He coughed a little, went to the bathroom, and spit something into the sink. He acted like I'd upset him. Had I overreacted? Was that regret I felt? Guilt? I shook it off.

I sat down on the bed next to Jess. Thomas appeared in the door, shaking his head. "What are you doing?" he asked. "I mean, other than being your usual jerk self." He must have heard the whole thing.

I set the book down on the side table. "Do you really trust him?"

"Is there a reason not to?" When he wasn't acting completely dense, another one of Thomas's irritating habits was to answer my questions with his own questions.

"Doesn't it bother you the way he tells us when to go to bed or when to take a bath? It's not like he's our parent."

Thomas tilted his head a little. "In case you haven't noticed, our parent hasn't been around for a while." God, he was so matter-of-fact. Did he never miss Mom?

"Yeah, but why do we even need one?"

He spoke, shaking his head. "For one, we've got a place to sleep. Another thing would be food. Vic cooks" — he paused to look at the ceiling — "amazing things." I rolled my eyes. The Vic thing again. "He lets us live here, even if it is a funeral home. He takes us places, buys us stuff."

I'd known for maybe a year or two that my brother secretly hated me, but he never said anything. Now that we were living with someone else, he apparently felt, what's the word … empowered to say whatever he thought.

Honestly, Thomas's words stung. I'd spent most of the past three years or so doing the shopping, cooking, cleaning ... stealing, for all of us. If we'd had any money at all, I could have easily kept doing it. Minus the stealing, of course. Did Thomas just not see what I'd done? Did he not appreciate it?

"You like cleaning that much?" I asked.

Thomas continued: "Are you blind? There's nothing he's said or done or asked us to do that's been remotely unreasonable."

I spun around, my legs hanging off the bed. "It's like he's taking over Jess. Can't you see that?"

His eyes narrowed. "What I see is that logic is a foreign concept to you."

I stood up fast, Thomas taking a step back. "Screw logic, I'm talking about reality here."

He swallowed hard, like he was trying to keep his food down. "You only do what you want!"

"Fucking hell, you just have no clue, do you? *Everything* I do is for us! My life would be so much easier if I didn't have to—"

Worry about you *guys.* But I didn't say it.

I had spread my arms wide to make a point and had kind of frozen in that stupid pose. My heart was pounding, my eyesight blurring even more than usual. Thomas, looking a little alarmed, took another step back into the hall. I swallowed hard, wincing at pain in my throat and elsewhere.

Jess's little voice came from behind me. "Why are you so upset? Was it because I told on you?"

I turned to see her contorted face. "Mom's gonna come back for us," I said. "We'll have a new place to live. Everything will be better." I yelled at Thomas, who was maybe halfway down the stairs. "No Delamorte, no rules, just us, our family."

Thomas moved back up the staircase a few steps. "Look, you can believe whatever idiocy you want. Just don't mess things up for the rest of us." He hurried back down the stairs.

"You mean for *you*," I yelled. "You're a selfish little shit."

Thomas coughed a couple of times. Had I made him sick? Good! I meant everything I'd said, or at least I thought I did. Hearing it out loud, the truth of my words melted away like ice cream in the park in July. I didn't blame my brother for running off. I was about to better my own record for the amount of sheer stupidity expressed in a single conversation.

I turned to face Jess again. She looked up at me, her eyes moving from side-to-side scanning my face. "How come you don't like Vic?" I leaned against the door frame, slid down to the floor, and sat there. "He's a nice guy," she said. "He really is."

"He put you up to this?"

She frowned at me. "You think I'm just a

dumb little kid and can't figure things out for myself? You think I'm stupid just like Thomas thinks you are."

"Wait, what?"

She marched into the hall. "I'm not stupid. I know what's going on." She disappeared down the stairs. My little sister had always supported me in everything. Had she given up on me? Like everyone else.

"Jess, I ... I didn't mean it like that."

In the hallway, staring down at the bare wood floor, I reflected on what I'd managed to accomplish: Push away the two people I cared about most in the world. As a bonus, I'd alienated the guy who was feeding us and giving us a place to live. Well done, Callie.

I slipped down the stairs to a quiet Underworld. The grandfather clock ticked ceaselessly. Delamorte's voice rumbled from the office. Thomas' voice whined from approximately the same location. I supposed Jess was in there also, all of them probably talking about what an idiot I was. So what? Let them talk. I headed out the back door and onto Evergreen Road.

It was like a half-hour walk to our old apartment. I went down a side street or two, not worrying too much about whether it looked safe. Not that I could see any signs of trouble without my now long-gone little kid glasses, the ones I'd lost during my fight with Pete.

I hopped a chain link fence that ran along the alley in back of our apartment complex, and stepped onto the faded, crumbling blacktop next to a trash dumpster. It'd been weeks since I'd bloodied Pete's face, and I wondered if the little shitball was still up there on the second floor hoping one day to catch sight of me. Pressing my body against the side of our building, I peeked around the corner up at the second-floor landing. No one was there, and no telltale wisps of smoke coming from the breezeway.

I looked around for a piece of wood or something I could use as a weapon in case I ran into good-ol' Pete. A large tree branch lay against the building, but it was too big, too obvious. What I needed was a baseball bat or my trusty box cutter.

With no bats or blades available, I stepped out into the open space of the parking lot with nothing but my hands and feet to defend myself. That was all I had the last time I'd met up with the resident shithole.

The wind picked up swirling trash around, and lifting sand and dust into the air and my eyes. I rubbed them with my hands and kept going. Alert for the sound of doors opening, people coughing, or concrete rumbling, I eased across the asphalt toward the stairs.

The cars in the lot were the same. The

same dents, the same windows busted out and covered with cardboard. Some of them hadn't moved from those spaces in months, maybe years, and were covered with the same dust.

A gust of wind pushed me to the side. Squinting, I looked up at a pale brown sky. For a moment there, it was like a full-blown dust storm. Grit covered my sweaty face and arms.

Keeping my eyes on the door to Pete's apartment above, I set my foot on the first step of the concrete steps. Birds cawed overhead as I moved silently toward the second-floor landing, a big part of me wondering what the hell I was doing. The door to Pete's place was shut, and there were no beer cans or smoldering cigarettes. Maybe Fat Jesus had kicked him out. I grinned at the thought of Pete living in a tent under some freeway.

I relaxed a little once on the third-floor landing. After a few steps, I noticed the door of our old apartment had a crisscross of yellow plastic tape. It was like what TV cops used at a crime scene, except this tape didn't actually say crime scene. What else could it mean, though? Did something happen there after we were gone? Mr. Gerard said the TV was gone. Had there been a break-in? Was Mr. Gerard the reason for the tape?

For some reason I decided to knock. I didn't know who I expected to answer. A ghost maybe? The landing vibrated as a set of footsteps bounded toward the door. My heart skipped a beat.

Was Mom home?

Dying Young

After a few moments, I realized the sound had come from the apartment across the breezeway. Directly behind me a little kid's voice mumbled something from the other side of the door. A slightly deeper voice spoke, then silence.

I felt let down, sad even. Did I miss Mom that much? I might have felt that way when I was younger, but certainly not lately. Not until that moment.

It was weird staring at the door of our old apartment. My brother and sister weren't inside. Realization dawned that this place wasn't our home anymore. It was nobody's home. Just a vacant cave, an empty shell.

I felt hollow, like an empty box of Cheerios on a hungry morning. I longed to be with my brother and sister. I wanted them to crawl all over me, to feel their bodies pressing against me like they did when we were little. But there was no doing that anymore. They probably wanted nothing to do with me. No matter what I'd done for them.

It wasn't fair. What had I done to deserve my wonderfully shitty life? Was I that bad of a kid that my life had to be so cursed?

Dad didn't have to go to Afghanistan. Why didn't he just stay home? With all of us? Maybe then Mom wouldn't have abandoned us. Forgot she even had kids. Left me in charge of two littles.

"How could you do that?" I said it out loud, to no one. "Leave your kids."

Leave *me*.

As I tiptoed down the stairs, the wind painting my skin with filth. The familiar image of my mother popped into my head. The one that always came to mind when I was angry or disgusted with her. The one with her smiling so carefree and innocent.

Whatever relief I felt being out of that apartment was washed away by a wave of sadness and grief that balled up under my ribs. There was something else mixed in with that sad, empty feeling. Guilt.

Sure, I took care of my brother and sister, but I'd also taken care of my mom. What if I was the one who abandoned her and not the other way around? I'd never even considered that as a possibility, not until that moment. Did I leave Mom behind? A wave of nausea oozed from my stomach up into my throat.

I stared at the concrete. A little black beetle made its way through a crack in the sidewalk. A horn blared, I blinked a few times and forced myself to move.

It must have been pushing a hundred degrees outside, but it felt more like two hundred. My throat felt scratchy and sweat trickled down my back. Damn, was I getting sick? My throat went from scratchy to sore in just a few minutes. I felt lightheaded, enough that I saw little dots. I leaned over until they went away. What I really wanted to do was lie down somewhere. Lie down and not have to get back up.

I head back the way I'd come. The wind died down a little, but the dust lingered in the air. Shuffling along the sidewalk, I came to an overpass across Old Home Road. Grateful for a place to rest, I leaned over the rail and watched the blurry cars below. Coming, going. They had real lives. Whatever life I had was missing so many pieces it was hardly recognizable as a life. My existence was like so many disconnected scenes from a movie. None of it had any meaning or made any sense.

I waited until the street was clear below, hocked back snot, and spit it off the overpass. One-thousand-one, one-thousand splat. Less than two seconds. It wasn't so long to wait if a person were to fall. Or jump. Not like leaping off a tall building or, God, falling out of an airplane. You'd have to wait so long. Like minutes or something.

What would you think about on the way down? Would you, like, try to fly or something? Would it hurt when you landed? Would you die instantly? Or would you pass out on the way down and not even be awake for the big moment? Whatever it was that had been you smashed into some mush inside your skull or splattered in the middle of some field out in the wilderness where no one would ever find you.

Or miss you.

"It is only a little ways down."

The voice was Lucy's. I turned to see, not the elegantly dressed funeral home beautician, but my dad in his Marine outfit leaning on the railing. "Hard to predict what would happen if one were to ... fall."

I glanced down at the dark asphalt street. A wind gust sandblasted my back and shoved me into the railing. It would have been easy to just keep going, over the guardrail and down.

I looked back at my dad or whoever it was haunting me on the overpass. "Why are you here?" I asked.

"Sometimes things happen, perhaps things one did not intend. I must be there when they do." A blackbird fled up and landed on the railing between us. "Ah," Lucy in the form of my dad said. "Someone has a grudge."

Car brakes squeaked. I turned to see a tiny, bright yellow Fiat pulled up next to me on the overpass. The window rolled down. I frowned and blinked until Pastor Priest came into focus behind the wheel. But, for a good second or two, I had thought it was my mom in the driver's seat.

"Looks like you could use a lift."

Her words shocked me a little. Did the pastor know what was in my head? I glanced back at where my dad had been standing but saw no one. Yep, I thought. I was without a doubt batshit crazy.

I climbed into the passenger seat without really thinking about it.

"Just out for a walk?" the pastor asked.

"Yeah, maybe, I guess."

The pastor's little yellow car had what could best be described as an altar on the gray dashboard. A small Buddha surrounded by fake flowers and plastic green vines occupied the space directly below the rearview mirror. Did she pray to it while driving? Was praying while driving worse than texting while driving?

"You don't look so well."

I leaned forward, holding my face in front of the air conditioning vent. "I'm okay," I lied. Truthfully, I felt like shit. "You ever go along in life believing something, then realize it was really all bullshit?"

"Hmm. All the time actually."

"What do you …?" I couldn't think straight enough to even finish the question. What was the question?

"I normally relish those moments. I rather dislike living a lie. I much prefer a truthful existence."

Truth pretty much sucked. So, my brother and sister didn't look up to me as much as I thought. They saw me as just another problem in their lives. Maybe they always had.

Talk about living a lie. Had I been in denial that much to not see what they really thought of me all those years?

Looking over at the pastor, I couldn't get past how much she looked like my mother. Was that what Mom might have been like if so much shit hadn't happened to her? She'd been my age when she'd popped me out. Had I just been part of the shit in her life? Just another reason she ended up an addict? Vague nausea derailed my thoughts.

"If I may," the pastor said. "You seem to be an angry person."

Jesus, where did that come from? "Is it that obvious?"

"I understand such things," she continued. "I have experienced many things in my life, many of them unpleasant. Some of them were quite destructive and painful, leaving me full of rage at both myself and others."

Studying the pastor's face, she didn't appear angry. She had the same placid look as when she delivered her sermons. "You don't look angry."

"I have found peace, but it took many years to do so and, as Paul said, the path was long and winding."

"Paul? From the Bible?"

"No, McCartney." She paused, then added: "The Beatles."

"I know who Paul McCartney was." My words carried more irritation than I felt, at least about what the pastor had said.

Peace was one of those words that had long ago ceased having any meaning for me. For me, it was mainly just a sound.

"If I may ask, what were you doing on the overpass back there?"

Nosy lady. I had no idea how to answer. It was a developing situation. I just shook my head. It was the best answer I could come up with.

At church the next day, the air conditioning must have been broken because it was hot as our old apartment with the windows shut and the oven on. I was sweating like some Rottweiler had been chasing me. It didn't seem to affect Pastor Priest. She calmly, peacefully, delivered her message as usual. Not that I heard any of it. My head felt thick, my brain foggy. I couldn't focus enough to make sense of a two-word sentence.

When the pastor was done, she yielded the podium to the song leader. On cue, everyone rose and started singing. I stood but felt dizzy and sick at my stomach. Fuzzy dots appeared and disappeared in my vision like bubbles in a grape soda. I swayed with the singing, but at some point, I just kept swaying and fell over into Delamorte. He guided me onto the pew like he was laying me down in the grave.

That was the last thing I remembered.

My body rocked back and forth. Three guys to my right, three to my left. Was I dead? Were those guys my pallbearers? Where were Thomas and Jess? And why was I awake if I was dead? Wasn't death supposed to be black nothingness? No awareness of anything anymore? If I was dead, it was a damn disappointing experience.

I thought I heard the voice of Pastor Priest mumbling something. The guys carrying me stopped and Delamorte appeared. A couple of my pall bearers let my legs and feet down while the others kept me propped up like a mannequin. Then, Delamorte and some other guy helped me into the hearse, which was appropriate since it felt like I was dying. Jess sat next to me in the middle of the front seat. Thomas got in the very back of the hearse and sat cross-legged as far away from me as possible.

Once back at the funeral home, I opened the hearse door and sat there a moment trying to find some energy. Eventually, I swung my legs around onto the driveway and tried to stand up, but it seemed like the world had tilted. I took a step forward, went off-balance and stumbled off to one side like I'd stepped in a hole.

I steadied myself enough to squat down on the driveway, my head down, almost between my legs. If I'd tumbled over, it would've been better than passing out standing up and doing a face plant onto the concrete.

On top of the dizziness and not being able to keep my balance, I felt sick to my stomach. God, I hated throwing up. By the time Delamorte got around to my side of the hearse, I was on all fours retching.

"We must get you inside," Delamorte said.

I let him help me to my feet, then drew my arm around him just to hang on. It felt weird touching him, feeling the muscle in his back, the warmth radiating beneath his slightly sweaty shirt. His scent, cinnamon and cigarettes, was strong. Jess tried to help, but I warned her off. "Stay away, Jess. You don't want what I got."

Thomas wasn't a concern as he'd exited the hearse through one of the side doors and gone straight inside as soon as Delamorte turned off the ignition. For him, I was just something to be avoided.

Inside, I got as far as the stairs, then sat down leaning my forehead on my knees. "Give me a second," I said.

Delamorte stood nearby, observing me. My stomach felt a little better, but I still teetered

on the point of gagging. My head felt thick and
heavy, like it was going to fall off my shoulders.
After a few moments, Delamorte gently took
my arm to lift me up. I was afraid to stand,
thinking I'd puke, so I shook him off. I turned
and began to crawl up the stairs on my own.

I made it to the hallway, paused to rest,
then just kept crawling across to our bedroom.
Delamorte and Jess both followed along, ready
to help if I asked.

I let the others steady me while I literally
climbed up the side of the mattress and into bed
still in my church clothes. How long did it take
to die? I hoped not long.

I fell asleep almost immediately. When I
woke up, my nose was stuffed up and my
throat felt like it had something growing in it.
Even my ears were clogged, especially my right
one. It felt like someone had me in a headlock.

One of the church members, who was a
doctor, examined me. She said I had this weird-
ass inner ear infection. Secretly, I suspected it
was due to some bug crawling in my ear back at
our old apartment. I imagined a creature with a
zillion legs laying its eggs deep inside my head
and they'd all hatched and were trying to get
out.

Getting sick was the stupidest thing. I'd
lived in a smoky little rat hole for months, slept
on the veranda sometimes, inhaled mold,
mildew, and all kinds of shit, got lice but

managed not to get really sick. I'd moved into some place with a decent bed and started eating regularly, and my health had gone to hell. It seemed I was dying from the poison of good food and the curse of continuous nights of uninterrupted sleep. So much for good luck.

My condition wasn't getting any worse, as in I apparently wasn't dying. I decided I was mostly glad about that. But I also wasn't getting any better. I'd be lying in bed feeling halfway decent, then dare to lift my head up. That was all it took for the world to start spinning and the nausea to lay me out flat again hoping I'd have time to lean over and throw up on the floor and not in the bed.

I tried to crawl to the restroom by myself once but barely made it across the hall before spewing whatever liquid I'd been able to keep down across the *dulce de leche* colored bathroom linoleum. Delamorte found me asleep on the bathroom floor in a pool of my own snotty-looking puke and helped get me back into bed.

If I thought about it, I'd cover my face with the sheet to keep from contaminating the room. Jess and Thomas both slept elsewhere instead of in the room with me so as to avoid catching whatever shit I had. I tried to force myself to worry about where my brother and sister slept but ended up drifting off to sleep.

Once or twice I'd wake up to find Thomas staring at me from the hallway. God, he could be such a little freak. Was he hoping I'd die so he'd be free of me? Jess, too, sometimes hovered outside my door. She didn't come inside, but I could see her legs extended into the hall where she sat reading.

Day after day cars and groups of people came and went. The sounds of murmuring, occasional sobbing, and soft music drifted up from the Underworld. There was one time I was so out of my head I thought I was the one who had died, and everyone was downstairs mourning me. I felt like a spirit hovering in the funeral home somewhere as people gathered in the Slumber Room to bid me farewell. I had no idea who those people would be, though, as I had no family or friends other than my brother and sister.

Sometimes I'd hear Thomas, Jess, and Delamorte laughing downstairs like some big happy family. Thomas could certainly live happily without me. Jess could make friends with anyone and do just fine. She knew how to get what she wanted. Thinking either of them needed me had just been another one of my many delusions. This should have upset me, but instead all I could feel was relieved. I hated myself for feeling that. Was I abandoning them the way Mom had done to us? Thinking that, I fell asleep.

I dreamed my mom was calling me. I wasn't sick in the dream, so I got up out of bed and followed her voice down the hall to the Forbidden Room. I searched for her in weird places like a goblet on the dining table and behind paintings propped up in the room. At one point, I noticed that the ancient black box, the one that looked like a coffin, had the lid off. Inside lay Delamorte, arms across his chest, his eyes closed. I walked over and his eyes popped open.

"Look in there," he said, his eyes gesturing behind me.

I turned around and was in the Preparation Room looking at a set of cold storage drawers. Lucy appeared in her long red dress with the Phoenix and pulled open the drawer. Inside was my mom, eyes were open, her face frozen with the same expression I remembered from the photograph. Smiling, simple and innocent. She was also, I knew, fairly dead.

Was she? Dead?

Cookies and Caskets

I thought my imaginary dad might visit me in my sickness, but he never did. He was the body part I didn't remember having. One I apparently didn't need. Or did I? I had no idea what having a dad would add to my life. Maybe he would have been a jerk. Or maybe he would have been just as much an officer and gentleman as he looked to be in his photograph. I decided I didn't much want to stay angry at my dad, you know, for dying. He was just trying to provide for his family in the best way he could.

The last two times I'd seen my dad, my crazy mind had dreamed up Lucy's voice for him. Where had that even come from? Why would I imagine Lucy talking through my imaginary dad? Something about that bothered me. But I couldn't figure exactly what it was.

* * *

It seemed like every few minutes Delamorte came in carrying a tray with some water and a bowl of clear broth. With the same care he used in cooking, he fed me sips of the broth.

"We must try and get your strength up," Delamorte said, repeatedly.

I hadn't bathed in over a week, and my short hair was more or less a mat of grease plastered to my head. I stunk of residual puke and old sweat over layers of even older sweat.

My own stench made me sick to my stomach. Delamorte started bringing up flower arrangements and leaving them in my bedroom. Honestly, I didn't mind. The smell of roses, lilies, daisies, and irises beat the hell out of fragrance *de* Callie.

Lucy came to visit me. She had on the black apron, like she'd just come from the Preparation Room. At least, I thought she was wearing the apron. It kind of seemed like she was wearing all black, right down to the gloves she had on her hands. Then again, maybe my eyesight was as shitty as the hearing out of my right ear, which was damn near nonexistent at that point.

"You're not afraid of catching this shit?" I asked.

She smiled, but only a little and out of one side of her mouth. "No chance of that."

Was she immune or something? Honestly, I didn't care. She unzipped a bag she had brought in with her, one of her black gloved hands pulling out a comb.

"No," I said. I was too weak to protest any more than that.

"Relax," she said. "Everything is cleaned and sanitized, by my touch if nothing else." That icy cold touch, freezing the lice on my scalp.

"Ti ... trate," I mumbled.

"Of course, my dear." She smiled again,

this time more fully as if she were genuinely amused. "Of course. It is not your time, and I know these things."

"What do you mean? Were you, like, a doctor in another life?"

"Not remotely," she said, matter-of-factly. What the hell did she mean by that?

She sat on the bed next to me and proceeded to comb my hair. "You will be fine," she said. "You, like the Phoenix, shall rise again and be transformed."

"Transformed? Into what?"

I literally blinked and Lucy was gone. Had she ever actually been there? I touched my hair, enough to tell it had been combed. The woman was damn good at disappearing. I mean, I was good at hiding, but not totally disappearing. I was a little envious.

* * *

I had little to do lying in bed day after day except think about things. Lucy's visit reminded me of the night I'd smelled Delamorte's weed. She'd asked Delamorte if I was his backup plan. I was too preoccupied with smelling his weed and hadn't stuck around to hear his response.

I'd suspected Delamorte of having some agenda inviting us to live with him. Was I right? Was he going to ask me to do something for him? Lucy apparently thought so. Back when I had my fresh haircut, Lucy had said Delamorte's request would be something, how did she put it, beyond my imagination. I mean, she'd been nothing but kind to me. Weird, but kind. She seemed to be a responsible ... person, and was an excellent lice killer. Lucy knew what Delamorte was going to ask, but she didn't seem all that worried about it. Did I have any reason for concern?

* * *

I woke up from a nap one afternoon to find Pastor Priest sitting in a chair by the bed. She was wearing a loose-fitting dark green button-down blouse over her jeans. Up close, her red-orange hair had a little silver in it but still looked as if she'd been through a tornado. Even with crazy, flaming hair, she reminded me so much of my mom.

She fiddled around in her bag and stood. Pulling out some herb-like leaves, she stuffed them in what looked like a tiny teacup. She snapped her finger and a little smoke rose from the herbs. She must have had a butane lighter or something to start the herbs burning. I couldn't see anything like that in her hand though. She pulled out a red candle from her bag and set it on the bedstand. After a moment it flickered to life. I still didn't see a lighter.

"Did you, like, just conjure flame?"

"Possibly," she said. "Or perhaps it's merely a self-lighting candle."

"A what?"

She rubbed her hands together. "Among other things, I am a practicing witch."

Great. Ghosts and corpses and one strange beautician had been part of my life for some weeks. Now witches. What next? Zombies? Vampires? Yeah, it was bizarro. But what about my life wasn't? I knew for a fact it could have been worse because it had been. At least up until recently.

The pastor laughed. "That's for healing," she said. "And some other things."

"Like what?" I asked.

She sat on the edge of the bed. "Our lives are not so dissimilar, Callie Valentine. I grew up in a home torn by anger, violence, alcohol and drug abuse. I lived with a relative or two, then ended up in foster care. I was fortunate. Someone found me, a wise woman who taught me much of what I know about how to live. She, too, conjured flame. Not of the candle, but in my heart. She was my resurrection and light. I left all of my past behind, as if I'd climbed in a rocket to a different world. To this day, I am amazed and very grateful for that escape. Now, I seek to help others do the same."

She stood, her hands folded in front of her. "You have friends here. Your task henceforth is to accept the help that is offered. If, that is, you can find it within yourself to do so." I nodded. I knew she was probably talking about Delamorte.

"How did you do it?" I asked.

"Do what?"

"Find peace."

She tilted her head, her forehead wrinkling a little and her gaze more distant. As if she'd retreated somewhere, some place long ago. Her pleasant expression dimmed, but only for a moment. "I may have mentioned it was a long, winding road. But, the secret for me was forgiveness."

"You mean, like from sin?"

"Perhaps, though not in the sense many tend to use that word. More like evils, injuries, both those done to me and those I did to myself. I had to find a way to forgive myself and others. And that was not an easy task to accomplish."

I thought of Mom and her many boy-friends, Pete, guys in the neighborhoods where we'd lived. People who'd hurt me and would have hurt Thomas and Jess if I hadn't gotten in their way. One of my frequent fantasies was bashing one of Mom's boyfriends in the head with a baseball bat. No, forgiveness would not be an easy task at all.

"Forgiveness," I said. "That's like kind of an unnatural thing, isn't it? I mean, especially when you know the person who hurt you would do it again and again if you let them. They're just that much of a piece of shit."

She smiled her peaceful smile. "Truly, the world would likely be a better place without certain people in it. But, short of murder, there is often nothing we can do to remove the affliction of their existence. The best we can do is remove ourselves from their sphere of influence."

Murder, I'd honestly considered. More than once. But I never could see a way to do it that wouldn't blow back on me, on us. The pastor's eyes met mine. I wondered if she knew what I was thinking. "We must survive first," she said. "Then we can prosper. I don't mean in that typical capitalistic, I win, you lose, eat or be eaten, everyone out for themselves sense of prosperity. I merely mean living at peace, with yourself, with others, with the world around you."

It sounded like a fairy tale to me, which made sense. Pastor Priest seemed a little like a fucking fairy godmother. "One thing more," she said. "Your brother cares very much for you. He's spent most days out in that hallway, reading, but also keeping an eye on you."

"Seriously? I thought he'd be glad to be rid of me."

"He may be angry with you at times, but that doesn't mean he doesn't love you. You're his family, he knows that. For those starved for love, a little attention and encouragement goes a long way."

She grinned, held out her hand, palm up, thumb and forefinger pressed together, then blew on it. "Blessed be."

Maybe it was her strange way of waving goodbye or maybe she was performing some kind of spell. "Blessed be" sounded like something positive.

* * *

Between the candle, the blessing, and maybe my immune system, after nearly two solid weeks of lying flat on my back, I could finally sit up without my head spinning. Jess noticed my upright position when she brought me a cup of water one morning. "Hey, you're sitting up."

I nodded. "So far, so good. No puking at least."

Delamorte and Pastor Priest walked up. They'd come from the direction of the Forbidden Room. What had the pastor been up to down the hall? Why did she get access to that room and not me? Did she know something about the casket or whatever the *device* was supposedly hidden there?

"Glad to see you are well," the pastor said. She glanced down at the candle and little teacup she'd left next to my bed.

"Yeah," I said. "The herbs, the blessing."

"No, my dear. The healing power was in you all along," she said.

Thomas came to stand in the doorway, his patented ear-to-ear grin plastered on his face. What was he so delighted about? "I see reports of your death were exaggerated," he said.

"My death?" I asked.

"We were looking at caskets for you online," Thomas added, grinning.

"We?" I asked, looking at Delamorte.

"Okay, so mainly me," Thomas said. "I couldn't decide if you'd look better in pink or silver."

He seemed genuinely happy to see me feeling better, so I played along. "God, anything but pink. Silver ... better yet, black."

The pastor mumbled something to Delamorte and went downstairs.

"I'd like the pink one," Jess said. "What color do you want, Vic?"

"None of the above."

"You mean just toss you in the ground and cover you with dirt," I said.

"Hardly, my dear. In the unlikely event of my permanent demise, I would prefer to be cremated and my ashes scattered to the four winds. For now, though, I am pleased we all can hang onto the miracle of life a while longer."

Lucy peered around the corner where she'd apparently been lurking in the hallway. She leaned one shoulder against the door frame, her arms folded. I couldn't see what she was wearing.

"Life's less a miracle than it is a fragile anomaly," Thomas declared. "On the other hand, death is the dominant force, the natural, normal state of entropy, disorganization, chaos."

"God, Thomas," I said. "How do you get up in the morning?"

He grinned. "Hey, don't get me wrong. I celebrate my fragile anomaly."

"What a perceptive boy," Lucy said. "He is quite delightful, Victor."

Delamorte closed his eyes, shaking his head slightly. Thomas ignored Lucy, same with Jess. For Thomas, that was normal, but Jess? She was glad to see most people, but at that moment she didn't give so much as a wave in Lucy's direction. A weird thought occurred. What if my brother and sister couldn't see Lucy? Was she, like, a ghost or something? No, I decided. Ghosts couldn't actually touch you. Could they? Let alone kill your lice. Lucy's form seemed to blur, and she was gone. Maybe I still wasn't right in the head.

My belly felt hollow as a chocolate Easter bunny, and I decided I might could eat something. That is, something besides the broth Delamorte had been feeding me.

Delamorte named off different foods, most of them fancy French things he cooked. I kept refusing everything, then out of the blue it hit me. "You got any vanilla wafers?"

"I will shortly," Delamorte said. He pivoted and marched downstairs.

"Just the ones from the store," I said. "You don't have to make them yourself."

"As you wish," he said.

"And some really cold milk," I shouted. "With ice cubes."

"You may be assured ..." His voice faded as he marched out the back door to the hearse.

I thought about asking Jess if she had any of Delamorte's pastries stashed in her dresser drawer. I decided not to bring it up. She had her reasons for hiding food.

Thomas lingered around the bedroom door, looking up, down, all around.

"What?" I asked.

"Oh, uh. Nothing, just ... I'm glad you're better."

Well, that had to be the first time Thomas had ever said he was glad about anything that had to do with me. What had gotten into him? I started to reply, but my brother had raced off down the stairs God knows where.

When Delamorte returned, I downed the entire box of vanilla wafers and most of the milk in the refrigerator. It was just cookies and milk, but it might as well have been a pepperoni pizza.

I was able to get up and walk around that day, but I had little strength, no endurance, and my hands shook. I had to sit down a couple of times going both up and down the stairs. I got dizzy taking showers, and going outside in the summer heat sucked away all my energy within seconds. So, I mostly stayed indoors.

After a few days I could make it up and down the stairs without resting and was able to eat most of the foods I'd eaten before I got sick.

Turned out Jess and Thomas had been sleeping across the hall in a tiny room, or maybe it was a small closet Delamorte had cleared out. When I got well, Jess moved back in with me. Thomas liked the closet just fine and chose to make it the only room he'd ever had that was his and his alone.

The room was about three times as long as it was wide, and the ceiling was angled downward on one side, but there was enough room for a twin bed at one end, a chest of drawers at the other, and a small desk with a chair in the middle. On one corner of the desk sat the Lego spaceship, the *Novus Stellar* as Thomas called it. At least he had a little space to himself where he didn't have to deal with his big sister all the time. Maybe that would help the both of us.

I thought of him sitting out in the hall during my illness, staring at me. I'd thought he was weird at the time. Maybe he was just worried. Did he care about me more than I thought? He was a good kid. He deserved a mom and a dad, but instead he'd gotten me. I decided I could at least try to be a better sister.

A week or so after my recovery, Delamorte presented Thomas with his own laptop computer. In exchange, Thomas was to tell Delamorte one new fact each day, something he didn't already know. Thomas didn't have to look anything up for his first fact.

"Oh," he said. "Well, did you know that nearly every galaxy in the universe has a black hole in the center?"

"I did not know that," Delamorte said, grinning. He kept encouraging Thomas to tell what he'd learned about space.

Five minutes or so later, Thomas had basically explained the origin of the whole damn universe and given us a description of one way it might all end. "Heat death," he said. "Stars and galaxies won't last very long. Our universe began in a one-second flash and will end in literally trillions of years of nothing but black holes and dark empty space. Compared to the entire lifespan of the universe, we still live in that one-second flash."

Delamorte shook his head. "That is one of the most terrifying, yet encouraging, things I have ever heard. Well done, Mr. Thomas. Well done."

Thomas's grin spread from ear-to-ear.

"It's fairly amazing we exist at all," he said. "I kind of like that."

I had to marvel how he managed to feel so amazed and excited about anything at all. I mean, considering the amount of shit in our lives it would be normal to basically hate everything and everyone. You know, pretty much the way I did.

Would Thomas know as much stuff as he did if our lives had been more normal? Would he have still retreated to the internet? Escaped into his own mind? Maybe he would have had friends, learned to be more social.

Most people my age had best friends or friend groups. Maybe even boyfriends and girlfriends. They hung out at malls, were in some kind of activity together. Church, band, sports ... something. It dawned on me that, if we could manage to keep living with Delamorte, things might be changing. Could our luck be changing?

Were we finally going to have a life?

Mise en Place

Delamorte's rules weren't hard for any of us to follow, even my asshole self. Rules or not, I needed our time at the funeral home to continue. Certainly for Jess and Thomas, but also for me. I had no idea what a normal life would look like. I mean, on TV shows, most kids had at least one parent. So that would be different. Kids usually went to school on TV shows and movies, so that wouldn't change. But they also had friends, maybe were in clubs at school or played sports. All that was a foreign concept. Probably the main thing about living with Delamorte was I didn't want to have to go looking for another place to live anytime soon. Yes, we lived in a funeral home, but it was *our* funeral home.

One afternoon a few days after recovering from my strange ear infection, I was rubbing polish on a Briar Rose lilac-purple deluxe model casket with a pink velvet lining in a French Fold design. The eighteen-gauge steel reflected the ceiling lights at just the right angle to make it seem like the casket was surrounded by a bright halo.

It was work I'd come to enjoy. With the polish Delamorte provided, I could make the metal caskets in the Showroom shine like chrome wheels on a low rider. By the time I was done with them, people might decide they needed one. You know, for their home décor.

I felt prickles on my neck.

"Victor would like a word with you."

I nearly jumped into the Briar Rose. I spun around and found Lucy staring back at me. I might have been good at hiding, but Lucy defined stealth. I mean, she could creep up on a person and totally take them by surprise. Her voice was like someone had mounted a speaker inside, not just my head, but with every cell in my body.

My skin was still crawling as I followed Lucy into the hallway, past the grandfather clock with the swishing pendulum, and down to where she stopped just outside the kitchen. She cocked her head toward Delamorte who was arranging some items on the countertop.

"Come in," he said. "We have some things to discuss."

I glanced around, but Lucy had vanished. Since my strange sickness, I'd obeyed the rules like I was trying to get into heaven. Had I somehow managed to screw up again?

Delamorte pulled out a plate stacked two levels high with the colorful treats and set it on the kitchen table.

"Would you like a macaron?"

The cookie-sized pastries glistened in light streaming from the window. I grabbed a bright yellow one and took a bite. My mouth exploded with sweet, tangy lemon flavor.

We lived in a funeral home, yes, but one with a French bistro and bakery hidden away in the back. Not long ago, it would have bothered me that our meals were created by the same hands that injected people with embalming fluid. But the truth was I'd never tasted death or some weird chemical in anything Delamorte cooked or baked for us.

"How much sugar you put in these?"

"I believe the term you might appreciate is a butt-ton."

I nearly spit my macaron all over the table. He grinned and handed me a dishtowel. Wiping my mouth, I thought of the times during my illness that Delamorte had cleaned me up. I had to admit I'd been pretty much a jerk to him before I'd gotten sick, but since then I'd sort of mellowed or something.

"You know," I began. "Cleaning up my puke repeatedly ..." I'd started to say it had earned him my trust, but I wasn't quite ready to say that out loud. It was true, though. I felt differently toward Delamorte after he took care of me that way.

He grinned. "You can believe I have cleaned up much worse."

"Thanks," I said. "It's been a while since anyone took care of me when I was sick."

He nodded, then looked away like he was remembering something. I took a bite of another macaron, a pink peppermint flavored one this time. "What're you making for dinner?"

"We," he said, his focus returning to the here and now. "What are *we* making for dinner."

"You're gonna trust me with cooking something edible? My cooking experience is kind of limited. Like opening a can and pouring it into a pan to heat up."

"How does mac and cheese sound?"

Even with a belly full of macarons, my mouth instantly watered. "Uh, yeah. That sounds awesome."

"Excellent," he said, returning the plate of macarons to the fridge. "Today we shall learn about *mise en place*."

"Meezon who?"

"It simply refers to having everything ready before one begins cooking."

"Sounds kind of like prearrangements," I said.

He jerked his head around to look at me, then grinned. "Indeed, I suppose it is something akin to that in terms of cooking."

Delamorte put a pot of water on the stove and turned on the flame. I helped him set out a bowl of flour, some butter, like, three different kinds of cheese, and milk. When we had everything in place, Delamorte showed me how to make a roux for something called a béchamel sauce.

"As it is with much cuisine, this dish is all about the sauce."

I had just tossed some butter into a skillet when Delamorte cleared his throat and swallowed. "I have always enjoyed having a family."

"You were married? Had kids?"

"I have been married. I have had many children."

Delamorte just stared at the skillet like it was some favorite TV show. "Do not allow that butter to brown. Sprinkle some flour in it."

I did as instructed. Delamorte handed me a whisk, and I mixed the flour into the butter until it became sort of a bubbly gravy.

"Where are they?"

He ran his hand over his mostly bald head and held it there staring at the pan. "They are all gone."

"Gone, like, living somewhere else?"

He blinked a couple of times. "No."

That left only one alternative. Delamorte made a motion with his hand and wrist meant to improve my whisking technique. "There are some parts of my life story ... that are difficult to explain."

Was it hard for him to talk about that stuff? I'd heard a lot of sad shit from Mom's boyfriends. They'd lie to you and, when you believed them, they'd laugh at you for being stupid enough to believe what they'd said.

He glanced at the pan. "Do not let that burn. Pour in some milk and stir like your life depended on it."

I did, while Delamorte dumped a bag of macaroni into the boiling water. I decided it was time to tell a story.

"When I was eight, maybe nine years old, about Jess's age now, we lived in this ratty rent house somewhere up in Oklahoma. Me, Thomas and baby Jess, our mom, and her boyfriend, Robbie."

Delamorte looked me, then down at the pan.

"Robbie seemed okay, at first anyway. He spent time with us some, said he wanted to be like a dad to us. He smoked a lot just like you do, the same stuff."

Delamorte sighed.

"Anyway, late one night when Robbie and our mom were smoking something, he asked me to go out to the store and get him some Cheetos. He gave me a twenty-dollar bill and said I could keep the change if I got back in ten minutes." I paused a couple seconds, fighting back unexpected emotion. "'You scratch my back,' he'd said, 'I'll scratch yours.'"

I could feel Delamorte staring at me, but I didn't dare look up from the pan. I was deter-mined not to cry in front of the man again.

"I got the Cheetos and was running back

when this dark car slowed, and the window rolled down. Mr. Stranger Danger wanted to know why I was in such a hurry, and did I need a ride. I ignored the guy and kept running, all the while hanging onto those damned Cheetos."

Delamorte sighed. He dumped the first of the three cheeses into the pan. I kept whisking away and talking.

"The car stopped, the door swung open. Before anyone could get ahold of me, I ran across the street. I couldn't completely cross because of traffic, so I just walked along on the yellow center line like it was one of those tight ropes in the circus.

"Somebody yelled at me to get out of the street. I thought someone was comin' after me, so I didn't think I had much choice but to run into traffic. I remember car horns blaring, tires screeching. I'm not sure what hit me, but something did. The impact must have knocked me across the street because I ended up on the far sidewalk on my feet screaming."

Delamorte dumped the second cheese into the pan. The whisk in my hand kept moving as if on autopilot.

"People stopped, got out of their cars, all of them coming at me. They didn't know I was screaming because I'd lost the damned Cheetos, not because I was hurt so bad. I spied the orange bag in the gutter, grabbed it up, and ran off before anyone could call the cops or an ambulance.

"I burst in the door breathing hard, and proudly handed over the Cheetos. Robbie looked me over and, instead of asking if I was okay, said 'Well now, it looks like you're a little late gettin' back. You know what they say, no service, no tip.'"

Delamorte dumped the last of the cheeses into the pan.

"The bastard held out his hand expecting me to give him his money. I looked at him, grabbed the Cheetos from the table, threw 'em down and stomped on 'em four or five times. The bag exploded and by the time I was done, there was nothing but orange powder all over the kitchen floor.

"I woke up the next morning on that same kitchen floor, probably right where I'd fallen, orange Cheeto dust all around me. My leg and shoulder ached probably from being hit by the car, and I had this dull pain on the left side of my face. My mouth tasted funny, and I ran my tongue around inside. There was a gap between two of my teeth and a hole in my gum, on my left side of course. Robbie was right-handed."

I paused my whisking, ran my finger over the scar on my cheekbone, then lifted up my lip and showed him the empty space where my tooth should have been. There were more things Robbie, and others, had done to me.

Things I would never tell anyone about.

"I am truly sorry that happened to you," he said. "It is said that what is learned in childhood is like etching in stone." He continued. "It is also said: Write kindnesses in marble, injuries in the sand. Your story is still being written, but it is my hope your life here will be a story written in marble."

Delamorte drained the macaroni, then dumped it into the cheese sauce where I used a large spoon to mix it all together.

"Look, I really don't care what you do in your bedroom at night, just so long as you don't bother us with it."

"I do not intend to bother you more than is necessary. However, I will bother you some. I hope you will count on that as fact."

I nodded. *Rules. Whatever.*

"But you may rest assured," he continued, "that I will never, ever ask you to go out late at night and get me or anyone else a bag of Cheetos."

I managed to laugh. "Okay."

"Personally, I prefer pork rinds, though corn nuts will do in a pinch."

A gentle grin spread across his face. I could have gotten angry with him for what he said, but I knew he wasn't making fun of me.

"So, what now?" I asked.

"Life ... proceeds. We move forward. You as my family, I as yours. Until death parts us."

"Jesus, sounds like we're getting married."

About that time, Jess's face leaned around the doorframe. "I knew you guys would fix things." She'd apparently been sitting in the hallway the whole time listening. If she wanted, my little sister could almost be as sneaky as Lucy. I suspected the Stealth Queen was nearby as well.

Delamorte got some bowls from one of the cabinets. Something he'd said during our office talk a couple months earlier popped into my head.

"That conversation we had in your office. The one about rules." He nodded. "Did you ever have any intention of getting rid of us?"

"Not remotely," he answered. "But I needed you to believe that I might."

"So I would ... behave."

He nodded. "I worried that one or all of you might end up on the streets, shadows in broad daylight. That I could not abide."

Shadows in broad daylight. What did that mean? Something from Delamorte's past maybe? Homeless? Street people? Or, was it something else.

Thomas appeared at the door. He looked back and forth between me and Delamorte.

"What?" I asked. "You never saw a cooking lesson before?" He shrugged and sat down at the kitchen table. Jess joined him.

I served up the mac and cheese for my brother and sister. I was piling a mountain of cheese and pasta into a bowl for myself when Delamorte started coughing and excused himself to the hallway. After coughing for what seemed like several minutes, he strolled back into the kitchen. "Why haven't you gone to a doctor?" I asked.

"I doubt there is anything they can do for me. I have gone in the past, but they have always just given me something for symptoms but never sought to treat the root evil."

"And what is that exactly?"

"It is something I have been afflicted with before and I dare say will have again."

"Sounds kind of like a riddle," Jess said.

"It's not like you got a cold or something," I said. "You've had that cough since we first met. If you've got something really major wrong with you—"

"I do not want you to worry about it."

Delamorte started coughing again, pulled out a handkerchief, covered his mouth, and turned away. I rolled my eyes at him when he was looking at me again. "See, that's what I mean right there."

"I was merely clearing my throat."

Thomas and Jess both stared up at Delamorte. "I call bullshit on that," I said. "You're sick and you have been since we got here. If something happened to you, we'd end up in foster care. So, go see a doctor. Or at least let's go to the drugstore and get a butt-ton of nicotine patches and chewing gum."

"I will take that under advisement."

That pissed me off even more. I would not be dismissed so easily. "You're gonna end up in one of your own caskets before I can graduate and find us a place to live."

All three of them shifted their gaze at me. I wasn't even aware of having that thought before, getting a place to live on my own and taking care of Jess and Thomas. Was that something I could even do? Did they allow kids to do that? Was I really a kid, though? I hadn't thought of myself that way in years.

"Do you want to die?" I asked.

He paused. Too long. *Did* he want to die?

PART III

The Forbidden Room

Time passed differently living with Delamorte. Days, which once seemed unending, turned into weeks. The things I'd had to do at different times of day, like find food or keep watch for whether Mom was bringing home a guy, were no longer important. As in I no longer had to do them. This led to a certain amount of free time, and that led to thinking, wondering.

My chest throbbed with excitement or fear or both as I placed my hand on the doorknob of the Forbidden Room. I thought Delamorte might have locked it after my last trespass. Surprisingly, when I turned the knob, it was unlocked. I decided he couldn't have been all that concerned about nosey guests exploring or he would have locked the damn door.

I'd considered the possible consequences of defying Delamorte's wishes. Consequences wasn't even the right word. That made it sound like I was concerned about being punished. You know, like no TV or getting grounded. Whatever fear I'd had about him calling social services was long since dead and buried. So, given the lack of apparent consequences, I'd kind of had no choice but to check out what was in that room.

What was really at stake was the generally positive relationship Delamorte and I had developed in the weeks since I'd gotten over my sick ear.

On the other hand, the funeral home was my home now. I had a right to know more about it, didn't I? What was the worst that could happen? Another conversation about rules?

Delamorte was preoccupied with a customer down in the Preparation Room and probably couldn't hear what was going on upstairs. As I pushed the door open, the hinges screeched as loud as a car slamming on its brakes just before a wreck. Even if Delamorte couldn't hear me, there was always Jess or Thomas. I really didn't want to involve them in my illicit activity. Neither of them could keep a secret, and Jess had been following me around just waiting for me to screw up so she could tell Delamorte.

Not wanting to create any more telltale sounds of breaking and entering, I slipped through the opening, into a room full of dark silhouettes. Damn, were there no windows in the room?

I left the door cracked while I felt around for the light switch. Flipping it on, I found the room crammed full of furniture as before. There was a dining table with every plate, bowl, and cup imaginable all stacked up on cloth placemats like it was ready for a feast. There were chairs, a couple of couches, lamps, and racks of what looked like Halloween costumes. One corner of the room seemed excessively dark, but I didn't think too much about it. All rooms had shadows and dark places.

A closer look at the "costumes" showed them to be just regular clothes, but from maybe a hundred years ago. Or two hundred. You know, stuff with frills on the sleeves, coats that came down to the knees or below, and pants made of what looked like curtain fabric. I eased one of the coats, a dark blue one, off the rack and slipped it on. It felt heavy, like the weight of it could keep you from flying away in a hurricane.

Conveniently, there was a full-length mirror leaning against the wall by the door. Looking at myself, I thought I could fit in some painting of a bunch of guys signing some important document, like the Declaration of Independence or the Constitution. All I'd need was one of those white wigs.

I kept exploring. Shelves full of books lined the walls and even covered the windows, darkening the room. Stacks of paintings were propped against the bookshelves. Sculptures of heads, torsos, and full bodies littered the floor. There were objects from different cultures, some Asian looking, others more African, and still others I had no idea. It was like the contents of an entire museum had been stuffed into a bedroom-size area.

Something I hadn't noticed before was what looked like portable air conditioners whirring away on different sides of the room, sending what was probably ancient dust flying around tickling my sinuses. I pinched my nose shut, closed my eyes, and silently sneezed. When I opened my eyes, I was staring at the dark, oblong box lurking in the darkness in one corner of the room.

The top of the box was sloped up like a roof with a handle about a foot long centered on a narrow flat top. The container, probably over six feet in length, was covered with rusty metal ribs lined up vertically about every six inches creating a series of panels that framed carvings.

I touched it, then jerked my hand away when static electricity zapped my skin. Undeterred, I ran my fingers over the smooth wood, which felt like it had been rubbed with oil or grease. I stepped back, fingering the sticky substance from the box. It didn't look like the wood had been painted dark as much as blackened or burned. Like it had been through a fire.

There was a section about the length of my middle finger that ran along the top of the box that had pictures and strange symbols carved into it. Birds, people with animal heads, squiggly lines, and other things I had no idea what they were. I couldn't tell if it was some language or just some intricate designs. If it was a language, it was nothing like English.

I felt around for latches or some way of opening it up. A deep voice penetrated the room, freezing me where I stood.

"What ... are you doing in here?"

I spun around so fast it slung my brain against my skull. Dizzy, I staggered a step, then focused. Delamorte stood in the doorway, hands on his hips.

"Um, uh, I ..."

"You know, this is the one room I told you not to set foot in." He didn't seem angry.

"What about the Preparation Room?"

"All right, one of the two rooms."

I started to mention the door with the sign stating "Private" but didn't want to risk further irritating the man. Looking side-to-side like the guilty person I was, I finally remembered my plan if caught. "I'm sorry." I could have and probably should have just shut up. Yet I continued: "But mysteries bother me." I added a shrug as if to emphasize I'd had no choice in the matter.

He looked me up and down, enough for me to remember I was still wearing my Revolutionary War coat. "Have you satisfied your curiosity?"

I looked at each of my arms in the dark blue coat, then around the room. "What is all this?"

"Apparently not."

I thought he would usher me out of the room like the last time. Instead, he cleared his throat and moved closer to where I stood by the dark coffinlike box.

"I heard Lucy say something about piracy. This stuff your past plunderage?"

"What?"

"You know, your loot. Downstairs, in the kitchen a couple months ago. The pirate thing."

"Oh," he grunted. I took note of the fact he did not deny having been a pirate. "No, these are just a few sundry items I have collected over the years."

"Sundry items," I repeated. I'd heard that phrase but damn if I knew what it actually meant. How many years did he mean? Some of that crap looked, Jesus, as old as, well, Jesus.

"What are the air conditioners for?"

"Those devices are dehumidifiers. Most of these objects are quite old and must be kept at a certain temperature and humidity level to keep them preserved."

I looked around the room. "How old?"

He looked off to the side, like he was deciding how to respond. "As I may have mentioned, there are things about my life that I have been reluctant to discuss. The ages of and story behind nearly everything in this room falls into that category. That being said, perhaps now is the time to share some things with you."

"Okay, then. Start with that." I gestured

toward the black box.

He cleared his throat. "That, my dear, is a casket."

I knew it! I was living in a funeral home, after all. Probably a lot of funeral home directors kept caskets hidden in secret rooms. You know, just in case. Still ...

"That doesn't look like any casket I've ever seen before."

He sighed and eased over to the dark box. "It is a very old, very ... special casket." His voice seemed altered. It was like Delamorte had a foreign accent or something and, for a moment at least, I thought a completely different person had entered the room. His fingers caressed the wood like it was an old friend, and I got to thinking it actually *was* an old friend, you know, inside the casket.

Or maybe the yellowed bones of Delamorte's dead mother. Hoping not to get in too much trouble, I'd joked with him about that the contents of the casket first time I'd snuck into that room. But what if I'd been right? Did he visit her at night? Did they have conversations? Was Delamorte actually a big city funeral home version of Norman Bates?

Oh. My. God.

I told myself to calm down. Maybe Delamorte just preferred a vintage model casket and was saving it for himself. There had to be a good, noncreepy explanation for why the guy kept a casket upstairs away from all the customers ... and us.

"What do you mean by special?" I asked. He just looked at me, then over at the dark box. After a few moments, he swallowed a little too hard. What was he not telling me? Was I right to begin with?

"Delamorte," I said, "is there someone in that casket?"

He frowned at first, then seemed to fight off a grin. "Not at the moment."

Okay, that was good to know. "What is that carved on the side?"

"It is, I believe, a reference to an old poem."

"So it's some kind of language?"

"Yes. Those are Egyptian hieroglyphs."

"Like the pyramids?" Were there hieroglyphs in the pyramids? I had no idea. I kind of pulled the idea out of my ass. "What's it say?"

He took in a breath, let it out. Tracing the symbols with a finger, he recited the poem: "What has been, will be again. What has been done, will be done again. There is nothing new under the sun."

He looked up at me. "There is more to it, but you get the gist. In the Bible, it is attributed to Solomon. Some, however, believe it to have been written by the third in a line of Egyptian pharaohs known as Amenhotep more than three thousand years past."

"The casket is that old?"

Delamorte shook his head. "One cannot be certain. It was ancient when it came to me, and that was ... a very long time ago. How it has been preserved this long is a mystery."

"So, what's it for?"

He looked to the side again, contemplating something.

"Is that casket the device Lucy was talking about?" He frowned. "I heard you guys in the kitchen the first morning we were here."

He glanced at the ceiling. "She warned me about ears. Knowing her, she probably knew you were outside listening and hoped to instigate your curiosity."

"What do you mean 'knowing her'? What is there to know?"

"Let us say Lucy is not at all what she appears to be." Delamorte approached me, hands extended. I had no idea what he wanted, but felt no fear of him. Eventually, I realized he was asking for the blue coat. I took it off and rehung it on the rack.

"I will say again that you are not to come in here alone. I am hoping I will need to say no more." He moved to the door, hands folded in front of him like an usher at a funeral. I reluctantly followed.

"So, what you're saying is I can go in here, I'd just need supervision."

He sighed, then shook his head. "You have a way of misinterpreting my words to your own advantage." I failed to see why that was a problem. "You are not to be in this room under any ..." He paused. "Do not go in here unless I specifically ask you to do so."

What did he mean by that? Why would Delamorte ever ask me to go in that room?

The Vinyls

The summer passed like the lazy river at a water park. We planted a garden in the plot behind the funeral home. We, meaning Jess and I. Thomas supervised from the back porch when he could be pried away from his laptop. Tomatoes, squash, green beans, a few rows of corn. I'd never done anything like that before, and was quite proud of myself when the first seedlings jammed their way into the daylight.

About a week before school started, Mr. Gerard showed up with a gift. He stood in the hallway near the office and held out a cell phone. "Almost nearly new," he said.

"For me?"

"Yep. A present from Mr. Delamorte."

"That a Galaxy?" Thomas asked.

Mr. Gerard looked at the device, groaned a little. "I 'spect what you got there is somethin' of a hybrid. Parts of one or 'nuther more or less smashed together."

"Seems there'd be compatibility issues," Thomas said.

"Whelp, it works."

It was no fancy iPhone. Just something to call, text, play some games, get on the internet. You know, basic shit. I admired my almost nearly new phone, the only one I'd ever had. I'd always avoided making friends mainly because I knew I'd probably only be living somewhere for a few months. That, and I didn't really want anyone nosing around into our home situation. Once school started up again, maybe I'd meet people, do some late-night texting or some check out some chat room. Or, maybe I'd make a few TikTok videos. We hadn't had a computer at home for at least a couple years, so I didn't know really anything about making videos. Still, I knew some kids had their own channel. If I could get Delamorte to agree, maybe I could do some shorts on the funeral home industry. Like an expose. Or, maybe just how it all worked. Who was I kidding? Delamorte would never agree to that.

Later that day, I found Delamorte piddling around up in his bedroom closet. The smell of burning herbs and cigarettes lingered around that end of the hallway. I felt a little queasy, the scent taking me back to our old apartment with its dark places and secrets.

"Thanks," I said, leaning my head just past the door threshold.

The room was nearly as messy as ours had been that first night in the funeral home. Scattered about were stacks of newspapers, shoeboxes, some long dead flower arrangements, piles of books, and a few pairs of old shoes. The bed was unmade. It didn't look like anyone else had slept there the previous night. As in Lucy.

Ornate designs were carved into a

caramel-colored headboard that looked at least as old as our dresser if not older. Had it belonged to the Sun God also? I made a mental note to ask Thomas to look up who the hell was the Sun God. It sounded like some Egyptian dude.

Behind me, opposite the bed was a table, upon which sat a set of small drawers that reminded me of those old card catalogs they had at some school libraries. The ones that couldn't afford many computers. I checked to see if Delamorte was watching, then opened one of the drawers to find a bunch of little cards. Each card had the name of some object on it, a piece of furniture, a painting, something like that, along with dates and places. Had I found a catalog of Vic's antiquities? There seemed to be more cards than there were objects in the Forbidden Room. Had he sold some of them? Maybe he had other storage rooms elsewhere.

Delamorte stepped from the closet. "I apologize for the clutter."

I closed the little drawer, and spun around waving my phone around. "I appreciate the, uh, gift."

Delamorte nodded. "Some may argue such a device is more a liability than an asset, but in my thinking that argument is, as you might say, lame. In this day and age, having a portable means of communication is a necessity."

A tall object sat on Delamorte's bedtable with a hose attached. The thing looked like a series of small Aladdin's lamps stacked on top of each other. "What is that?" I asked.

Delamorte turned that way. "That is what some call a *hookah*, others a *shisha*. I use it for smoking ..." He looked up, moving his hand dismissively. "Various things."

"Various things, huh?"

Delamorte started to grin but quickly wiped it off his face. Turning, he opened up one side of a tall heavy-looking wood cabinet that stood opposite the windows. He was blocking my view so I couldn't see what was in there. Was he going to show me his stash of weed? He probably had it neatly organized and labeled in containers. You know, *mise en place*.

Instead, he pulled out a square piece of cardboard about the size of a medium pizza box, only a lot thinner. The outside was decorated like some of Mom's old CD cases.

"Vinyls," he said. I shrugged. "That is precisely the reaction I thought you would have."

He stepped to his left to where a rectangular piece of more modern furniture sat closer to the door. The thing looked like a low desk, though there was no chair to sit on. "This was known as a stereo console. It plays regular radio, both AM and FM frequencies, but also has a turntable. Some refer to it as a record player."

From the square piece of cardboard, he pulled a black circular object with some kind of label in the middle. Holding the disk carefully by its edges, he flipped it over in his hands a couple of times.

"This is a thirty-three-and-a-third RPM record. I believe it is that one-third that makes the difference." He grinned at me. I shrugged my shoulders again. He twisted his mouth around, then shook his head. "It is also known as an LP."

Curious, I stared at the thing in Delamorte's hands. He angled it toward me. "This one is a classic." He looked at me like I was supposed to recognize the name. I mean, the group Blood, Sweat & Tears was vaguely familiar from listening to Delamorte's oldies radio station in the hearse, but otherwise I'd never heard of them.

"Won a Grammy for Album of the Year back in the day."

He lifted the lid up on the console, placed the record on a silver spike that was dull on top. Next, he moved a small armlike thing over the record and set it gently on top of the spinning vinyl.

"You might recognize this one."

A second later, a harmonica played a simple tune, rising, then falling. Trumpets played and soon some guy was singing how he wasn't scared of dyin' and didn't really care. The tune sounded like dance music, like one of the Broadway or movie soundtracks Jess used to listen to back when we had a computer and could stream music. It was less rock guitar and more trumpet and trombone, except at the end where there was this cool harmonica part.

At first, I thought the song was gonna be some depressing death thing, but it ended up sounding kind of encouraging.

Life goes on with or without you. I kind of liked that.

"What's that called?" I asked.

"And When I Die."

"Whoa, whoa, whoa! Who said anything about you dying? We just got here. You are not allowed to die on me. On us."

Delamorte closed his eyes and lifted his chin a little. "That, my dear, is the name of the song."

"Oh."

"The author of the song, Laura Nyro, was a young woman who was just about your age when she wrote it."

Had she been like me? Had she, too, wandered cemeteries looking at the ages of people when they died? Wondering how much time she had left to live? Delamorte moved across the room to his nightstand, opened it, and pulled out a harmonica. "It has been some years since I played this."

Delamorte lifted the instrument and blew as he slid it across his mouth, producing a quick scale of notes. Then, holding the harmonica with both hands, he proceeded to play those opening notes of the song we'd just listened to, rising and then falling. He stopped playing suddenly, breaking down in a coughing fit so bad he leaned against the wall.

"When are you gonna go to the doctor?"

"There is really no need for that. I know what it is that ails me. It has afflicted me in the past and will likely continue to do so for time immemorial." He made it sound like he had a cold or something, but that cough was not due to a cold.

"Yeah, you said that before. But what ..."

As he pulled his hand down from his mouth, both of us stared at the shiny red splotch on his palm.

Colds didn't make you bleed.

The Fall

Summer ended. School started, and everyone fell into a routine. Delamorte drove us all to school and was there waiting for us at the end of the day.

Thomas and Jess didn't seem to mind climbing out of a hearse in front of their schools. I, on the other hand, had Delamorte drop me off on a side street around the corner from my high school.

Thomas was in advanced classes in the seventh grade, exactly where he was supposed to be, and was learning to play the cello. When he wasn't practicing or messing around on his laptop, he spent a lot of time with Delamorte. What did they have to talk about?

Jess, a fourth grader, had already been invited to the birthday party of some girl she'd gotten to know the previous year at the same school. She was on the inside socially right where she belonged.

Pastor Priest had noticed my squinting and blinking all the time and had taken me to get some new glasses. Having them was like waking from a fuzzy dream and seeing the world in crystal clear reality. It was a life-changing experience socially, if nothing else.

Armed with my new glasses, I started noticing things I hadn't before: Like a girl massaging a guy's crotch in the stairwell, a drug deal or two by the lockers, a boy stepping out of a restroom with some girl adjusting her bra in the background, and a girl smoking a joint outside a window. I even saw a signup list for volleyball posted on the door of the gym. One of the coaches noticed me looking at it. "You interested in playing?" he asked. I nodded for some unknown reason and he took me to his office where he gave me a stack of papers to take home.

The following Monday I was practicing with the volleyball team. About half the girls on the team knew each other and were all talkie-talkie. The other half were in the same boat of anonymous wannabes I was and sat around quiet as ghosts.

Some of the girls looked like they were thirty-years-old, my height and taller, breasts like watermelons. Jesus, how would I ever deal with things that big on my chest? Secretly, I was afraid of having big breasts. Mom's were what you'd call average, but on Dad's side of the family who knew? Maybe my *abuela* had big boobs. If I was a so-called throwback height-wise, my breasts might be also. I feared my chest could be a ticking time-bomb.

Volleyball practice was a mix of humiliation and triumphs. Over a couple of weeks, I learned all the positions but had no skill whatsoever. I'd end up doing a face plant or otherwise crashing awkwardly onto the court. If I did manage to get a hand on the ball, it would fly out of bounds half the time.

"You looked like one of them deer on ice going for that ball," one girl said. She had short, dark hair, even shorter than the Peter Pan thing Lucy had given me. She had a cute nose, but that was the only feminine thing about her. It was obvious she lifted weights. I mean, it would have taken two of my biceps to equal one of hers. Her arms had more ink than my last English essay. I hadn't paid a whole lot of attention to her before she started flapping her lips. "You ever see a deer on ice?" she said to no one in particular. "Dumbest-looking thing ever."

I decided volleyball was not for me and quit. I stayed in athletics though because it gave me a chance to get better. Probably not volleyball, but maybe just get stronger, faster. So, I mainly stayed in the weight room or was out on the track. And, I stayed to myself, avoiding any possible conflict, especially that mouthy bitch from volleyball.

In the following weeks, Delamorte did better at concealing whatever it was he coughed up. Still, old worries arose like movie zombies in a graveyard. Where would we live if something happened to Delamorte? Then again, there was no sense in worrying about a situation that hadn't happened and might not happen for a long time.

Like not worrying that your mom might never come home one day.

There were warning signs with Mom. Staying out later and later, ignoring us as if we were ghosts. The way I'd imagined her addiction it was like falling through dark water looking up at the shapes at the surface, unable to swim back up. At some point, she'd lost sight of us and just quit trying. Was it the same with Delamorte? His age, his illness, his constant smoking, him not going to the doctor about anything. Had he quit trying to live?

I couldn't help but wonder what life would have been like had Delamorte showed up on the scene sooner. Honestly, it was a stupid question that had no answer. Water that has passed, I decided.

Short of tying him up and taking him to the doctor, there was nothing I could do about Delamorte. I decided to ignore his illness as much as possible. If he could do it, so could I. *Like I'd done with Mom.* But, as with Mom, I could ignore reality so long.

One Friday evening in the middle of September, reality hit me like a pencil jammed in my eyeball. Delamorte had been too tired to do any cooking, so we ordered out. He didn't eat anything himself, just sat at the kitchen table watching us cram our faces full of pizza. His expression, pleasant at first, shifted. He frowned, staring off into the center of the giant-size pepperoni centerpiece on the table in front of him. He blinked his eyes repeatedly as if considering some problem he was facing.

"What're you thinking about over there?" I asked in between bites of pizza.

He took a breath, winced, cleared his throat. "Oh, nothing much."

"Looked like you were trying to solve some major world problem," I continued.

He grinned, winced again, pushed himself up from the table and excused himself. A few moments later, we heard a bump, a bang, and a grunt. We hurried out into the hallway.

In front of us, Delamorte lie unconscious in a heap at the foot of the stairs. Jess and I knelt on either side of Delamorte. Thomas stayed back looking as if someone had just slapped him in the face.

"Hey?" I semi-yelled. "You awake?"

No response. Fighting off a sense of panic, I placed two fingers against his neck feeling for a pulse. Nothing. *Shit.* I kept adjusting my fingers, pressing harder, lighter, trying different places. Jesus, was the guy going to up and die on us just like that? After what seemed like minutes, I found the sign of life I was looking for. I tilted my head back and sighed loud.

"Is he okay?" Jess asked.

"His heart's still going." Delamorte's

chest rose and fell.

"He'll be okay," Jess said. "Won't he?"

"We need to get him up to his room," I said.

Jess had started crying silently, just tears rolling from each eye. Thomas sat on the first step of the stairs, elbows on his knees, staring at Delamorte. He hadn't gotten sick to his stomach in months. Hopefully, that wasn't going to change.

There was no way we were going to be able to move Delamorte anywhere even if I could rouse Thomas from whatever state of shock he was in and the three of us worked together. I yanked my phone from my back pocket, and texted Mr. Gerard.

After what seemed like an hour sitting around watching Delamorte breathe, I texted Mr. Gerard again. I'd just pressed the Send button when I heard his old pickup truck hissing in the driveway out back. He strode in the back door, the edge of his long, dark outer coat trailing behind him. He stood near us, placing his hands on his hips, the pearl-handled revolver dangling just below his belt.

He sighed, then went over to Delamorte and squatted down. "How long he been like this?"

"Just a few minutes."

"Y'all gonna hafta assist me a little."

Thomas remained frozen on the stairs.

"Get over here, T." My brother snapped out of it enough to finally move. Together, Mr. Gerard, Thomas, and I lifted Delamorte up. I brought one of his arms over my shoulder and Mr. Gerard did the same. Delamorte seemed almost weightless and hollow, like a scarecrow. Was that how corpses felt if you had to move them around?

Mr. Gerard spoke. "We might could make it up them stairs wif him, but there be a easier way."

Turning left, we made our way down to the Private Room. With Delamorte still unconscious and hanging on our shoulders, Mr. Gerard dug around in his pants pocket for the key to the door, the pearl-handled revolver flopping around as he did so.

"I suggest yer brother and sister meet us upstairs."

Jess ran up to wait for us. Thomas stared at us another moment, then plodded up the stairs after his little sister. Off to the side in the Private Room was an old-fashioned elevator, the kind with a cage-like door.

The two of us carried Delamorte onto the elevator platform, and Mr. Gerard pulled the door closed with his free hand. He pulled a lever and an unseen piece of machinery started up, producing a familiar sound I'd heard many times lying awake in my bed at night. It had not been a conveyor belt to hell after all, just a rickety old elevator.

The platform lifted slowly through the ceiling into the darkness. After a few moments, the elevator stopped. The only light was what filtered up from below. I could barely make out Mr. Gerard's arm pulling back the cage door.

"Careful of the darkness," he warned.

"Don't you mean what's in it?"

"Like I said."

I heard the dehumidifiers churning up ancient dust only a few feet away and knew we were in the Forbidden Room with all the artifacts and the dark casket with the hiero-glyphs. Blind, we carried Delamorte across the room toward the hallway. I sensed the casket there in the darkness as if it were a living thing. Warm and electric.

I could hear Mr. Gerard feeling around on the wall in the dark and an overhead light popped on, blinding me for a second or two. When I could see again, I glanced over my shoulder at the casket. Did it somehow "know" that Delamorte was near death?

We shuffled into the hallway where Thomas and Jess fell in behind us. We shifted Delamorte's weight around a little every now and then to make him easier to carry. Moving down the hall, each step produced a creaking that started at a high pitch and ended with a low moan. It made the funeral home seem tired, in pain even.

Like it was ready to lie down and die.

Thomas and Jess watched as we got Delamorte into bed and pulled the covers up. I turned on the light next to the bed. Mr. Gerard twisted his mouth around a moment, pivoted on one foot, and looked at us. "Let him sleep. See how he is in the morning." Without so much as a nod in our direction, he marched down the stairs and out the back door. I was pretty sure he didn't have a date. The guy probably just left his beer somewhere and didn't want it to get hot.

Later that night after the others had gone to bed, I got up to go check on Delamorte. I had no way of knowing my understanding of the world was about to be flipped on its head.

Lucinda

The door to Delamorte's room was open, which was odd. He normally kept it shut. I moved toward the open door until I stood in the doorway to Delamorte's bedroom.

Not wanting to disturb him, I didn't turn on the light. I entered as quietly as I could, silently stepping toward where Delamorte lie on the bed. He wheezed every now and then confirming he was still alive.

Moonglow filled the room with pale blue light. Standing at the foot of the bed, the features of the room — the cabinet, the chairs, the old stereo, even the windows — all receded as if pulled away from me. The walls fell away, and it felt as if the room had expanded. It was like I'd stepped into a huge warehouse or basketball gym.

A breeze from somewhere blew against my cheek. Thinking it was the air conditioning unit, I looked up at the ceiling. Instead of the ceiling fan and a vent, countless stars spread out above me like the core of the Milky Way galaxy.

Standing there, I had the impression of something moving under my feet, like sand on a seashore being washed away by the tide. Looking down, I saw what seemed to be every star, planet, and galaxy flowing toward Delamorte's bed. Wrinkles in space formed, and I realized what I was looking at was literally fabric. As in the long train of a dress. The cloth depicting the universe moved toward a chair that had appeared next to the bed. A few moments later, a dark shape formed, eventually becoming the silhouette of a person seated in the chair. One with great posture. "Lucy?" I asked.

"I can feel your heart pounding all the way over here," Lucy said. Her pale blue eyes, icy cold as ever, glowed in the darkness.

I coughed a little, stars shooting around in my eyeballs. Feeling dizzy, I sat down on the edge of the bed.

"Keep breathing," Lucy said. "Or you'll pass out and we ..." I either did pass out or fell asleep, but not for long. "Wake up, human. We still need to talk." Lucy again. I blinked a couple of times, sat up, and found her sitting on the bed next to me. Like uncomfortably close. I scooted away from her.

Titrate, titrate, titrate.

"Ask," Lucy said. The dress containing the galaxy, or galaxies, poured over the edge of the bed and across the floor. Staring at it, I could imagine floating alone somewhere in the universe, gazing at every heavenly body ever formed.

Lucy's torso seemed to hover in midair near the edge of Delamorte's bed. Her piercing pale blue eyes stared directly at me.

"Wha, what is ... is that a dress?"

"This old thing? Just something I picked up in a thrift store."

I started to ask what thrift store, then realized she was being sarcastic or facetious or something. I decided to ask something a little more relevant. "What are you?"

She cocked her head. "Obviously, I am just an ordinary beautician."

"Uh, obviously not. You're some hallucination, or, or supernatural ... thing."

"Supernatural?" She closed her eyes, or at least I thought she did, shaking her head a couple of times. "Far from it, my dear."

I really hated it when people or ... dark creatures in Delamorte's bedroom... called me that. At least she didn't call me "sweetheart."

"What are you then?"

"There is nothing supernatural or even magical about me. I am as natural as life itself. Indeed, I am as old as life itself."

"I got no idea what the hell you're saying."

"We evolved with this universe."

"We?"

"My ... kind."

"Are you, like, a person?"

She looked down at her torso, still oddly floating at the end of the bed, held out her arms, and inspected them. "I certainly appear to be."

"Yeah, well, you certainly weren't a person a minute ago. You were just some starry, galaxy cloth thing running under my feet."

Lucy nodded. "I am, shall we say, prone making dramatic entrances."

"What are you doing here?" I asked.

"Merely keeping my eye on the prize."

"I still got no—"

"Really? No idea?" She sighed or at least made a sound like a sigh. "There can be no life without ... death." She smiled out of one side of her mouth. "Catching on?"

"Nope." As soon as the word was out my mouth, an idea began to form in my mind. It was kind of unthinkable.

"What was it you used to call Victor, before you came to live here and made friends?"

I had to think. "The Grim ... Reaper?"

Lucy closed her eyes a second and bowed her head slightly. "Pleased to make your acquaintance."

I laughed. "I'm dreaming ... aren't I? I fell asleep somewhere. I'm really in my bed, or, or ...? This is one of those dream things where you can't wake up. Right?"

"You are so full of life it is utterly obnoxious. I can see why he enjoys having you around. And yes, my dear, I'm afraid you are wide awake."

Shit.

"I am content to remain mostly in the shadows. I only appear this way because of my great love for Victor."

The memory of an overheard conversation way back last summer popped into my head. "I heard you guys talking in the kitchen that one time. You said something about taking *her* form. Whose? Who are you supposed to be?"

"One of Victor's great loves from long ago. It either pleases him to gaze upon me in that form, or it causes him grief because he realizes I am not her."

"What do you look like for real? A skeleton or something else gross and, excuse my French but, fucked up?"

"A skeleton? Really? Not everything looks like you do. I look like … nothing. Or, maybe a shadow that is a little too dark or perhaps is in the wrong place. It is more what I *feel* like."

"What do you mean?"

"Unease. Like something nagging at the back of your mind but you can't quite place what it is."

I'd felt that way before, a lot of times actually. Had I been luckier than I thought? How many times had I met Lucy or her kind and just not realized it. I remembered having the thought that Lucy defined stealth, that she could creep up on you without you ever knowing. *Holy shit!*

Lucy pushed herself up from the bed,

dragging the stars and planets with her until they fell down onto the floor.

"You said something about your people. You're not the only one? There's more than one of you?"

"We are many."

That reminded me of some Bible story I'd read during some church service years ago, about a man possessed by demons. Legion, they called themselves, for they were many. I always thought that was a cool story. I kind of felt bad for Legion because they all got driven into a herd of pigs and ran off a cliff to their death. Jesus, all they were looking for was a place to live. Like all of us.

"Are you like ... demons or something?"

She turned to look at me. Even in the dark room, I could sense she was smiling. "No," she said. "Demons are a fantasy creation of humans. I am, we are, energy. Conscious energy. We become visible matter when and if we so choose."

I just shook my head. "Why are you telling me all this?"

"What Victor has not told you is a source of great frustration for me."

"What? What hasn't he told me?"

Lucy cocked her head to one side. After a few seconds, the image of the old casket appeared in my mind. "The casket?" She nodded her head. "It's the device, isn't it? The casket?"

"Victor must be the one to explain this, but yes. You are correct. A-plus to you."

Okay, so the casket was the device. But what kind of device?

"He is a fool in many ways," Lucy said. "He would be the first to tell you that, but I would certainly be the second."

I could relate to Delamorte in that regard. An obvious question occurred. "Why are you even here in this place?" As soon as I asked the question, I knew the answer. "Delamorte."

"I have pursued him for a very long time. So long, in fact, that ..."

Things came together in my mind, leading to a fucking weird conclusion.

"You're ... in love with him."

She smiled. "That is oddly perceptive of you."

"Oddly? Why oddly? Do you think I'm stupid or something?" Death was really pissing me off.

"Not remotely, my dear. It is simply that you have a propensity to act first and think later. I know this because impulsivity attracts my kind."

I started to say something in my defense, but the memory of my running into traffic toward the GrabNGo flashed in my mind. Lucy moved around to Delamorte's side of the bed.

I pushed myself up slowly, leaning my hands on my knees, waiting for the dizziness to return. It didn't, and I came to stand on the opposite side of the bed, Delamorte lying between myself and Death.

Lucy stared down at him. "He is going to ask you to do something," she said. "It is important that you do exactly as he says."

"Do what?"

"Why anyone would want to go on living in this world, I have no idea. Yet it is what Victor desires. He must be the one to explain. He will struggle with telling you and I would enjoy seeing that."

"I don't understand."

"I will be around to answer questions you might have, but only as long as Victor breathes. You are on your own after that."

"But ...? How do I ...?"

All of her facial features faded into darkness. Her voice, though, persisted. "Until then, I shall keep close watch over my love."

God, this was getting weirder and weirder. I'd finally met the actual Grim Reaper and discovered he was a she. Or maybe a them. And they ... were in love with Delamorte.

Lucy vanished. The galaxy of stars flowing along the floor faded and the bedroom grew dark. Standing there alone with no one but the sleeping Delamorte in the room, I felt kind of let down. One minute I was part of some great universe, then next just some tiny person in a funeral home. I searched for Lucy in the corners of the bedroom but found only regular gray shadows. Nothing darker than it should have been.

I stopped by the restroom to pee, then went to bed. I didn't worry about ghosts coming up through the floorboards anymore. I'd met fucking Death.

What did I have to fear from mere ghosts?

Death of Denial

Bright light poured through our bedroom window. Jess was still asleep next to me. The hall outside our door was quiet. No sounds from the kitchen made their way up the staircase. The funeral home seemed dead.

It was Saturday so we had no place to be anytime soon. I rolled out of bed and stood in the middle of the room. What if Delamorte just didn't wake up? The memory of meeting Lucy in his bedroom in the night rose in my mind slowly like the float in a toilet bowl tank as it refilled. Did that really happen?

What did Lucy mean about doing exactly as Delamorte said? But, more worrisome, what if Grim Reaper Lucy had claimed Delamorte in the night? After a few months of food, a nice bed, and more peace of mind than any of us had in our lifetimes combined, were we about to be on our own again? Part of me wanted to face it straight up, like with Pete the Perv. But denial had always been somewhat of a superpower for me. Dealing with shit directly? I had no idea how well I could do that. What if I somehow fucked everything up? Ignoring it, though, all that did was tie my stomach in knots.

So, Delamorte was going to ask me to do something. The fact Lucy, corpse beautician and resident Death Angel, told me about it probably should have worried me. But it didn't. I mean, she wouldn't be telling me about some pervy thing Delamorte wanted from me as a last request. Would she? Seeing him drive around the neighborhood in the hearse all those months ago, I'd thought Delamorte was into some sexual death fetish thing. Damn, was I right? I mean, Death sure hung out in his bedroom a lot.

A sound from Delamorte's room pulled me from the edge of a swirling cesspool of weirdness. Had he survived the night? Or was it just Lucy banging around in there, doing whatever Death did in her spare time. Memories of the noises Mom and her various boyfriends made in bed streamed through my head. With Lucy's icy touch, how would they even— Jesus, surely not.

Shaking the thought from my head, I threw on some jeans and a T-shirt and eased into the hallway. Delamorte's bedroom door was closed. Had Lucy closed it?

I tapped on the door. Nothing.

Maybe he was just asleep. I knocked again, a little harder. Gripping the doorknob, I waited hoping for an invitation to enter. My hand had just begun to sweat holding onto the brass knob when Delamorte coughed and cleared his throat. "Just a moment."

I leaned my head against the door and breathed a sigh of relief. I thought of the first night we'd spent in the funeral home. Delamorte had made pancakes and sausages with syrup and had given me that homemade ointment to use on my sore neck. My clothes were covered in Pete's blood and Delamorte had washed them for me. I didn't trust the man much back then.

"Come in," he said faintly.

Delamorte was sitting up in the bed, the covers pulled up not quite to his chest. He looked tired, but otherwise seemed normal.

"Good morning," he wheezed. "What has you up so early?"

"Do you really have to ask?" I asked, coming to stand next to his bed.

He cleared his throat. "I have no memory as to how I came to be in my bed. Perhaps you were concerned because something happened last night?"

"You passed out. Mr. Gerard and I used the little elevator to get you upstairs and into bed."

"I see," he said. "And you wished to ascertain whether I was still breathing."

"I see you are ... still breathing." I sat down on the edge of the bed. "How do you feel?"

He looked up at me, a grin of resignation on his face. "I await my fate and will greet it with open arms. That being said, the process can take an inordinate length of time for completion."

I must have looked clueless because he

smiled a little more. "One can get impatient waiting around to die."

"Yeah, that's kinda what I thought you meant. So, now that we're all settled here, you're going to die."

He sighed. He'd had a cough for months. I'd seen blood on his handkerchief. Still, it seemed too soon for him to be dying. Didn't people sometimes linger for years before dying? Then again, maybe he'd already been in the lingering phase when he showed up at the front door of our apartment.

"Are you sure you're dying? There's no chance—"

"One knows," he said.

He talked like someone who'd been through the whole dying thing before, like it was no big deal. As if he were sitting around in the waiting room at the doctor for the nurse to call him in for an appointment. Damn, how could he be so carefree about death? It was the end. Wasn't it? Shouldn't he seem more bothered by that fact? I sure as hell was.

"Can I get you anything?" I asked.

"Maybe some fresh water."

I got the glass from next to his bed, filled it with water from the faucet in the hall bathroom, and brought it to him. He leaned forward and took a sip and swallowed, grimacing a little as he did. "Thank you, my dear."

At least he could still drink without any

help. I couldn't even do that when I'd been sick the previous summer and Delamorte had taken care of me. He coughed some, picked up a handkerchief and covered his mouth. He wadded up the handkerchief so I couldn't see if there was any blood on it.

A sad expression drooped over his face.

Jess marched in, swept past me to the bed, leaned down, and hugged Delamorte. "Are you okay?" she asked.

"For the moment."

"You don't look okay," she said. "You look ..." Jess's voice trailed off. Thomas stood at the doorway rubbing his eyes. He took a deep breath, then let it out. No hugging for my brother, but I could tell he was relieved Delamorte was awake.

I had considered telling my brother and sister about Lucy, but Thomas would want proof. He'd ultimately conclude I'd been hallucinating or dreamed the whole thing. Maybe I had. Jess? Who knew how she would react. Then again, neither of them had acted like they were even aware of Lucy's existence. Neither had acknowledged her when she was present. Could they even see her? If that was the case, why could I see Death and them not.

Delamorte pushed himself up in the bed a little. "I suppose now is as good a time as any to have a certain conversation." Thomas came closer. All of us were silent, waiting to see what he had to say. "As you can see, I am quite ill. From past experience, I can tell you that I will not recover."

"You realize that makes no sense," Thomas said. "You must have recovered in the past or you wouldn't be here to tell the story."

Delamorte nodded. "I realize some of my words will be truly confusing and difficult to comprehend."

I understood everything he was saying. Hearing him say it was a different story. Irritation washed over me. "You know, we wouldn't be having this little talk if you hadn't smoked your whole damn life."

Delamorte closed his eyes a moment and sighed. "The timing of your arrival has been less than optimal." He frowned and winced. "I simply did not think my physical decompensation was so far advanced. I believed I would have more time to help you set a course. I can see I was mistaken." He genuinely seemed disappointed. It was hard to stay angry with him looking that way.

"You're going to die?" Jess asked.

Delamorte took her hand. "It is not what I want."

It wasn't what I wanted either. There were so many practical reasons for wanting to keep him alive. But all of them together didn't seem to add up to the emotions roiling through my body. There was something else.

There was no other conclusion I could think of but that I cared about what happened to Delamorte. And not just because of the uncertainty about where we would live if something happened to him. I cared, because I liked him.

I didn't feel that way about Mom at the end. I could feel sorry for that carefree, happy person in the photograph I had in my mind. Not for that shell of a person I'd cleaned up and dragged to bed time and again. The one who abandoned us.

My dad hadn't exactly abandoned us, at least not on purpose. He didn't mean to go away. But losing him was so beyond my memory as to be little more than unemotional fact. Delamorte had cared for us like we were his family. Had I added him to the list of people I was trying to take care of? Did I feel the same about him as I did about Thomas and Jess? I guess, I kind of ... did.

Was that how you came to love another person? God, what had happened to me?

Hope and Fear

Delamorte was eventually able to get up and around the day after he'd collapsed. There were corpses to embalm, viewings to arrange, caskets to sell. He even cooked meals for us. Sometimes, at least. He once even managed to add an additional item to his daily activities.

He moved slower than usual, though. I'd find him in the kitchen or the office sometimes, just sitting, staring off. I couldn't tell if Lucy had been with him, but I knew she was there somewhere. Waiting patiently.

"Shit!"

I'd slammed on the brakes of the hearse at an intersection where the stop sign was sort of hidden.

"Language, my dear. There is always a better way to express oneself."

"I have no idea of any other way to express my ... utter shock and ... disappointment ... at the location of that damn stop sign."

"See what I mean," he said. "You are capable of such eloquence."

"That's the first time anyone has ever referred to anything coming out my mouth as eloquent. Eloquent swearing maybe, but not, you know, normal conversation."

"Keep your hands at ten and two," he

said. It was my first and, as it turned out, my only driving lesson with Delamorte. We stayed on side streets mainly. "Begin to apply the brakes a couple of houses before the stop sign." He said this after I'd slammed on the brakes at the last minute at the previous intersection. We eventually ended up in a shopping mall parking lot. Delamorte looked nervously out all the windows of the hearse. "Many in such places as this do not observe their surroundings sufficiently to safely operate their vehicle."

I practiced parking and backing out. Finally, we just sat in the hearse in a parking space as far from the mall entrance as possible. I thought Delamorte might light up a cigarette, but instead he cleared his throat.

"Do you recall the poem written on the casket?" I nodded. "I said there was more to it. A portion of it goes thus: 'I have seen everything that is done under the sun' and 'all is vanity, all is meaningless.'" He emphasized the words "vanity" and "meaningless" with, well, more emotion than he normally expressed. "My words, or at least the way in which I say them, may concern you, but there is a point."

"Which is?"

"The wise poet was mistaken. There is something that is not in vain. Kindness. Love, if you will." The word "love" reverberated in my brain. Delamorte said it in a way that gave it more power or magic. "If one finds a way to be kind to others, that is clearly not vanity. Jesus, at his most basic, was a kind man, condemning no one except those religious authorities who, often for their own gain, placed undue burdens on others."

Jesus apparently wasn't very kind to demons, especially Legion. But maybe that story was just hearsay.

"The Buddha lived long before my time." *And Jesus didn't?* "He sought self-enlightenment, but humanity benefitted from his wisdom of kindness."

Kindness was one of those words that had long ago lost any meaning for me. Anyone offering kindness usually wanted something in return or just wanted a good laugh when you stupidly trusted them. Lucy said Delamorte was going to ask me to do something. Had I been right all along? Was his kindness offered only in return for something else?

"You once asked me why I invited you into my home. The three of you have provided me with meaning in life and sufficient reason to continue onto the next. I admit to a certain selfishness to my motivation. That being said, I merely wished to be kind. To you, Mr. Thomas and young Jess."

Okay. "That's it? All that to say you were being kind."

"Well, yes. Practicing kindness is the easiest and best life to live. If, as in your case, one has but a single life to live, one must make it count and find a way to be kind."

A single life to live?

"Like that's not the way it is for everyone? I mean, we all have just one life. Right?"

Delamorte just looked at me, a grin trying to form. He wiped his mouth as if trying to erase the smile. Was I somehow amusing to him? Whatever.

The problem, the way I saw it, was that not everyone deserved kindness. I mean ... assholes. Then again, if everyone was kind to each other, would there still be assholes? There was a new asshole motto in there somewhere.

I realized my hands were still gripping the steering wheel at ten and two. I took a deep breath and dropped my arms to my sides. So, Delamorte was being kind. Beats me why he thought that was worth a parking lot conversation.

"I'm glad to see you understand I was not pursuing you for the purpose of self-gratification. Clearly, there was no financial gain."

"Yeah," I said. "Clearly."

"As I have spent a near unfathomable amount of money on food over these past several months."

"If you weren't such a gourmet chef, it wouldn't have cost so much. I mean, a good hot dog, one of them Kosher ones, and some potato chips are pretty damn tasty and filling. And, you know Cheerios for breakfast would have been just fine. You didn't have to go baking all those rolls and pastries." I wondered for a moment whether Jess was still hoarding food in her dresser drawer.

Delamorte cocked his head to one side, kind of like Lucy did at times. "If one must eat, eat well."

"Yeah, I get that. You could make all those profiteroles you want... Hey, before anything, you know, happens to you, could you maybe write down the recipe for those things? And maybe the fricassee. "

"I most certainly could."

"Oh, the macarons, too."

He tried taking a deep breath but ended up coughing. He probably needed to get back to bed. Clearing his throat, he continued. "Back to those words inscribed on the casket ... whether by Egyptian pharaoh or Canaanite king, they reflect a certain pessimism about the invariability of the human condition. Living and dying, love and hate, wars and pestilence, ignorance and poverty. For centuries, nothing seemed to change. It had gotten to the point that I questioned whether I wished to continue living in such a world."

Was that the reason he kept smoking his life away?

"But over the course of my most recent

lifetimes I have begun to question the inevit-
ability of suffering, of repeating the same errors.
Change is happening faster than one can keep
up with. Never has there been more reason to
hope, and because of that, more reason to fear."

"Fear what?"

"That progress will be thwarted. That
some cataclysm will occur that sets humanity
back centuries. A great war, a plague, perhaps
some unexpected celestial event. Or, and this I
fear is more likely, that greed will triumph,
ignorance will prevail, poverty will remain or
worsen."

"Why do you think things are better? I
mean, to me, people seem the same, mostly
looking out for themselves. Rich people have all
the money, everyone else has shit. Ya got a war
thing in Europe, war in the Middle East, nuclear
bombs laying around everywhere. People living
and dying on the street, drug addicts, pervs and
crazy people all over the effing place."

Delamorte tilted his head slightly,
probably at my ineloquent effing. Hey, I edited
it. What did he want?

"Perhaps I have hope because I have seen
worse. I have seen times when people died by
the thousands, instead of the tens or hundreds. I
have seen pestilence. I have quite literally seen
streams of blood and bodies in the street. I
realize this still occurs, but it is not common.
People are increasingly horrified by what

happens to others, not just down the street from them, but on the other side of the planet.

"Yes, this is a most exciting time to be alive. People are sharing their knowledge, their food, their lives and stories all across the globe. And they do it in, as they say, real time. It is as if we all live in the same neighborhood now. We are more connected than ever, and I long to see the outcome. I look forward to my next life more than I have most others."

Whatever train of thought I was on stopped dead in its tracks. "You keep talking like that, about living more than one single life. You believe in that reincarnation stuff?"

He cleared his throat. "I fear what is yet to come may be somewhat difficult to grasp."

I decided then was as good a time as any to bring something up. "As if meeting Miss Death in your bedroom the other night wasn't a challenge to my mentality." He frowned. "Yeah, Lucy. I know her little secret."

"That she is the Collector?"

The Collector? That sounded so much creepier than the Grim Reaper. The fact Delamorte didn't deny Lucy's true nature was strangely comforting. I mean, maybe I wasn't as batshit crazy as I thought. Then again ...

"She, uh, didn't use that word, but yeah."

"Lucinda is an ancient entity, but one I have grown fond of." He stared out the front of the hearse. "She is my constant companion."

According to what she'd told me, she was more than just a companion. I glanced around the hearse when I thought Delamorte wasn't looking, searching for extra dark places Lucy might be hiding.

"I trust you will keep that to yourself."

"No friggin' way! I'm tellin' everyone I see, calling the newspaper, the TV people."

He looked concerned for a moment.

"What am I supposed to say? I met Death. She lives in a funeral home, of course. She's like my best friend now. Her number's in my list of phone contacts." I didn't even know if Lucy had a phone. But, did she even need one?

Delamorte did his own eye roll. "It seems you have elevated sarcasm to an art form."

I grinned. "So, I'm eloquent now?"

He started to smile, then started coughing again. Wiping his mouth, he returned the red stained his white handkerchief to his pocket. I guess he thought there was no point hiding it anymore.

How much time did he have left until Lucy collected him?

Mr. Gerard

Mr. Gerard showed up one day after school in early October with some tacos for us, an oxygen tank for Delamorte, and a whole roll of cherry Lifesavers for Jess. He handed off the Lifesavers, smiling almost like a normal person. He carried the tank up the stairs on his shoulder, and I could hear him moving around up there setting it up.

Delamorte's bedroom door clicked shut, which I thought was a little weird. The only other time he and Mr. Gerard had been alone behind a closed door was the first time we'd come to the funeral home. Mr. Gerard had come out of that meeting carrying an envelope stuffed with papers or maybe cash and wearing his full Grinch grin.

Upstairs, someone raised his voice. It must have been Mr. Gerard as he was the only one in that room with any energy. I left Thomas and Jess in the kitchen with their tacos and crept up the stairs avoiding all the spots known to be especially creaky until I stood outside Dela-morte's door listening.

"I will make it more than worth your while." The voice was Delamorte's.

"But ya won't be 'round to see to it I'm recompensed."

"Trust me, Gerry. You will be taken care of, if you will continue to help me just as you have all these years."

"Is my name anywhere in this document?"

"There is no need to include you in my will. We have our own agreement. You will be pleased with your compensation."

"But there's nothin' in writin'."

"What I am asking of you is technically against the law in this day and age. It cannot be documented as if it were a regular contract."

"Ya 'spect me to take the word of a dead man."

There was silence for a few moments. "I expect you to carry out my instructions to the letter."

Mr. Gerard responded, aggravation in his voice. "This is some bullshit."

Footsteps pounded over the floorboards coming toward where I stood listening. I was in my sock feet but was able to hop across the hall and slide into the bathroom just as Delamorte's bedroom door opened. A second later, I stepped into the hallway acting like I'd just finished doing my business on the toilet. Mr. Gerard glanced my direction, then stared down the hallway at the Forbidden Room for a couple seconds before trotting down the staircase. A few moments later, the engine of the old gray pickup fired up, the sound of hissing pistons fading after a few seconds.

* * *

Delamorte reduced the amount of work he did at the funeral home. I'd only seen three or four corpses delivered over the course of a week. Delamorte spent long periods resting or napping in his bed.

Mr. Gerard dropped by one Saturday afternoon. I remember because it was Texas-OU weekend. Not that I was a big college football fan. My dad was, though. I remembered sitting in his lap watching games.

"Delamorte's asleep," I said.

"That's no problem. Just need to do a little, uh, inventory." He eased up the stairs to the Forbidden Room. Curious, Thomas and I followed.

"These objects appear to be ancient," Thomas said, surveying the contents of the Forbidden Room for the first time. "Some of this, maybe all of it, belongs in a museum."

"That'd be the last place Mr. Delamorte would want it," Mr. Gerard said. "For that matter, neither would I."

"Why?" I asked. "They have sentimental value or something?"

"From my understandin', he's collected these items over a very long period by somewhat mysterious means for the purpose of sellin' 'em in a time of need."

"So, he's making money off them," I said.

"Well, we are, yes. I earn a small

commission off the sales." He glared at the door to the hall. "Very small actually. Seems to be gettin' smaller all the time what with inflation and such." He glared at me. "I 'spect my employer has other concerns besides payin' fair compensation."

What the hell did that mean? Delamorte's words, about greed winning out. Was he thinking about Mr. Gerard?

"Where do you sell these things?" Thomas asked.

"There be auction houses that'd love to get their hands on some of this stuff. Places in New York City, London. They tend to ask too many of questions about the origins of the artifacts that I don't have the answers to and Mr. Delamorte seems reluctant to provide."

"So, what do you do instead?" I asked.

"It's taken some years, but I have managed to put together a small group of buyers who cater to private collectors."

"Sounds like the black market," Thomas said, grinning a little.

Mr. Gerard looked at him a moment, then cleared his throat. "That's rather a derogatory term fer a legitimate business enterprise."

Thomas's eyes got big. "You sell this stuff on the—"

"Like I said, I sell to private collectors." Mr. Gerard placed his hands on his hips, his topcoat parting enough to remind us he was armed. I tilted my head and shot Thomas a look telling him to shut up and leave it alone.

"I still think some of this needs to be in a museum," Thomas mumbled.

"Maybe so," Mr. Gerard said, picking up one of the smaller paintings in an ornate gold frame. "And should you come into ownership of similar artifacts, you are more than welcome to make such a donation to tha art world. However, I strongly advise against this cause it represents a terrible waste of resources."

Mr. Gerard kept moving from one part of the room to another, inspecting other pieces of art. "There's not much to this life but grief and pain. Everyone's out for his own good and I don't blame people for that. Truthfully, that's tha only way to be. Doing things for strangers is just a fool's errand, unless you're getting' somethin' outta it."

It was an attitude I was familiar with having lived it for some years. Thomas looked up at me, shaking his head a little. Mr. Gerard noticed. "I take it you disagree. Well, that's the prerogative of youth. You'll understand when you get older" Every now and then, he'd peer into the hallway. Was he checking to see if Delamorte was awake? Or was he worried about someone else? Lucy perhaps. He'd been utterly terrified of her every time I'd seen them in close proximity to each other.

"My guess is there's nothin' in this room that's less than two hunerd years old," Mr. Gerard said. He ambled over to the old casket, running his fingers along the edge. "At least one item is prob'ly much older than that."

Thomas acted as if he'd only just noticed the casket. He went over to take a closer look. "Wow, this wood. Is it mahogany?"

"Darned if I know," Mr. Gerard said. "It's value, though? Well now, that's incalculable. I 'spect, however, I could find more than one individual willin' to place a value on it, especially if I was to get a bit creative in providing a historical context for the box."

"You mean lie about its origins?" Thomas said.

"Perhaps this is the burial box of some beloved Christian saint or a famous emperor or king of the ancient world."

"Amenhotep," I said.

Again, everyone stared at me. Thomas frowned.

"How did you—?"

"Just something Delamorte said."

Mr. Gerard shook his head. "Sticking him in that old casket and destroyin' it would be a terrible waste of a valuable resource." Thomas and I looked at each other.

"Him?" I asked. "You mean Delamorte? He wants to be buried in that thing?"

"That is correct."

"I thought he wanted to be cremated, his ashes scattered to the four winds," I said,

"He hasn't specified the manner in which his remains shall be disposed of, only that his lifeless body be placed in that casket."

Mr. Gerard pulled out his phone and started taking some pictures of the artifacts.

"Why you taking pictures?" I asked.

"In the event these items need to be liquidated, I'll have some visuals for potential customers."

Thomas got down on his knees, inspecting the casket. "So, if these are hieroglyphs, that would make it—"

"Three thousand years old." Once again, the others stared at me. "Delamorte," I said.

"Really," Mr. Gerard said. "That is helpful and perhaps lucrative information to know."

"These pictures on the sides are interesting," Thomas said. He was referring to the square-shaped scenes running in sequence under the border with the hieroglyphs. "It looks like the same person in all of them."

I leaned down to take a closer look. "Huh," I said. "I hadn't noticed that."

"The women are different," Thomas said. "See, this one in the red dress holding the silver platter is dark-haired and that one over there in the armor carrying the sword is blonde. And there are kids in some of the scenes, but they all look different."

I have had many children.

There was one scene of the man, a woman, and two children seated around a table with a pair of candelabras The table in the center of the room was set for six people with every conceivable plate, knife, fork, and type of spoon. Several candelabras dotted the table, but in the center was a tarnished silver plate. Were the silver plate and candelabras the same as the ones in the pictures on the casket?

The man in each of the panels on the casket looked a lot like Delamorte. Was it a relative? His great-great-great, add a few more greats, grandfather or something? But relatives didn't all look exactly alike. The longer I looked, the more certain I was the man in the panels of the casket was, in fact, the same guy.

The house creaked. Mr. Gerard's Adam's apple bobbed up and down as he moved to inspect the hallway. Knowing what I knew, I kind of enjoyed the thought of Lucy confronting him unexpectedly. I could imagine him jumping up startled, screaming like a little girl. I grinned at the thought.

"Huh," I said. "Wonder if Lucy's downstairs?"

Mr. Gerard's face fell. He was downstairs in his old pickup truck less than a minute later.

We had leftovers that night, meals Delamorte had prepared over the summer months and left in the freezer. Afterwards, Thomas retreated to his closet bedroom. I guess he didn't want to feel completely alone as he left the door open. Across the hall, I found Jess in bed with a chapter book. I had a fleeting notion of wandering over and looking in her dresser drawer to see if she was hiding any food.

I went to the restroom, then came to stand outside Delamorte's door. Music quietly played on the other side. Voices spoke softly. Lucy was visiting.

Delamorte was soon to join the list of dead adults in our lives. What would happen then? I'd turn seventeen years old in the spring, not technically an adult. If I had a job and money, it might not matter how old I was.

The biggest problem with that plan was somebody who didn't know me might think we needed an adult around. Maybe I'd get an office referral at school for something stupid and some idiot assistant principal would feel some strange responsibility to call social services. You know, just because he or she could.

We were in much the same situation as we had been earlier in the year. Just in a nicer, better smelling place.

It seemed my life was running in reverse.

PART IV

Decomposition

The funeral home shut down for good a couple weeks before Halloween.

It had been days since Delamorte did an embalming. No one had gathered in the Slumber Room since early-October, and the smell of flowers no longer permeated the air of the Underworld. Instead, the house smelled of dust and mildew no matter how much we cleaned. It suddenly seemed as old and decrepit as it really was.

Outside, the garden withered. The green bean vines were bare, and the squash leaves drooped on the ground. The tomato plants looked ragged, only one or two with any fruits and those were tiny and blemished. The air smelled of decaying leaves and wet dirt. A layer of dust gathered on the old hearse.

Fear of the unknown poked me up under the ribs. I had no idea what was going to happen. Delamorte had passed out nearly a month ago. What was I supposed to do if I found the man, you know, dead? Was I supposed to call 911? Was there a special number you called when there was a dead person in your house?

"Hello, how may I assist you," the operator would say.

"Uh, yes, we have a dead person that needs collecting."

"I see. Let me get your name and address, phone number, age, number of orphaned children in the house, your entire fucking life story ..."

Jesus!

As soon as I called anyone, our new lives would effectively end. We'd be jerked out of our schools and tossed into foster care. I don't know what I'd been thinking before. There'd be no chance to find a place of our own. Probably no more advanced classes for Thomas. None of the same friends for Jess. We'd be back to where we were at the beginning of summer. Cursing-at-Pete-from-the-parking-lot nowhere.

A thought formed in my mind. What if I just didn't call anyone? That would be the easiest thing. Do nothing. We could keep living in the funeral home, maybe indefinitely. Then, when I turned eighteen in less than two years, we could figure out what to do next.

But how long could we keep Delamorte's corpse a secret? Maybe for a few days, even weeks until someone from church decided to come check on us. What would we tell Pastor Priest? Delamorte went out of town? Maybe he was on an extended trip to ... where? Europe? The Middle East? He kind of looked like someone from that part of the world. It could work.

I went into Thomas's closet room one day after school. Taking a deep breath and letting it out, I told him my idea of not telling anyone if Delamorte died. My brother literally put his hands over his face and moaned.

I shouldn't have even brought it up. My brother just could not handle Delamorte dying. He'd lost a dad and probably a mom. Losing one more person would be more than he could handle. What was I doing, thinking he could actually help?

He moved a finger covering one eye to look out at me. "You have got to be kidding me," he said, his voice muffled by his hands. "Have you no idea what happens to a body once it dies?" Thomas asked as if what happened to dead bodies was common knowledge.

"I know there's some decomposition thing," I said.

He opened his laptop, fingers flying over the keys. "Look," he said. "It only takes twenty-four to seventy-two hours for internal organs to decompose ..." Images of dark, decomposed bodies spread over the computer screen before me. "Three to five days for the body to bloat and this bloody foam to ooze out of the nose and mouth."

He typed a few words into the search bar producing a whole new set of images of former people, their lips gone, gums receded, faces nearly skeletal.

"Damn, T. You don't have to —"

"I'd say you've got major issues right there. If for some reason you waited around a week or ten days ..." He typed in a different search phrase, then spun the screen around for me to see the hideous results. "The body turns green, then red, and this gas accumulates in the abdominal cavity and sometimes the corpse can actually explode."

"Stop!" I turned away from the computer screen. "Jesus fucking Christ! I get it, not a great plan."

Apparently, Thomas was so used to my swearing, he didn't react to it much anymore. Delamorte would have encouraged me to be more eloquent, but the images Thomas showed me were effing gross. He'd apparently come to terms with Delamorte dying enough to investigate the nastier details.

"I thought Delamorte dying would upset you."

"It will. When it happens. It hasn't happened yet so this whole discussion is entirely hypothetical."

"Funny, I was thinking it was pretty damn real, but maybe that's just me."

He shifted in my direction, gesturing, first at me, then in the general direction of Delamorte's room. "You actually thought of just letting Vic's body stay in there?"

It suddenly struck me how decomposition was kind of a metaphor for our lives in the funeral home. Our lives might be okay for a little while. After that, it was going to get real ugly.

"So, what are we gonna do then?"

My brother rolled his eyes. "You know, there's a reason they have funeral homes."

It was like a slap in the face. We *lived* in a damn funeral home. There was like equipment for dealing with dead people. In the Preparation Room there were six cold storage compartments where Delamorte kept corpses, at least when the mortuary was still operating. I had a fleeting thought about whether he'd forgotten anyone in those compartments. He'd accepted some corpses from the county, homeless people who didn't have a family that would wonder what happened to them. Had one of them been left in a compartment to rot? I shook the thought from my head.

"We could get him downstairs and keep him in one of the storage compartments," I suggested.

"What storage compartments?"

I realized then that Thomas had never laid eyes on the inside of the Preparation Room. I had been the only one brave or, in my case, stupid enough to go in there.

"Come on, let me show you something."

Thomas followed me downstairs. As our shoes clomped past the kitchen, Jess, who'd been doing some homework at the table, joined in behind us.

"What're y'all doing?"

There was no point in trying to deceive my little sister. She'd immediately know we were lying.

"I'm showing Thomas the cold storage drawers in the Preparation Room."

"You're not supposed to be in there," she said. "But you're going in there anyway, which means ... no. You're not, are you?"

"I'm not what?"

"Going to put Vic in there?"

How the hell did she figure that out? My mouth opened and I shook my head a little in disbelief. She must have seen my expression. She twisted her mouth up a little. "I'm not stupid. I heard most of what you were saying upstairs."

I looked over at Thomas. "Clearly you've got competition for smartest person in the family."

"Clearly," Jess said before Thomas could respond.

"Okay," I said. "Here's my plan in the event Delamorte ..." I paused, not really wanting to say it.

Thomas and Jess said in unison, "Dies."

"Yeah, that. If we can get him on the gurney, we can use the elevator to get him down to the Underworld and put him in one of these."

"For how long?" Thomas asked.

"I was thinking it would have to be until I graduated high school."

"Are you serious!" he said. "That's like three years!"

"Excuse me," I said. "It's like less than two."

Thomas opened his mouth to say something, then closed it. Either he had nothing to say or ... he was editing his words. Why would Mr. Judgmental do that?

"I'd be like eleven," Jess said.

"I could get a job. And we could find our own place to live."

Thomas looked off in the corner of the Preparation Room, rubbing his hands together. "Honestly, I have no idea if that could work. It just seems we'd be in, I don't know, a precarious situation again."

I didn't want to ask for a definition of precarious from my little brother. From the context it assumed it meant something like dangerous. "Yeah, but still better off than at our old apartment."

Thomas raised his eyebrows, but eventually nodded. "I ... can see your point."

I felt, I don't know, gratified or something that Thomas didn't find enough flaws in my idea to shoot it down completely. It irritated me, honestly, that I felt that way. Did I really need the approval of my twelve-year-old brother that bad? Then again, maybe I was just relieved we weren't going to fight about it.

"People will start to ask questions," Thomas said. "Lucy and Pastor Priest. Mr. Gerard would certainly wonder what happened to him."

I didn't worry about Lucy, but the pastor might be someone to worry about.

"Mr. Gerard scares me a little sometimes," Jess said.

I had totally forgotten about Mr. Gerard. He'd been really helpful to us in the past getting all our stuff from the apartment. He'd shown kindness to my little sister. Maybe he could help with Delamorte's body and keep the whole thing quiet.

And ... and he might could sell some of the stuff in the Forbidden Room for us to pay the bills, buy food, whatever we needed. He was already preparing to do that very thing. All those photos a few days earlier? We would definitely need Mr. Gerard's help to pull the whole thing off.

* * *

For the next few days I brought Delamorte broth and crackers before and after school. He was able to sip the broth on his own, so I didn't have to feed him the way he'd fed me the previous summer. He'd have some good days where he'd get up and move around a little, but there were some bad days when as far as I could tell he never made it out of bed and just slept all day.

Our whole situation at the funeral home seemed to be balanced like an egg on a kitchen countertop. The damn thing could roll any direction at any time. Roll the wrong way and splat. I had a basic plan, but it was dependent on Mr. Gerard's cooperation. It felt a little — okay, a lot — out of my control. If I thought about it enough, my heart would start to flutter and I could get sick to my stomach. Standing around waiting tended to do that.

On the other hand, running helped calm my nerves. After enduring the humiliations of trying to play volleyball, I'd started lifting weights and then running during my athletics class. At least I could focus on my breathing and other parts of my body besides my flipping heart and burning belly. Breathe in, breathe out. Arms more at my sides than up close to my chest, shoulders twisting back and forth.

When I was in motion, I could better control my thoughts and not allow them to boil into panic. So, I'd been running a lot more lately, mainly around the cemetery, until one of my knees started bothering me a little.

I stopped at one point during my run one day to massage my left knee. I needed some of Delamorte's dragonfly wing goop. Rubbing my knee, my thoughts came together to form a conclusion. I needed to know exactly what to do with Delamorte and that damn casket. Those were the prearrangements I needed.

When I got home that day, I jogged up the stairs and straight into Delamorte's bedroom. Fortunately, he was awake.

"We need to talk," I said.

Prearrangements

Delamorte slipped off his oxygen mask, set aside some papers he'd been reading, and took off his reading glasses. The smell of sickness was stronger than it had been in past days.

"I am actually glad you barged in."

"Sorry," I said. "But I really need to know what is going to happen. I need to know ... the plan."

"I would imagine so."

He folded his hands on his lap and looked at me expectantly. I was eager to get things off my chest, so I sort of blurted it all out. "What am I supposed to do when you ... stop breathing."

"You mean when I die?"

The harmonica part of the Blood, Sweat, & Tears song went sailing through my head. "Well, yeah, since that's apparently happening whether I want it to or not. Do you want to be buried in that old casket down the hall?"

"It is what must be." He was silent a moment, studying me. "There is, however, more to it than a simple burial."

"That's what Mr. Gerard said."

"You spoke with him about it?"

"Not much. He wasn't very talkative."

He worked his mouth around, then swallowed. "Once deceased, I must be placed in the casket that is in the room at the end of the hall."

"Mr. Gerard isn't going to do that?"

"My faith in Mr. Gerard has dwindled to something less than the proverbial mustard seed. I fear I am no longer able to trust him to do as I ask in this regard no matter the payment I would guarantee him." He shook his head. "I realize it is, as they say, a 'big ask.' One would have to handle my body after it has become inanimate."

Was this what Lucy had said was going to happen? Had Delamorte wanted us to do this all along? Maybe he'd had his doubts about Mr. Gerard for months, and he'd moved us in with him so we could do this ... thing.

Would it be so bad? Better than some of the other personal services I'd imagined him asking for. Stuffing a dead body into a casket? I suppose I could agree to it, but there was no reason to actually go through with it. Delamorte would be dead. He wouldn't care one way or the other anymore. Honestly, keeping him in cold storage seemed like the better plan.

Delamorte seemed to space out a couple seconds. Then, with a suddenness that startled me, he looked me in the eye. "Oh, and once I am in the box there must be an application of fire." He said it quickly, almost as an afterthought. Like, of course there must be fire ... *as we all know.*

"I'm sorry, what?"

"The casket must be set aflame in order to work properly."

Was that what Mr. Gerard meant when he said there was more to it than just putting Delamorte in the casket?

"What do you mean, to work properly? What is it supposed to do?"

"The casket is a device, an ancient one, that I have used many times before."

Many times before?

"Let me ask you this. Do I seem to be in full possession of my faculties?"

"Yeah, you seem pretty sane. I mean, other than what you just said."

He closed his eyes a moment, nodding. "There are some things that simply must be witnessed to be believed. What happens to me in that old wooden box is one of those things."

In terms of my beliefs, I was fairly sure nothing was going to happen if he ended up in that old casket. But, the application of fire made a little sense. He'd said he wanted to be cremated. "So, the fire thing. You want cremation, right?"

He sighed sharply. "No, that is not the case. There is no provision in my will for a trip to the crematory. That would beg too many prying questions from a variety of sources." He paused a moment. "Perhaps the easiest thing to do would be to place my remains in the casket and light everything on fire here and let the funeral home itself be devoured in a conflagration."

I blinked a few times trying to understand what he was saying. "You want to burn down the funeral home?"

"Few questions would be asked about an old house burning down."

What did he think was going to happen to us when he died? We'd camp out in the cemetery? Live in the effing woods? "You know … I was kinda thinking we could maybe *live* here after you're gone," I said. "Since our alternatives are basically the same as before you moved us in with you."

Delamorte leaned his head back on the pillow. "Yes, of course. I apologize. I had suspected that, but it unfortunately slipped my mind." His mind? What was left of it anyway.

Delamorte placed the oxygen mask over his face again and took a couple breaths. He removed the mask and waved in the general direction of his bedroom door. "I must not be thinking clearly as there is also the matter of the antiquities down the hall."

"A funeral pyre." The voice belonged to Thomas. I turned around as my brother stepped into Delamorte's bedroom.

"Sorry," I said to Delamorte. "Guess I should have shut the door."

Delamorte nodded his head at Thomas. "A similar method has been used in the past."

"Really?" Thomas asked.

"Yes, a group of Vikings once decided I merited some honor and placed me in the casket, loaded me onto one of their boats and set the entire thing on fire. The boat burned down to the water. Fortunately, the casket had sufficient buoyancy that I ended up floating along a river all the way to the North Sea. Roused from what seemed a brief sleep, I slid the lid back enough to see out and found myself afloat on the high seas quite literally without a paddle. Fortunately, the current brought me to shore on an island off the coast of Scotland before my renewed self died of thirst and my remains rotted in that wooden box."

Out of the corner of my eye I could see Thomas looking at me. I looked at him enough to see he was grinning a little. I couldn't tell if he was amused or incredulous. Honestly, I was beginning to think Delamorte had a talent for pulling stories out of his ass.

He pushed himself up in the bed again. "One would need to find a place where a fire of that magnitude would not arouse much attention or concern. The last thing you would want is some volunteer fire department showing up to extinguish the flames of hope."

"Flames of hope?" Thomas asked. "I'm sorry, I didn't hear everything you were saying earlier. What exactly are you trying to accomplish?"

"He wants to be put in the old casket and for someone to burn it up."

Delamorte raised his eyebrows. "I think you will find that quite an impossible task."

"What do you mean impossible?" I asked. "Why are we even—"

Delamorte held up his hand, the magic hand of silence. "The old casket is indestructible, at least by flames." His eyes shifted to the doorway where Lucy had appeared.

"As I recall," she said, "someone once tried to burn up that cursed casket of yours in a foundry." Thomas looked at me and Delamorte, then behind him. He turned back to face us frowning. Lucy continued: "I believe they thought it was evil, a device of Satan, and should be destroyed."

"Who did?" I asked.

"A priest," Delamorte said.

"Did I miss part of the conversation?" Thomas asked.

I looked at him. "I need to ask you something, T. How many people are in this room right now?"

He looked at me like I was nuts. "Three?"

"You, me, and Delamorte, right? That's all."

"Who else would there be?"

Luch and I both looked at Delamorte. He took a breath, coughed a little. "I can explain, but now is perhaps not the optimal time."

I had wondered if I was the only one in my family who could see Lucy. I guess I had my answer. Honestly, I was probably okay with them not knowing everything about Lucy. I mean, would my logical little brother be open-minded about Death as a literal creature? And Jess? Would she try to make friends with Lucy or be terrified? Honestly, I'd be curious to know the answer to that. Was Death inherently good or bad? That would probably depend on your outlook on life.

Lucy eased onto the edge of the bed opposite Delamorte. He was a fairly handsome man even though he was dying, and Lucy was damn attractive despite being, you know, Death. They actually made a good-looking couple.

"The priest was a reasonably good person," Delamorte said. "He merely lacked in wisdom."

Thomas shook his head. "I still have no idea what you're talking about."

"I'll explain later," I said. "Maybe." I had too many questions to allow stories of Vikings and priests to distract me. "So, you're saying that old casket doesn't burn up if you light it on fire."

"That is the case."

"Then ... what happens to you?" I asked.

"What I am about to tell you is not to

leave this room. Are we agreed?"

"Absolutely," I said, though I would have said anything to hear more about the secrets of the casket. Thomas nodded in agreement.

"I have been in possession of that box for many cen—"

"Are you certain," Lucy interrupted, "you want them to know *everything*? It will change them, you know."

"It is what must be." Delamorte continued: "The casket has been with me for a very long time. It has, shall we say, restorative capacity, though I do not know by what mechanism."

"What do you mean?" Thomas asked. "I don't understand what you're saying."

A few things came together in my mind. The side panels on the casket, the same man in each picture. The hieroglyphs. What has been will be again.

"Yes, I realize I am being unclear. I am, as they say, beating around the proverbial bush. I will just come out and say it. It is a device—"

"That will bring you back to life," I said.

The Big Ask

Lucy clapped her hands silently. "They really are bright children, Victor."

"Yes, once I am deceased."

I examined his face for any trace of humor but found none. He seemed, well, dead serious.

Thomas looked down at the floor a moment, then sat on the very end of the bed. "So, you're hoping to be resurrected."

Delamorte nodded. "That is how it works."

I waited for Thomas's usual skepticism, for him to laugh at how ridiculous the whole idea was. Instead, he sat there deep in thought.

"How would it be possible to come back alive once all the life processes in your body have ceased? I mean, all your cells are dead. They're never going to work again. Why do you believe this will happen?" Thomas asked.

Lucy looked directly at me. "Remember the ashes." I knew she was talking about the Phoenix.

"Because it has happened many times previously," Delamorte said.

"How many times?" Thomas asked.

"I believe I am up to forty-eight?" Lucy, looking a little miffed, nodded.

"Forty-eight!" We turned to see Jess sitting cross-legged in the doorway.

"How long have you been sitting there?" I asked.

"I heard something about Vic being brought back to life in some casket down the hall, life processes, Vikings, and an unwise priest." Great. So my little sister basically knew everything.

"The number of panels on the side of the casket represents the number of times I have been restored."

Thomas did some mental math. "If you lived an average of, say, sixty years each lifetime that would make you ..."

"For various reasons, it is actually closer to an average of forty years per life." I think all of us frowned at him. He must have seen the questions. "I managed to die young a few times. Killed in battle, murdered once or twice, plague. The plague actually got me twice, as I recall."

"Back to back," Lucy said. She stared off, a halfway pleasant look on her face. "It was such a joyful time. Such a purposeful existence for my people."

Vic glanced at Lucy, then over at me. "At least it was easier to plan for than dying in one's sleep." My mouth hung open, my head shaking. "Let me tell you, being murdered in your sleep is a logistical nightmare. One must have all one's, as they say, ducks in a row all the time in the event of catastrophe."

"Yes, one must always be on call," Lucy

said, looking at her fingernails.

Thomas tilted his head, frowning.

Delamorte continued: "One important rule is to stay away from things that explode. It would be virtually impossible for anyone to place my remains in that casket when my parts are scattered all over everywhere." Jess let loose a belly laugh. "I am pleased your sister can see the humor in it all," Delamorte said, grinning out of one side of his mouth.

"That would still make you in the neighborhood of two thousand years old," Thomas said.

"I do not know my exact date of birth, but that is likely a fair approximation."

I had no idea what to believe. Delamorte was either a lunatic after all or he was making up shit off the top of his head just to mess with us. Or ... or, he was a very old human being.

The presence of Grim Reaper Lucy kind of argued in favor of the very-old-human theory. Was that why she appeared? To add credibility? To make sure I believed Delamorte enough to do what he would ask. Belief, was that what was required? It was sounding like Santa Claus and the Easter Bunny to me.

"Is there any proof of this?" Thomas asked, still struggling as much with his doubts as I was.

"All the proof you need, indeed all that I have, is what lies in that room at the end of the hallway and, of course, my presence before you."

"And mine," Lucy said. I glanced at Thomas and Jess to see if they responded in any way to Lucy. Nothing.

Thomas frowned. "The antiquities?"

Delamorte nodded. "I have collected those items over the centuries from many different places, knowing they would serve mainly as a means of financial support should that be necessary but also as witness to the truth of what I am saying."

"That ... actually makes sense," Thomas said. "I mean, it's more feasible for you to have collected them than to have bought them." I could tell Thomas really wanted to believe Delamorte.

"What if he stole them?" I asked.

Delamorte looked shocked. "Do I look like a thief to you?" Thomas and I looked at each other, then at Delamorte. "Apparently my appearance and your experience with me are not as convincing a testimony to my character as I had hoped."

"My dear," Lucy recounted, "you were a pirate for many years."

Delamorte was silent. Realizing the others couldn't see or hear Lucy, I tried to supply the missing parts of the conversation. "Didn't you tell me you were a pirate?" Thomas and Jess stared at me. "You know, that time I went exploring the room at the end of the hall?"

Delamorte nodded, eyeing Thomas in particular. "Yes, I believe I may have mentioned such."

"Together with your great love," Lucy began, "you plundered the China Sea and Indian Ocean for decades."

"But you weren't alone, right?" I asked. You had like a ... partner or something."

"Indeed," he said. "With the greatest pirate in the history of the world."

"Like Blackbeard or something?" Thomas asked.

"Zheng Yi Sao. After the death of her husband she was known as Ching Shih. At one time, she commanded three hundred ships under the red flag and upwards of forty-thousand pirates."

Lucy looked down at herself, then back at me. "I assume her image." I nodded. I remembered overhearing her talk about that with Delamorte after our first night in the funeral home.

"We digress," Delamorte said. "By placing me in that box when the time comes, all your questions as to my sanity will be answered." He looked at each of us. "Through the long years of my life, I have consistently found one person who has acted in my interest at my death. There have been people, young and old, who have been my helper, my *complice*. Mr.

Gerard was to have taken on this role, but he has abandoned me to pursue his own interests."

That's what it sounded like from the recent conversation I'd overheard between the two of them.

Delamorte fixed his tired eyes on me. "Tell me ... do you have faith?"

"You mean like religion, God and all that?"

"Not entirely, no. I refer to the concept of trusting a person to do what they say they are going to do."

"I trust some people, just mostly not everybody."

He nodded. "That is understandable given your life experiences. What I am asking is for you to trust me enough to do exactly as I say."

It seemed the conversation had taken a turn from vague and impersonal to specific and very much directed toward me. Delamorte stared at me, eyes intense and penetrating. "Let me ask you, Callie Valentine, do you have any love for me in your heart?"

The way he said the word "love" vibrated through my skin, into muscle, and down to bone. It was a word or action I'd not heard or seen much in my recent life. Something kindled in my body, like an oven pilot light igniting. Who was I kidding? Of course, I would place him in that old casket. I should have just said yes and gotten it over with. Instead, I let the question of love stay in my head too long, burrowing deep down into a grave where my hope had been long ago buried. My eyes blurred.

"I take your tears as an affirmative."

"I'm not crying," I said. "I think it's just allergies. This room is so full of dust."

He pursed his lips a little, swallowed, then continued. "I have seen the character you possess in spite of what you have endured in your short life. So I ask you this: Will you place me in that casket at my death and set it aflame? Will you be my *complice*, Callie Valentine?"

Jess stood, dramatically nodding at me, her eyes huge. "Do it!" Jess, the true believer. Thomas raised his eyebrows, but said nothing. Even Doubting Thomas looked like he was encouraging me to agree to Delamorte's crazy request.

Part of me wanted to run out of the room. But as I looked at Delamorte, the flame in my body burned and the desire to believe him felt overwhelming. I chose not to fight the feeling. Hell, I cared about the man. Enough to do exactly what he was asking no matter how weird it was.

"I would be honored to be your assistant, your *complice*."

At least I wouldn't have to worry about keeping Delamorte in cold storage for some years.

He nodded. "Thank you."

I took a few seconds to get it together enough to say anything. "No problem," I said, then added, "Vic."

His face lit up with a smile the size of Texas. "How I have longed to hear that from you."

"I know," I said. "Sorry for being such a dick about it."

Delamorte nodded, acknowledging what was probably my last bit of resistance to having a relationship with the man. His smile faded, and he swallowed hard.

"One additional thing," he said, "and this is vital. I must be in the casket within twenty-four hours after I have taken my last breath." He was breathing kind of heavy like I might if I'd run up and down the staircase a bunch of times. He placed the oxygen mask back up to his face and took a couple breaths. "Am I clear on this requirement? I need your assent."

"Twenty-four hours. Got it." Something inside me was screaming, *No, I don't got it.* Love or not, this is crazy fucking nuts. "What should I do if Mr. Gerard has other ideas?"

Vic's lips tightened into a straight line before speaking. "You must thwart him at all costs."

"I would offer to assist," Lucy said. She

looked at Delamorte, a hungry smile on her face. "But, I will be preoccupied."

Mr. Gerard may have been several inches shorter than me, but he was undoubtedly stronger. Pete had been a drugged-out idiot. Mr. Gerard was a wiry, energetic, determined, and apparently fairly smart guy with an attitude. I was pretty sure he knew shit about how to take care of himself that I did not. If it came down to a physical struggle, could I win that?

"I have told you these things in confidence. You had best keep them to yourself. There are some who would interpret my words as instability of the mind."

Geez, ya think? I had no intention of *ever* telling anyone what I'd just heard. I mean, what if some authority person heard we were living with a guy who thought an old casket would bring him back from the dead. They'd jerk us out of the funeral home and toss us in foster care so fast ... It'd be like falling off the Old Home Road overpass. One-thousand-one, one-thousand splat.

So what if Delamorte believed in the power of some magical box? Did that even matter? I mean, people had their quirks. A lot of church people believed they would be resurrected after death.

No big deal, right?

The Empty Room

Delamorte didn't know his exact birthday, and we'd never had a party or anything to celebrate. So, a couple days after his wild story about the casket, I decided we should do something. I put to use what culinary skills I had learned from Delamorte, gathered some flour, eggs, and sugar and followed a simple recipe on YouTube and baked him a birthday cake. Jess even helped make a frosting.

I had no driver's license, never done driver's ed, and never actually driven solo before. That didn't stop me from taking a risk and driving the hearse to the grocery store to get candles. I had no idea how old the man actually was so, remembering Thomas' estimate, I bought a two and three zeros.

After dinner, the three of us marched up the stairs, cake in hand, lit the candles just outside Vic's bedroom, and knocked.

"Come in," he said.

We strolled in, cake aflame, singing "Happy Birthday." His face lit up and he pushed himself up in the bed, folding his hands in front of him.

"I have never celebrated my birthday. For the vast majority of my lifetimes, it was simply not done. You certainly did not need to go to all this trouble. I am not someone who needs recognition in this manner, my lives are not worthy of such honor even if I have had many of them. Nevertheless, I appreciate your effort. Thank you, children. Thank you."

I portioned out some slices of the cake onto paper plates, and we sat around Vic eating it. He couldn't eat much of it, but he did comment on my baking. "Very nice texture. You used both vanilla and almond extract, correct? And plenty of oil?" I nodded. "I can tell. Very nice. You would make an excellent *cuisiniere*."

It surprised me how good it felt to hear him say that. When we were done, Jess took the plates down to the kitchen.

Delamorte had confined himself to the side of the bed closest to the window. Various papers and a magazine or two were spread over the opposite side of the bed. He set his plate down on the bedstand, turned, and picked up what looked like a piece of leather folded over on itself and wrapped with a little cord.

He pushed himself up in the bed so he was leaning against the ornate headboard, grimacing in pain as he did so. He undid the leather and pulled out some thick sheets of paper and unfolded them before him. "I am leaving you the hearse."

"Wait," Thomas said. "If you're coming back, won't you need it?" He wasn't grinning. Did my brother actually believe Vic would be resurrected?

He shook his head. "I believe I will ply a

different trade next time around. I have found that, once freed from the drudgery of one life, it is much preferred to not immediately step back into that very same drudgery or quagmire from which one has just escaped." For some reason, the image of our old apartment flashed in my mind. I'd considered trying to rent a place there, but it would be kind of the same thing as what Vic said. A return to the quagmire.

"Thanks," I said, grinning. "I mean, I still need a driver's license, but really, thank you."

"You have become like a daughter to me. Of course, you can sell it or drive it. It is your choice."

The word "daughter" vibrated through my body. It produced the same warm feeling as when Delamorte had used the words "milk" and "chocolate" months ago and "love" more recently. The word "daughter" was like a drug, one that made me feel somehow bigger, like my life meant something. Delamorte had acted a lot like what I'd imagined a dad would act over the past few months. Giving me my first car was just another one of those things.

"I think I'll keep it around a while," I said.

"Being able to give love and care to someone else has been a potent salve for a broken heart and burdened conscience."

"Like that dragonfly wing goop, but for the soul."

He grinned. "Yes, my dear. I had not thought of it that way, but yes."

"Can I get you anything?" I asked.

He shook his head, leaned back, and closed his eyes. Thomas got up and left. I followed a few moments later, shutting the door to his bedroom as I went into the hallway.

I noticed the door to the Forbidden Room open and went down to see who else it was had violated Delamorte's rules.

Thomas knelt next to the old casket. "And here I thought I was the only one who had no boundaries," I said.

"Do you think what Vic says could be true?"

"You're the rational one," I said. "What do you think?"

"He spoke about having an in-person conversation with Karl Marx, but that would have had to be over a century ago. And that dresser in your room? The one Vic said had belonged to the Sun God. That was Louis the Fourteenth, I looked it up." I knew I could count on Thomas to answer that question. "He was King of France more than three hundred years ago."

"Do you think Vic was there then? Three hundred years ago?"

"There are more things in heaven and earth than you have dreamt of in your philosophy, Horatio."

"Okay, first, don't call me Horatio, and second, that's a quote or something?"

"Shakespeare. Hamlet."

"Didn't know you were such a Shakespearean scholar."

"Vic said it that one morning in the kitchen so I looked it up." He'd said it just after we'd moved into the funeral home. I barely remembered it, but Thomas had apparently latched onto the idea.

"It makes sense," Thomas continued. "I mean, we haven't learned everything about our universe yet. Dark matter, dark energy. They're called dark simply because we don't know what they are."

"So, you're saying it could be true? What he said about the casket?"

"Look at this thing," he said, running his fingers over the wood. "It's almost like you can feel its age." My brother was right. I'd felt the same thing when I'd touched the casket before. I placed my hand on it and instantly felt something and it wasn't just age.

"Do you feel that?" I asked.

"Feel what?"

"There's a vibration in the wood."

Thomas waited, his eyes moving back and forth. "Yeah, yeah! I can feel it too."

Did the ancient box have power? Was it really what Delamorte said it was? A means to resurrection? If that were true, I shouldn't be worried about anything. Not where we would live, what we were gonna eat, or honestly not even social services. I shook my head a few times to erase the thought and the stupid hope that went with it.

I started to go, but Thomas stopped me. "Hey," he said. "I ... " His mouth twitched like he couldn't figure out how to say what he wanted to say. "Thank you," he blurted out finally.

"Um, okay."

He swallowed. "For taking care of us."

My mouth literally fell open in shock. My judgmental brother, critic of every breath I'd ever taken, thanking me for something?

"I've been thinking a lot about everything you've done for us since I was little, too little to remember apparently."

"The diapers?"

"Yeah, the diapers."

"Vic talked to me about it some."

"The diapers?"

"Well, not exactly. He said I needed to put myself, the way he said it was 'behind your eyes' and see what you see." That sounded like something Delamorte would say. "I imagined if it had been me having to do what you did, I don't think I could have done it. In fact, I know I couldn't have done it."

I thought about all the late nights in various apartments and rent houses, barricading our bedroom door to keep out whatever shithead had wandered home with Mom. Stealing Mom's SNAP card while she slept so we could go to the grocery store. Discovering the library, helping with homework, reading to my brother and sister.

I hadn't started doing those things all at once. I guess they kind of accumulated, along with the weight of having to do all of them. I realized for the first time how nice it felt not having to do them all. I'd have felt even better except for my new responsibility of what to do with Vic's dead body.

"Don't get me wrong," Thomas said. "I still think you're kind of a bully. But at least now I sort of understand why."

"Is that some kind of weird ass, sideways compliment?"

He looked away, then back at me. "Just appreciation."

"I started taking care of you guys when I was younger than Jess. I didn't get a lot of things right. I mean, I messed up a lot. I'm just glad you don't remember a lot of it."

"Oh, I remember some things."

"Like what?" Honestly, I didn't want to know.

"Maybe later. Right now, all I wanted to say was, you know, I kind of get it."

I nodded, relieved not to have to listen to Thomas' list of horrible memories of me. "I don't know, T. You might have surprised yourself," I said. "You might could have done better than I did."

"Maybe so, but I didn't have to. You did. So, thank you for that."

"So, you still think I'm a bully, but you're thanking me for it?"

"Well, no, that's not ... "

"I know. I was just messing."

He opened his mouth to say something else, but closed it.

It surprised me how good it felt hearing Thomas say those words. Good like waking up at night, freezing cold, reaching around and finding a warm blanket. It was a relief knowing my brother appreciated me. At least, he didn't hate me as much as I thought. Maybe he'd attend my funeral after all. Him and Jess both.

* * *

Vic's illness worsened. About half the time I had this feeling lightning was going to strike down out of the sky. Or some meteorite was going to land on my head. If not the climate, one of Lucy's kind or bad luck out to get me, it was animals or people. I kept imagining dogs and pervs lurking around every corner. I'd promised Vic something, but doing it worried me. There were so many gaps in the plan.

I stayed busy most of the time. Either running at the school track or around the cemetery or just messing around the funeral home. I still did a lot of the cleaning around the house. It kept my mind off other things, things that would eat a hole in my brain if I let them.

Death was closing in all around me.

* * *

My muscles were starting to evaporate off my bones from lack of punishing them. So, I went up to school the next couple of Saturday mornings to work out in the weight room and do some running.

After school, I mostly spent time with Vic in the afternoons. Sometimes Thomas or Jess would join, but mostly it was just me and Vic. I asked him one day about the pictures on the sides of the casket.

"I may have mentioned that I do not fully understand how the device works. That being said, I believe those images are meant to depict relevant scenes or perhaps a summary of each of my lives."

"So the man in the pictures, it is supposed to be you?"

"It is as you say." I nodded, looking around the room, thinking.

"And the others? The women, the kids?"

He studied me a moment. "Wives, mothers, sons and daughters."

"Do you remember them much?" I tried to ask it kind of nonchalant, kind of like Pastor

Priest had asked me about my dad.

He looked around the bed covers, like he was surveying landscape from a mountaintop. He swallowed, spoke. "It is hard to speak about it." I nodded, he continued. "It would be more difficult, perhaps, if I could remember more details about them all. Unfortunately, over the many years the details of each have faded from memory."

"You have no albums, no photos?"

He looked up at me, eyebrows lifted. It took me a second. "Oh, right. No cameras."

"There were times I undertook to write things down, but parchment and vellum fade and rot. All I possess now are vague outlines, echoes of voices, and all of them have blended together like ingredients in a recipe. Little is left of the individuals of whom I was once so fond. Even in my recent lives, with more durable writing material, looking over my journals is like reading someone else's story. The emotional connection to them has grown cold. Still, I find myself missing a particular child without fully recalling them. It is like being in a constant state of grief without fully understanding why."

My own memory of my dad, the one I'd mostly manufactured, had muddled in my head as I'd gotten older. I was even staring to forget what Mom looked like before she was an addict.

"Were you able to keep track of your

grandchildren? Like maybe raise them? The same with their children, like one generation after the other."

He took in a breath, held it, let it out. "That would have involved letting a great many persons in on my little secret."

"The resurrection thing."

He nodded. "In those times, I would have been labeled a heretic son of Satan for not dying." I thought at first he was making a joke about it, but his expression collapsed into something reflecting sadness, then anger followed by sadness again.

I'd lost a mom and a dad. For Vic, his life had been one lost family after the other. Was that what immortality was like? Just a constant ache of grief? If that was true, why did Vic keep getting into that casket life after life?

* * *

I picked up Thomas and Jess from school the Wednesday before Halloween. Thomas had been kind of a jerk about my driving without a license, but he didn't refuse to get in the hearse when I picked him up from school.

We got fast food on the way home. As I passed the white paper bags out to Thomas and Jess, I couldn't help but remember how much we'd craved fast food the day I'd robbed the GrabNGo. How things had changed.

We didn't get back to the funeral home

until late afternoon. I was walking toward the back door when something felt, I don't know, off. Like it did when we'd come home to our old apartment and ran into Fat Jesus and his eviction notice.

First, there were light-colored scrapes on the concrete driveway that hadn't been there before. Some of the shrubs at the corner of the home were smashed down. I went over and found depressions in the ground like something with large tires had rolled over it. On the porch, some of the gray paint on the flooring had been scratched as if some heavy thing had been dragged across it.

Thomas and Jess had already gone inside and headed upstairs. I stepped into the hall and had the same feeling as outside. I scanned the hallway looking for anything that might be wrong. Easing toward the kitchen, I found that the door to the Private Room was ajar. Usually, that door was shut and locked.

I pushed it open to look around. Inside, boxes of toilet paper and paper towels sat on shelves along with cleaning supplies, some tools, and boxes of old clothes. The gate to the elevator was open and there was a lot of dust and debris on the floor. Had it been there when I'd ridden up with Mr. Gerard and unconscious Vic the night he'd passed out?

I stepped into the elevator, slid the cage closed, and pulled the lever engaging the machinery that lifted me upward into the Forbidden Room. I opened the cage door, felt around for the light, and flipped the switch.

Other than wads of dust, a few splinters, and some thin strands of cloth, the room was completely empty.

The casket was gone.

And When I Die

"Fuck!"

The word echoed off the walls of the bare room before being absorbed by the dust. It was obvious to me who had taken the stuff from the Forbidden Room. Mr. Gerard had done it while we were all at school and Vic was lying helpless and probably asleep in his room down the hall. Had the guy been watching us? Waiting for us to leave that morning?

The little shit!

It wasn't until after we'd eaten lunch that I got up my nerve to go in Vic's bedroom.

"I heard you curse earlier. Had something occurred that prompted such a crude outburst?"

I sighed dramatically. "Sorry, I guess I should have yelled something like 'oh snap, look at this room where all Vic's antiquities used to be. It's so empty now.'"

His expression went from pleasant to blank. He looked in the direction of the window. "Mr. Gerard, I presume."

"I'm pretty sure."

He looked dejected and, after a moment, resigned. He'd gotten so thin. His face looked almost skeletal. "Perhaps I have lived long enough." His eyes fluttered shut and I left him to rest.

I wanted to go look for Mr. Gerard, the

casket, and the other stuff he'd stolen but had no idea where to begin. I mean, I didn't even know where the guy lived. I tried to keep myself busy vacuuming and cleaning the funeral home so I wouldn't have to think about it. Sitting around doing nothing just wasn't an option.

Pastor Priest stopped by that afternoon to visit Vic. I left the two of them to talk in his room but made my way upstairs when I heard the pastor talking out in the hall.

"We'll see how everything turns out," she said. "Maintain your faith in humanity if nothing else."

"Thank you," Vic said to the pastor, "for your understanding and your help."

She eased past me into the hall. I followed her downstairs. "Pastor?" She turned to face me, eyes searching mine. The sight of her red hair, even with the few gray ones, froze me for a second. My parallel universe mom. "You wouldn't happen to have any spells for handling impossible problems, would you?"

I explained to her about the missing antiquities, including the casket, and my suspicions that Mr. Gerard had taken all of it. I didn't know how much she knew about the casket, so I left out the resurrection part and the part where Vic asked me to put his dead body inside the old box. She listened intently and nodded when I finished.

She smiled warmly, and went into the kitchen. I followed and we sat at the table. The pastor cleared her throat. "I have found that pulling a problem apart into smaller pieces often reveals a completely different situation. One that is more manageable. Cognitive psychologists refer to this as 'unpacking' a problem."

"You sound like a therapist or something."

"I am a licensed professional counselor."

"Didn't you say you were a practicing witch?"

"I find they are often one and the same."

The image of a cackling old woman stuffing children into a hot stove was burned into my consciousness. "How so?"

"Both practice healing. It's just that one of them got a bad rap, mainly due to misguided religious fervor and people's insatiable need for entertainment." I frowned. "Burning women at the stake attracted huge crowds." She smiled gently. "Pure blood lust."

The pastor stood. Searching the kitchen cabinets, she found a jar. Placing it on the kitchen table, she fished around in her clothes, checking places that didn't seem to have pockets. A moment later she pulled out a small stone and dropped it into the jar.

"Carnelian," she said. "For motivation

and confidence." Her eyes scanned the kitchen. "Mr. Delamorte is a chef. He should have a collection of ... Ah, yes."

The pastor stepped over to where Vic kept his dried herbs.

"What are you looking for?"

"Whatever I can find. So often, the best spells are concocted on the spot from available materials. Improvisation is key, the energy of the desperate moment acting as a powerful binder."

I had no effing idea what she was talking about. She examined the herbs, pulled out some lavender, and dropped it into the jar. "Is there any mint or lemon?"

I went out to the back porch. The day was fading, the shadows getting longer. I picked a few leaves of fresh mint that grew in the ground near a faucet and added those to the mix. I found a lemon in the fridge, grabbed a peeler, and dropped a couple pieces of lemon peel into the jar.

"Now, is there maybe some ribbon?"

"Ribbon?"

"Yes, like you might use for gift wrap."

I spied an apron with red trim hanging on the wall. Grabbing it, I tore the trim off and handed it to the pastor. "Hmm," she said examining it. "This will do nicely." She handed the red cloth back to me. "It is best that the beneficiary of this spell perform this part on her own."

She had me tie the red trim from the apron around the top of the jar. The best I could do was pretend I was tying my shoelaces into a big bow.

"Perfect," she said. "Now, repeat after me. 'I am big, I am strong, feelings of doubt be gone.'"

I did as the pastor said. She nodded her approval. "This is merely a ritual, it has no true power other than what you assign to it. As far as the decision you face, I advise you once again to pull the problem, or the question, apart. Find what is doable, or knowable, and act on it as you wish. The rest may very well take care of itself."

I stared at her, the image of my mom overlying the pastor's face.

"You have kids?"

She smiled. "It's always seemed ridiculous to bring more children into a world when there are so many already in need of a parent. If I wanted to take on that responsibility, I would seek out one of those in need before trying to produce another life myself."

I nodded, filing her words away for future reference.

* * *

It was finally Halloween. The sun's orange glow stretched from the window in Vic's room across his bed. Shadows grew in every corner. "I hope I have done right by you, that I have given you what you needed." He cleared his throat, weakly. "I just wish it could have been more."

His face was paler than it had been even earlier that day, his breathing labored. His body seemed to have sunken into the mattress as if it were eating him alive. I started to leave to let him rest, but he stopped me. "Stay with me," he said.

I sat down on the edge of the bed looking at him.

"I will find the casket," I said. "I promise, as your *complice*." My words sounded empty, mainly because I had no idea how to do what I was promising.

"Do not put yourself in harm's way because of me. I fear Mr. Gerard can be fairly dogged in his ... pursuit ... of monetary gain." He began coughing, wincing in pain. He felt around, found a handkerchief, and wiped blood from his mouth. I helped him put on his mask and got the oxygen flowing. "He feels wronged by me in some way," he said after a moment. "Perhaps wronged by everyone."

Thomas appeared at the door. "Everything okay?"

"What do you think?" I said with more snark than I meant to let out. I was afraid he might retreat to his room. Afraid because I didn't want to be alone there watching Vic die.

And I was sure that's what was happening.

As in that very night.

Relief washed over me as Thomas came and sat against the end of the bed. The golden light streaming from the window faded to a pink orange. Jess came in and sat next to me. She wound her arm around mine and leaned her head against me.

"What happens when we die?" Jess asked.

"You cease to exist," Thomas said. He was usually so matter-of-fact about things he equated with science. Not this time. There was a bitterness in his voice.

"Jesus, T," I said. I motioned toward Vic.

"What do you mean?" Jess asked.

"Just what I said, There's" — he glanced at Vic, then back at Jess — "There's no more you."

"What about heaven?" Jess asked. "Can't we go to heaven?"

"That's a figment of someone's imagination to make us feel better," Thomas said.

"I don't want Vic to die forever," Jess said. "We have to put him in the casket so he'll be alive again." Her face contorted, tears appearing in both eyes. "Please, can we put him in it?"

"We're—" I glanced at Thomas. "I'm going to."

Thomas looked at me, shocked. "I'm

going to help. Not because I think it will bring him back to life, but because that's what Vic wants."

Jess wiped her eyes. "It *will* work," she said. "The casket will do just what Vic said it would and he'll come back to life." I leaned into her, she into me. She really wanted to believe Vic would come back. Honestly, so did I.

Early evening crept into the room, bringing with it a light blue color a little darker than the old hearse. Normally, we all would have dressed up in our costumes to go Trick or Treating somewhere. The New Life Church of the Resurrection was having a Trunk or Treat thing with people handing out treats from their cars. I'd considered getting Lucy to make up my face like a Katrina. Instead, though, we were sitting around waiting for Vic to die.

I had no idea what to expect. Dad died a long way off and Mom just sort of disappeared. This was different. We were going to see it all happen right in front of us. I wasn't certain whether I liked that idea. Part of me just wanted to retreat somewhere. Pretend it wasn't happening. But I couldn't. I had no real choice but to watch.

Thomas left, returning a couple minutes later with his Lego spaceship. He leaned against the opposite wall and slid down to the floor, silently taking the ship apart piece by piece. He barely had enough light to see what he was doing, but I didn't think he cared. The spaceship was not the reason he was there.

Jess got up to use the restroom. A couple minutes later she came back with a chapter book and crawled up on the bed and sat cross-legged next to Vic's feet. I found a chair, pulled it up closer to Vic's bedstand, where I switched on the lamp.

Light divided Vic's body nearly right down the middle, warm yellow on one side and deep purple on the other. Like he was on the border between life and death. I searched the corners of the room, finding shades of deep blue and dark gray. Just normal shadows. Vic's closet, on the other hand, was unnaturally black.

Lucy was in there. Watching. Waiting.

Vic's eyes were closed, but the pulsing on the side of his neck persisted. There was some life still left in him. At one point he cleared his throat and I thought he was about to say something. His head moved from side to side, then was still again. The persistent ticking and chiming of the grandfather clock marked the passing hours.

It was nearly midnight. Darkness loomed, pressing against us from all sides. Jess and Thomas slept, and my eyes were dry and heavy. Vic's head moved a little and it sounded like he grunted. I leaned closer. Jess awoke and pushed herself up. I heard the click-clack of Thomas's Lego blocks, then he was standing next to me.

Vic moaned. It lasted a few beats until it sounded like groaning. It became more rhythmic, to the point I thought it might be a song. It only lasted a few seconds. Then his eyes opened wide, searching the room.

"We're here," I said.

His facial expression was serious. It almost looked like he was going to say something. He blinked a couple of times and closed his eyes.

She appeared almost immediately.

Lucy, elegantly dressed in deep purple satin, every shadow in the fine cloth seemed exaggerated like a cartoon outline. Standing at the side of the bed, her face solemn, posture straight as a door frame.

Jess stirred. "Who is that?"

Thomas stammered. "What's happening? Why is ...? How'd she ...?"

"Shhh," I said.

So, my brother and sister could now see Death.

Lucy's dress billowed as if caught by some invisible wind. As she moved, the purple satin turned to smoke, shades of gray at the edges roiling off her like storm clouds that flowed over the entirety of the bed.

A chilly wave ran over me, head to toe. I reached for Jess and pulled her over to me and out of any harm's way. I had no idea what Lucy was capable of but didn't want to take any chances. What if she got overly excited and decided to *collect* all of us?

Lucy moved across the bed toward Vic, inching closer until the full-length of their forms were touching. The expression on her face looked like anticipation, hunger, maybe even lust. She spoke, her voice low: "Again, we embrace, my love. Will you stay with me this time?"

What Lucy was doing to Vic, had it been that way for my dad? My mom?

"What's happening?" Thomas asked. The pitch of his voice was high, like he was scared. Having no answer for my brother, I put my hand on his arm. Maybe a minute later, no more, Vic's breathing became inconsistent. His chest would stop moving a moment or two, then he'd gasp. This happened maybe a dozen times, until finally he just stopped breathing.

Lucy, mostly dark vapor at that point, became one with Vic until she was no longer visible. Jess gasped and she gripped me around the waist, Thomas pressed close from behind. Vic's body seemed to deflate and flatten into the bed. I looked for the pulsing on the side of Vic's neck. Nothing.

His skin quickly faded from pale to a light gray color and the corners of his mouth turned down. I'd never seen anyone die. I stared at Vic until it sank in. He wasn't going to move again. Ever. He was gone.

"Is he ...?" Thomas asked.

I nodded. "I think so, yeah."

I wasn't sure how my brother would react. I remembered how upset he'd been when his goldfish died back in the fourth grade. This time, though, he seemed almost relieved.

Jess escaped my grip and crawled over to Vic. "Wait, Jess."

"It's all right," she said. "She's gone."

Did Jess know what Lucy was? Had they had their own conversation or something? I saw no sign of Lucy, so I wasn't too worried when Jess laid her head on Vic's chest. His being dead didn't seem to matter to my little sister. Her huge blue eyes moved from side-to-side, then she sat up.

"It's like he's ... empty," she said. "Like he's not in there anymore. Is that because his soul left?" I had no idea how to answer that question. The whole idea of a soul was so damn religious and churchy. What the hell did it even mean? Were we just biological processes like Thomas thought? Was there nothing more?

"I don't know, Jess."

My face felt cold and tight like my skin was being pulled back to my ears. My stomach felt queasy. I forced myself to breathe and keep breathing until the queasiness went away.

It might have been natural, but I hated

seeing Vic that way. Him dying was only the beginning of what lay ahead. Now that he was gone, I had no choice but to do one of two things. Get him in that old casket and set it one fire, or put him in one of the cold storage drawers indefinitely. Which one would it be?

I did as Pastor Priest advised and tried pulling the problem apart. Either way, I was going to have to get Vic downstairs and into cold storage. If, and that was a huge if, I went looking for and somehow found the old casket, I had a time limit to deal with. Twenty-four hours.

Reaching into my back pocket, I pulled out my phone and opened the Clock app. Since the app didn't allow me to set the timer for twenty-four hours, I set it for twenty-three hours, fifty-nine minutes, fifty-nine seconds. Then I thought it had already been a little bit since Vic died, so I changed the minute setting to fifty-five minutes, then fifty-four. A little extra just in case. In case of what? In case I decided to be a good *complice*.

I moved the chair from the side of the bed over to where Thomas's spaceship lay in pieces on the floor, unfinished, kind of in limbo waiting to be assembled once again. Jess slid off the bed, came over, and put her arms around me. I held her as long as she wanted. Thomas, who'd been staring at Vic's body, finally turned away and looked over at me.

"What exactly happened?" he asked. "I mean other than him dying. What happened to Lucy?" I really didn't want to have that discussion at that moment.

"She took him, didn't she," Jess said.

"What do you mean?" Thomas asked.

"There are more things in heaven and earth ..." I quoted.

Thomas nodded. "Apparently."

"There's something else," I said. "Come on."

Thomas and Jess followed me down the hall toward the Forbidden Room, the floor creaking as we went. I pushed open the door.

"What happened to all the ...?" Thomas paused, then finished in a whisper. "The casket."

"Yeah, the casket," I said.

"Somebody took it?" Jess asked, her voice reflecting shock and the beginning of panic.

I nodded. "I'm pretty sure Mr. Gerard helped himself to all of it."

"What do we do?" Thomas said.

If we were going to do as Vic asked, we had to find that damn casket. In fact, I had less than twenty-four hours to find it, load it in the hearse, get it back to the funeral home, and put Vic in it. I had no clue what I was going to do after that.

I needed to find Mr. Gerard but had no

idea where to look. I didn't even know his full name. Was Gerard his first name or last? I remembered hearing Vic call him Jerry. Was Gerard then his first name? And where did he live? How far away? He might have lived way out in the country for all I knew.

"It's probably time for bed," I said.

Jess didn't fight bedtime. I hugged her and gave her a kiss on the top of her red curls. "It'll be okay, won't it?"

"Yeah," I said. "It will." I turned out the bedroom light, and pulled the door almost closed.

"I just need to rest my eyes a little," Thomas said. My brother looked like a zombie, his eyes nearly shut, his head bowed a little. He headed to his room. I knew he wanted to help, but he was up way later than usual on a school night. Plus, he'd just lost ... what? A good friend? The only dad he'd ever really known?

I went downstairs. It was dark in the Underworld, so I started turning on some lights. It was unnaturally quiet. I don't know what I expected. People in the chapel? A wake?

I texted Mr. Gerard. *Vic died. Where are you?* It couldn't hurt to tell the guy what happened. Who knew? Maybe he'd bring back the casket.

I shuffled over to the back door and pulled aside the curtains. Looking out the window, all I could see was my own reflection in a black background. I reached over and flipped off the hall light. My face vanished, replaced by the silhouette of the hearse parked in the driveway.

Twenty-three hours, thirty-three minutes.

PART V

Graveyard Cheerleader

It was close to one o'clock in the morning and was as dark outside as the wood of the old casket. I just wanted to leave Vic at peace. I wanted to let *myself* be at peace, as in sleep. But, there was something I needed to do.

I forced myself to move, lifting my hand, taking hold of the doorknob, turning it, and pushing open the back door. I thought about switching on the porch light but decided it would be better to work in darkness. My luck some cop would be driving along, see me, and decide I was trying to rob the place. I'd been a creature of the night back at our old apartment. I'd had little choice. Things were no different that night at the funeral home.

I grabbed a windbreaker from one of the hangers on the wall by the door and put it on. It smelled of cigarettes and a little of cinnamon, so it must have been Vic's. I stepped out into the chilly fall evening. It was kind of wet, dew forming on everything. I reached into my pocket, found the keys to the hearse, and unlocked the back.

The door had a layer of moisture on it and my hand slipped off the cold, slick metal as I pulled open the back of the hearse. Vic had me replace the gurney in the back of the hearse after we'd finished with it a week ago. Putting it back in the hearse was easy. Just slide it in until it clicked. Getting it back out again was another thing altogether.

I started messing with levers and other moving parts trying to get the gurney to come loose. I might as well have been punching the metal stretcher with my fist for all the good it did. I bent down trying to see what was actually holding the gurney in place, but it was too dark to see anything.

Stepping back, I kicked the back of the hearse. After a moment I sat against the rear bumper, breathing hard, my eyes blurring. My body shook, but not with cold. What was I even doing out there? Inside me a scream welled up. Not wanting to wake Jess or Thomas, I ran down the driveway, blindly across the gray street and deep into the dark, lonely cemetery.

In the quiet, with no one to disturb but the dead, I let it all out. Repeatedly, until I was hoarse. I fell to my knees, the moisture from the damp grass oozing through my jeans. Vic, my dad, my mom, all of them had abandoned me. Why did I have to do this thing by myself? Why did I have to *live* by myself?

My entire body throbbed with rage at all the pathetic adults in my life. People who were supposed to take care of me, not the other way around. Clouds of steam blasted from my mouth and nose into the night air like fire from one of the dragons on Lucy's red dress. After a few moments, my breathing slowed, anger chilling to a lump of cold hard reality. I was never going to be able to get the gurney out of the hearse much less find the casket. I should have watched Vic more closely when he was unloading customers. *Stupid!* All I had to do was pay a little more attention.

I was fucking useless. I couldn't fix my mom, get her to rehab, convince her to be a parent. I'd failed as a daughter. And living at the funeral home, I'd never gotten Vic to go to the doctor and now I was going to fail as his *complice* because I didn't pay attention to some little detail.

If I'd worn a few more dresses, put on a little makeup, started acting like an actual girl. Would Mom still be around if I had? Maybe if I'd done what I was told a few more times I'd still have a … still have a dad. A real one, not the fake hallucination that kept haunting me.

I sat back on the wet grass, leaning against one of the few upright headstones. stared at a nearly full moon.

There was nothing I could do about that now. Water that has flowed by will not return. There was no changing the past. I was stuck with life the way it was. I was stuck … with *me*.

Tendrils of foggy mist threaded their way through the graveyard. I felt so damn helpless.

You're not helpless.

The voice was clear and distinct enough I

didn't think it was just in my head. But it had to be my imagination. There was no one else there. I looked around and noticed the name on the grave marker I'd been leaning against. Raymond Thibodeaux. He'd been the first corpse I'd met at the funeral home. Was his ghost giving me encouragement?

Get up, baby. Move.

I noticed a dark form by one of the scattered cemetery trees three or four rows of graves away. I thought it was just the tree's shadow, but it seemed extra dark. Darker than it should have been. Was it Lucy? No, she was occupied, wrestling with Vic's soul or something. This was different.

The darkness by the tree faded to a foggy gray mass. The air around me was still, yet that little patch of mist floated toward me. As it moved, it changed from a blob to something longer, more upright. Like a person.

Then I saw her, plain as day. Standing a couple headstones away, wearing the same outfit from the picture in my mind. The one where she had that innocent smile.

I got to my feet. "Mom?"

"Hey, baby. Don't you have something you need to do?"

I smiled. "What're you doing out here?"

My mother's face seemed to go out of focus, then sharpened again. It wasn't real what I was seeing. Just a ghost or yet another hallucination. The only other ghost I'd seen was that of my dad, someone I knew for a fact was dead. Did that mean Mom was also dead?

"Are you ...?"

Mom continued to smile, then winked at me. "Best not ask too many questions."

She didn't move like a normal person, there was no bounce in her step. She flowed more than walked in the direction of the funeral home.

"Whatever you have to do, you can do it. I'm pulling for you." She looked over her shoulder. "You comin'?" The fog in the cemetery thickened suddenly, swallowing her.

"Mom?" I called. "Mom, wait. I'm sorry." I yelled, hoping to somehow reconjure her. "I'm sorry, Mom. I didn't mean to ..." But, she was gone. I was alone. Again.

I hadn't meant to leave her, but what was I supposed to do? My brother and sister needed someone. I couldn't wait for Mom to get better. I had to go on, with or ... without her. I wanted to ask her for ... what? Forgiveness? I let that word settle in my head. Yeah, I guess that was it. Forgiveness. I repeated the word, testing its meaning. It felt warm and delicious, like something Vic created in the kitchen. I wanted to savor it, to grab it in a bear hug and pull it into me the way Lucy had become one with Vic at the end.

Cold air caressed my shoulders. I

couldn't stay out there in that cemetery all night. I had to keep going. I had to do this thing, whatever it ended up being.

Rubbing my face hard with both hands, I took a deep breath and let it out as slow as I could. I started to walk, then jogged, back through the rows of graves to the hearse.

I remembered what Pastor Priest had said about solving the impossible problem. Break it down into small pieces, do what you are able to do and the rest might take care of itself. With teeth clenched, I tried jiggling a couple of moving parts on the gurney.

I don't know how I did it, but the gurney came loose and slid out the back until the legs automatically extended on one end and snapped into place. It was like some invisible force had pulled it from the hearse. Maybe the ghosts of gurneys past or spirits of the long-departed or maybe my own mom had followed me from the cemetery and seen fit to lend an unseen hand. Then I remembered I didn't really believe in ghosts or souls. Definitely not those belonging to inanimate objects. I also realized I was on a slight incline and decided the invisible force was actually just gravity.

"Fuck you, asshole," I said, really to no one in particular. The hell with eloquence. It was a matter of principle. The gurney was caught on something, so it didn't come all the way out. Spurred on by unexpected success, I felt around until my fingers found a little latch. I lifted it and the gurney came completely free, the other set of legs snapping into place as I pulled it out the back.

"Son of a bitch!"

The elevator was just big enough for the gurney to fit, and I had it lined up next to Vic's bed a little before two o'clock. I figured out how to collapse the legs again to make it easier to slide Vic from his bed and onto the padded surface. I was really getting the hang of the mortician thing.

His body was cool to the touch but still flexible. I pretended he was only asleep as I pulled him off the bed in stages. Head and upper body first, legs last. *Shit!* One of Vic's eyes had opened a little. It freaked me out at first, but the more I looked at him it seemed like he was peeking at me.

"Yeah, I'm doing it," I said.

I had no desire to have Vic's dead eye looking at me while I worked, so I reached over and quickly pushed his lid shut. "Rest," I said.

I needed to raise the gurney back up but, as Vic said, it was a two-person job. I didn't want to disturb Thomas, and to be honest I really did want to do it all by myself. So I bent down and alternated pushing and pulling the gurney down the hall, into the Forbidden Room, and onto the elevator.

Once back in the Underworld, I got Vic

to the Preparation Room and over to the lowest of the cold storage drawers. Parking the gurney next to the drawer, I opened it and shoved him into the drawer in stages the same way I'd gotten him onto the gurney.

I adjusted Vic's arms so his hands came together over his waist. Most of the dead people I'd seen at the funeral home had their arms and hands placed like that. I stared at him for a moment. Was he really gone? Would he kick at the door of the storage drawer in the middle of the night? Wanting to be let out?

I squatted down and placed my fingers against the cool skin of his neck. Still nothing. He seemed at peace. Enough I felt okay sliding the drawer shut.

I felt dead tired. As tired as I used to be keeping watch for Mom late at night. But this felt different. Keeping watch for Mom had been a labor of hopelessness. Getting Vic into cold storage, I felt a warm flicker of excitement. I had no idea why.

I turned off all the lights with the exception of the kitchen and made sure all the outside doors were locked. I sat at the kitchen table, staring at the jar of herbs and the carnelian rock. My plan was to start my search for Mr. Gerard's pickup truck in the morning, hoping that he didn't keep it locked away in a garage somewhere I couldn't see it.

The kitchen light seemed to suck the

moisture out of my eyes, and I laid my head down to rest on my arms stretched over the kitchen table ...

I was driving the hearse or maybe just sitting behind the steering wheel with Vic in the passenger seat next to me. We were looking out the windows at the scenery, which happened to be stars, ringed planets, spiral galaxies, glowing pink and purple clouds, all against a background of black.

Glancing into the rearview mirror, I saw the face of Mr. Gerard with his Grinch grin. I turned around to see him sitting up in the old casket. His mouth moved, his voice the one from the song "And When I Die." As he sang the lyrics, he leaned over the side and picked up the lid to the casket and, still singing, pulled it over the top of him as he lay back.

The music from the song continued playing as the rear of the hearse flipped open and the casket containing Mr. Gerard slid out. The dark box floated away into a stream of furniture from the funeral home, the gurney from the hearse, packages of toilet paper, several paintings, a gold candelabra, and old tapestries unfurled like magic carpets.

"Hey."

I turned back to the front of the hearse to find Vic had somehow morphed into Jess.

"Hey!" she said.

The darkness of space faded to an empty

black. A chill along my spine spread over my entire body and the smell of old grease and orange-scented dishwashing liquid hovered around my nose. I forced my eyes open only to shut them again in the face of the bright light of morning.

"Are you okay?" Jess asked.

"Yeah, I'm fine." I looked around at the kitchen wishing I could return to the hearse in my dream to be with Vic on a tour of the galaxy. According to Thomas, everything that can happen, does happen. At least, somewhere. Was there a parallel universe where hearses flew through space and Vic was still alive?

I found my phone and saw it was already seven-thirty. Jess had thirty minutes to get to school, Thomas about an hour. And I had ... I looked at my phone timer ... sixteen hours, twenty-eight minutes, forty-seconds to find Vic's casket, get him in it, and set it on fire some place where no one could see.

Easy peasy.

Into the Fog

I sent Jess upstairs to get washed and dressed and followed behind her. Thomas had no desire to get up, and I couldn't blame him. The world had changed. Nothing had the same meaning as the day before.

He sat on the edge of the small bed in his closet room. "Did you ... get him, um, in the ...?" Thomas trailed off.

I nodded.

"Can we have a service or something?" he asked. "We even had a little service for my fish when it died. Don't you think Vic deserves as much as a goldfish?"

"Yeah, sure," I said. "But I've got to find the casket."

Thomas wiped his eyes, then shook his head. "There's ... there's no way. You don't even know where Mr. Gerard lives."

"I know he lives within eight minutes of the funeral home."

He blinked at me. "How?"

"Because it took him eight minutes to get here when I texted him to help with Vic that one night. I checked my texts."

Thomas looked off, his eyes shifting from one side to the other. "So that narrows it down a little bit."

"I plotted how far I could drive in eight minutes and I'm going to start searching for places that far from the funeral home." Who said you don't ever use math in the real world?

Thomas looked up at me seeming the slightest bit amazed. "That's pretty ... smart."

"Don't act so damn surprised. I did better in geometry than any other math class I've ever had."

He stood up, grabbed a shirt from his dresser and started slipping it on over his head. "I could help with the search."

Honestly, having the company would have been nice. But who knew what I'd find out there? Mr. "Gunslinger" Gerard had that revolver strapped to his waist and I didn't want Thomas to get hurt. The best, safest place for him and Jess was at school.

"You and Jess are my *complices*. If I haven't tracked down the casket this morning, maybe you could help me look for it this afternoon."

Thomas grinned a little, then nodded. "Okay. But, be careful. You don't have a driver's license."

"I am aware of that fact," I said, realizing I sounded a little like Vic.

It was foggy that morning, but not so bad you couldn't see anything. I'd mapped a route that was basically a circle eight minutes, or about two miles, in all directions from the funeral home. A lot of the area eight minutes away would have put me in the middle of some wildlife refuge or at the bottom of the Trinity River. That narrowed my search to an area the shape of a pizza with three slices missing on one side.

I looked at the timer on my phone. Twelve hours, thirty-seven minutes, fourteen seconds.

* * *

I was back at the funeral home before noon sitting at the kitchen table with nothing to show for it. All I managed to do was run the hearse out of gas. I'd hiked to a convenience store and used my last three dollars to buy enough gas to get me back home. A tow truck driver had stopped to help. He showed me how to pour a little gas directly into the carburetor to get the old engine started.

During my futile search earlier I'd driven past a bunch of little businesses. Cafes and donut shops, electronics and appliance repair places, and a pawn shop or two. There hadn't been anything that even slightly resembled Mr. Gerard's truck.

I got to thinking, what if there'd been more traffic the night Mr. Gerard had come to help? Or less. Maybe an accident had clogged an intersection and made it take longer for him to get to us. Any of those things would have screwed up my guess as to time and distance. I needed some way to narrow my search.

Once back at the funeral home, I felt jittery like just before I'd robbed the fried pies from the GrabNGo. I thought about running up and down the staircase or going for a run around the cemetery, but those things wouldn't help me find Vic's casket any faster. After about a minute of feeling like my skin was going to crawl off my bones, I stood up fast enough to knock the chair backwards into the cabinet under the kitchen sink and went into the hallway.

It was the first time I'd been there at the funeral home all by myself. Well, Vic was there, but he wasn't making any noise. God, it was quiet. I stepped into the hallway just to be moving ... somewhere.

The silence was aggressive. I had to think why. I walked silently along the thick carpet until I stood in front of the grandfather clock. Normally, it would have been ticking loud enough to hear upstairs. Not anymore. The clock had stopped at exactly twelve. The same time Vic had died.

After a few seconds of attempting some sort of cosmic reflection at this strange coincidence, I heard what sounded like mumbling. I followed the sound down the hall to the Preparation Room. A voice, more real than imagined, was coming from the other side of the door with the No Admittance sign.

The jittery feeling I had in the kitchen

turned into a wave of cold prickles. The only person in there was Vic. Had I somehow made a mistake? Was he trapped in the storage drawer, freezing? *Shit!*

I put my hand on the doorknob and threw open the door. Inside off to the left, the cold storage drawer where I'd put Vic had been pulled out. Next to him someone sat cross-legged hunched over his face. And it wasn't Lucy.

Pale face, flaming orange-red hair, all the ear piercings. It took a couple seconds, but I recognized the person as Pastor Priest.

"Hey," I said.

Pastor Priest looked up. "Oh, hi."

I half expected the pastor to ask me what I was doing in the Preparation Room and to shame me for not following the rules. Then again, she probably didn't know about that particular set of rules. I moved a few steps closer.

"How did you know?" I asked.

"He texted me."

I frowned. She smiled gently. "Before, not after. Although receiving a text from a deceased person would certainly be an interesting experience."

I stood opposite the pastor, Vic laid out between us. The scent of nicotine and cinnamon wafted up from his corpse.

"Did he tell you to do this?" she asked.

"Put him in the storage compartment?"

I shook my head. "No, it just seemed to fit with the ..."

I did not want to use the word "plan." The last thing I wanted was for a pastor witch person, even if she was my friend, to start asking questions about what we were up to.

"Moment?" she asked. "Mood?"

Was the pastor adopting some authority role? Was she judging me, accusing me of ... what? Corpse abuse? Maybe she wasn't as open-minded as I thought.

"I thought it would buy me some time."

"For?"

"To do what he asked me to do."

"Which is?"

Her questions would have been irritating, if not for the fact she reminded me so much of my mom. "How many details do you need?"

"I don't really," she said. "Mr. Delamorte said to help you in whatever way you might require." She stood, smiling down at Vic. I relaxed. The pastor was still my friend it seemed and not eager to criticize. "I am aware of the casket and its purported function."

"You ... you know that it's supposed to ..."

"Bring Mr. Delamorte back? Yes. At least, as far as what he told me."

"So, what do you think of that? Kind of

crazy, huh?"

She looked at Vic, then up at me. "Crazy is a rather vague term. Insane. Nonsensical. Chaotic. The word could mean any of those things."

I looked down at Vic's face frozen in apparent sleep. "Yeah, pretty much all of that."

She looked off toward the door, then up at me. "How resolved are you to complying with his wishes?"

"Up until last night I'd say I was pretty resolved."

"But?"

"Last night, it all seemed impossible. Even more since I went looking for the casket this morning and came home with shit to show for it." The pastor grinned a little and nodded. "I did what you suggested, though, pulling the problem apart."

"And?"

"It actually helped. I mean, I had a strategy. It's just, I need more information or something to find Mr. Gerard."

Together, we slid the drawer closed, returning Vic to his dark, chilly waiting place. We went back into the warmth of the hallway, coming to stand in front of the silent, still grandfather clock.

"I would love to help," the pastor said, folding her hands in front of her. "Where should we start?"

I'd started to say I had no clue, but an electronic noise further up the hall distracted both of us. Together, we eased over to the office door and flipped on the light. No one was there, so I thought it was probably just some computer alert that had made the sound. Opening the top drawer of the desk, I found a collection of papers and letters.

"If I might ask," the pastor said. "What are you looking for?"

"Are you sure you want to know?"

"I believe so, yes. That is, after all, why I asked." That was something I kind of liked that about the pastor. She could quietly be a smart ass.

"Anything that might help me figure out where Mr. Gerard lives."

She nodded. I started pulling out stuff from the desk drawers and the cabinets that lined the wall. It was mostly old bills in there, receipts from casket and chemical companies, office supply stores, gas, electric, water, internet. A solution to my problem might be somewhere in that mess of papers.

"Pastor, if you want to check through one filing cabinet, I'll start working through another."

"Melissa," she said, smiling. I filed her name away, but doubted I'd ever find myself calling her by that name.

We found some utility bills. Gas wasn't

much, like forty dollars a month. Water was around a hundred, internet seventy-something. The electricity, though — that was crazy. Vic had been paying nearly two thousand dollars a month for that in the summertime. Added all together, there was no way I could earn enough working at some fast-food restaurant for minimal wage to pay for everything. If we lived at the funeral home, that is.

By mid-afternoon, we'd gone through every cabinet looking for some trace of Mr. Gerard but found nothing. Eventually, I had to leave to pick up Thomas and Jess.

The pastor hopped into her little yellow Fiat. "Later this evening, I can perform a Prayer for the Dead. If you will allow me, that is."

"Why not," I said. "I'm not sure of when or even what exactly is happening tonight, but I will let you know."

We exchanged numbers, adding someone else to the short list of contacts in my phone.

"Will do." I slid into the light blue hearse, and we both left.

* * *

"So, you didn't find anything?" Thomas asked as soon as he got in the hearse.

"Nope," I said. I didn't mention running out of gas. Yeah, his attitude toward me may have changed, but I didn't want to tempt him into falling back into the habit of lecturing me about paying attention or planning or some other skill he thought I lacked.

By the time the three of us got back to the funeral home, it was nearly four o'clock. I'd wasted nearly the entire day. Starving, again, we raided whatever was in the pantry, but it was mostly raw materials in there. Flour, sugar, salt, and pepper. Buried in the freezer, we found some of the profiteroles Vic had made last summer. Less than a day after Vic died, we were searching for food again. Just like we had at the end of our time at the old apartment. The pastries were just shells with no crème inside. I had nothing to make any crème, so I just crisped them up in the oven and we ate them plain.

I resisted the urge to ask Jess if she had anything stashed in her dresser drawer. It would embarrass her. Whatever was going on in her head, I was no therapist. Stashing food like that wasn't hurting anyone.

All of us stared off in different directions as we ate the profiteroles. I couldn't speak for my brother and sister, but I was lost in my memories. Why couldn't things have stayed the way they were last summer after my illness. A full refrigerator, no pervs, and ... no dead Vic to deal with. And, for me, the freedom to do absolutely nothing if that's what I had wanted.

Eight hours, ten minutes, fifty-five seconds.

* * *

I turned Vic's bedroom upside down looking for anything I could find on Mr. Gerard. In the closet, I glanced at the darker spaces to make sure they were merely gray and not unnaturally black. God, was that going to become a habit? I mean, how could it not?

I dug through shoe boxes, the pockets of his shirts and pants, coats and jackets. I went through his bedstand drawers, and all his vinyls, but found exactly nothing.

"I've got an idea," Thomas yelled from down the hall in his little closet room. Eager to escape the futility of my search, I went to see what he had in mind. "There are websites where you can use a car license plate number to find out an owner's address."

"You know his plate number?" I asked.

"I know it ends with 1388." It figured somehow my brother would remember the numbers part of it. "I remember the 13 because that's how old I am. The 88 was easy because that's the year Mom was born."

My brother was right. I didn't remember the year Mom was born, but the math worked out. She'd been sixteen years old when she had me. God, what would that have been like? Having a baby at my age. Yeah, I'd changed a butt-ton of diapers, but going through the whole pregnancy thing, actually forcing another human being out of a shockingly small opening in my body. Nope, I had not done that and had no desire to go through the experience.

"What are you doing?" Jess asked from behind me.

"Trying to remember the license plate on Mr. Gerard's truck," Thomas said.

"All I remember is fish," Jess said.

"That's too many letters and numbers," Thomas said. "It can only be seven combined. I remember the four numbers at the end. We need the three letters at the first."

"What do you mean fish?" I asked.

"You sure it wasn't a type of fish?" Thomas asked.

"You mean like trout or salmon or something?" I asked.

"No, I don't remember either of those," Jess said.

Thomas's fingers pounded his computer keys. "Maybe it's literal," he said.

"Like?" I asked.

"Like this." Thomas had typed in the plate number FSH-1388. The screen showed the following: 1972 Ford F100 Ranger.

I remembered the truck had the oval shaped Ford sign on the front and the brand name written on the tailgate. "Can you get an address?"

"All these sites have paywalls."

"Meaning?"

"We'd need a credit card," Thomas said. "Did Vic have one?"

Earlier that afternoon when I'd been looking through all the paperwork in the office, I thought I'd seen a Visa logo somewhere. "Hold on," I said. I ran down the stairs, stumbled and grabbed the banister to keep from falling, and jumped the last two steps to the floor. I sprinted past the chapel, the still Grandfather clock, and the Preparation Room like I was running from the GrabNGo after stealing the fried pies, skidded to a stop, and all but leaped into the office.

I'd left all the folders I'd pulled from the file cabinets strewn around on the desk and the carpet of the office floor. My hope faded after two or three minutes of pushing around papers, opening and closing folders, and rechecking drawers.

I stood up to go back to Thomas's room and spied the corner of a folder under the desk. I raked it out with the toe of my shoe, picked it up, and opened it to find the Visa logo at the top of the first page. I thumbed through the file and found an envelope, inside of which was what looked like a brand-new Visa credit card. I took the card and was about to race back upstairs to Thomas's room when the doorbell rang. I'd never heard the doorbell at the funeral home before. It was one of those old-fashioned kinds. Ding-dong, ding-dong, dong-ding, ding dong. If it weren't dead, I'd have expected the grandfather clock to start chiming the hour after all the dinging and donging.

I stood there, still as a body on a slab. After a moment, I approached the door, running through the usual possibilities in my head. Mormons? Jehovah's Witnesses? Some young guy selling cleaning products or maybe Bibles? Was it the pastor again? Maybe with a spell for finding out information? Then again, if it was her, wouldn't she have just come inside without ringing the bell?

I opened the door a crack thinking I'd see a couple guys with white shirts and long, thin black ties. Instead, an older woman with short, almost gray hair stood before me dressed in jeans and a white blouse. I could immediately tell she wasn't selling anything. A lanyard hung from around her neck holding an ID card displaying the seal of the great state of Texas. It felt like someone had punched me in the gut.

"Hello," she said. "My name is Dale Johnson. I'm with the Department of Family and Protective Services."

You fucking kidding me?

The Pawn Shop

It took a good five seconds or so to silence all the swear words flying through my head and threatening to explode out my mouth. *Eloquence, eloquence.* I finally edited it all down to a single word. "Okay."

"May I have permission to come inside?"

I swallowed hard. What was she? A fucking vampire? "Uh, well," I stammered. "This isn't a good time. We ... I'm right in the middle of a ... project ... that I really need to finish ... for school."

"Is your parent at home?"

"Not right now. He's out right now." I couldn't exactly say he was at work, although it would have been technically true.

"I'm following up on a report the Department received earlier this year."

I nodded. *Fucking Pete!* But, how was that even possible. He didn't know where we lived. Did he? It must have been someone else. Mr. Gerard? Had Delamorte called social services after all? Surely not Pastor Priest.

"I took over an abandoned caseload. The investigating worker resigned abruptly and not all of her cases got distributed to other workers to follow up. Yours was one that sort of fell through the cracks."

If it fell through the cracks, why didn't they just goddamn leave it there? I opened the door a little wider, keeping my foot up against the bottom in case the woman decided to not take no for an answer and barge inside. Where would she go looking and what might she find?

"We'd like to close the case, but just needed to follow up with your parent or possibly guardian to make sure everything is fine."

"Everything is fine, it's going to be just fine."

She nodded. "You seem nervous. Is everything okay? Do you need help?"

I opened the door fully, enough to let her see all the Underworld she wanted without setting foot beyond the door threshold. "I'm fine. Just a little stressed about my project."

She nodded again, then handed me her card. "Well, if you would have your parent or guardian, what was his name again?"

"Victor ... Vic."

"Yes, have him give me a call and set up a time to meet so we can get your case closed."

"I will."

"Thank you," she said and walked off to her car parked in front of the funeral home.

I sighed and shut the door. It took a few seconds to remember what I was doing before the bell rang announcing the entrance of damn social services to our lives. I decided not to say anything to Thomas about the visitor at the door.

"Who was at the—"

"Look what I found," I interrupted.

He took the card and plugged in the number. "What's the zip code?"

"What?"

"It's asking for the zip code associated with the account."

I had no effing clue. I'd had no need to know the zip code for anything before. I ran back downstairs, found the credit card file and brought the whole thing back in case they asked for some other stupid shit I didn't know.

Thomas finished putting in the credit card information and a few seconds later we were staring at five addresses the system had pulled up. One, Beeville, was in a town in Texas I'd never heard of. The other, Uvalde, I'd most definitely heard of because of the fact an entire class of fourth-graders were shot by some idiot with a gun a few years back. Those kids were only a little older than Jess. Our situation was kind of bleak, but nothing like that kind of nightmare hell.

Both those towns were hundreds of miles away. The other three were close around the east side of Dallas. I copied down the addresses, jogged downstairs, and was outside almost to the hearse when I heard Thomas's voice.

"I want to come," he said. "I'm your *complice*, right?"

I turned around. God, he looked so

expectant, and he was my *complice* just as he'd been when I'd robbed the GrabNGo. It was weird how my perception of my brother had changed. He wasn't the whiney little boy he'd been only a few months ago.

I didn't know what I was going to have to do to get the casket once I found it. Would I have to fight Mr. Gerard? What if there were other guys there? More guys with sidearms or shotguns or some automatic weapon like that piece of shit shooter had at that school in Uvalde?

"You don't want me to go, do you?"

"T, it might get dangerous. I mean, the guy wears a gun." Seconds passed, the two of us staring at each other. I actually would have been glad for my brother to join me, but there was a problem. "Jess needs you to stay with her while I'm gone. That's what I need my *complice* to do." He looked down at the concrete driveway, then back up at me. Jesus, he looked so disappointed. I remembered what Pastor Priest had said about a little encouragement going a long way. I walked over to him.

"Thomas?"

"Yeah?"

"Thanks for helping find Mr. Gerard's address. You did most of the work. I'd have nowhere to even begin to look if not for you."

He acted like he wanted to say something, then sort of lurched toward me and grabbed me in a tentative embrace. I stiffened. I wasn't much of a hugger and my brother hadn't hugged me since he was a preschooler. After a moment, he stepped back. We looked at each other probably thinking the same thing. How hugging was both weird and nice at the same time.

"Hey," I started, "why don't you research how to make one of those funeral pyre things?"

He managed a little grin. "Sure, I can do that." He turned to go back in the funeral home, but paused. "Be careful. I don't want to be ..."

He didn't finish, but I knew what he meant. He didn't want to be what I'd been, do what I'd done. Take care of someone else.

I remembered Vic's lesson on *mise en place*, having everything in place and ready to go before I started cooking anything. Well, my *mise en place* kind of sucked at that moment, mainly because I had no idea what I was doing. There was no recipe for casket recovery.

Then something hit me. Part of *mise en place* was gathering the utensils you were going to need. I had no need for whisks or spoons, but maybe ... I jogged over to an old shed where Vic kept a lawn mower and garden tools. I flung open the wooden door, searching for anything I might conceivably need. Off in a dark corner, a rusty crowbar was propped against the wall. I could definitely see myself using a crowbar at some point. Grabbing it, I turned to leave. Lying in the dirt were what looked like tree trimmers, so I took those also. Not sure what I would use the trimmers for, but what the hell.

As I was leaving, I checked the timer on my phone. Six hours, forty minutes, seven seconds.

One of the places on the list was somewhere I'd already driven past earlier that morning. The pawn shop with the sheet metal gate and storage shed in the back. When we'd lived in our old apartment, I'd actually walked by the place once or twice on the way home from school. A Fiesta supermarket was only about half a block away, so I parked the hearse in the grocery store lot.

I needed a plan before I acted, which was a whole new concept for me. Remembering what Lucy said about impulsivity attracting her kind, I thought it best to have some idea what I was going to do. But to make a plan, I had to see what I was up against. So I got out and walked back toward the pawn shop.

It felt strange being in the old neighborhood, like going back in time but as a completely different person. Seeking to be as surreptitious as possible, I stayed on the side of Old Home Road opposite the pawn shop in case Mr. Gerard was for some reason just staring out the window. I needn't have worried. The windows were covered with black bars on the outside and blocked by boxes and wood slats on the inside. It was doubtful anyone would see me strolling down the sidewalk. Unless, of course, they were paranoid and all the time peering out from some crack in the slats. That description kind of fit Mr. Gerard so I tried to keep a hand over my face so he or any other assholes might not recognize me.

A narrow strip of dark asphalt about as wide as I was tall separated the pawn shop from a transmission repair place. I crossed the street about a block down trying to act like I was just minding my own business, not showing any sign of the desperation eating away at me from the inside out.

It felt like I was being watched the whole time, but the feeling was strongest walking in front of the transmission place. Was some guy in greasy overalls leering at me out from under a car he was working on? Could that be the place Pete worked? Shit, that would just be my luck. If he saw me on the street like that, would he come after me? Would I have to fight him all over again?

Lacking a box cutter or any actual weapon, I had an impulse to run like hell in the opposite direction. That's probably what I would have done in the past. But Vic gave me a reason to do exactly the opposite. So, instead of running, I ducked into the asphalt strip between the pawn shop and the transmission place.

Breathing harder than I should have been, I waited. I should have brought the damn crowbar with me. At least I would have had a weapon.

I squatted down behind a gas meter and waited. It was probably less than a minute, but it seemed like ages, when I finally lifted my head to look around. No one was there. At least, no one I could see. And that was always the problem. My new glasses weren't magic. I still couldn't see through walls or around corners or into someone's mind.

The pawn shop lot was surrounded by the same corrugated sheet metal barricade as the gate in the front, but there was also a chain link fence that came to about the level of my head. Razor wire wound along the top of the fence all the way down the side and around the back. The place seemed like a ... I searched for words other than fucking. *Veritable.* I'd heard the expression before, probably in some movie. A *veritable* fortress.

About halfway down the length of the fence, I saw a slight gap between two pieces of sheet metal. Glancing both ways, I stepped up to the hole and peered through the chain link. I couldn't see much, just the trunk of a huge mulberry tree, some old tires, a lot of rusty car parts, and a silver chain in the dirt.

I didn't have time to put two and two together. A long, dark face leapt up not six inches from my eye and bellowed, sending me literally into the air, arms flailing. Landing awkwardly, I lost my balance and staggered backward until I hit the cinder block wall of the transmission place, partially knocking the breath out of me. I let myself slide down the wall until my butt hit the asphalt.

The dog continued to roar at me through the gap in the fence. I wanted to unleash a shotgun blast of swear words at that goddamn animal, but I didn't need to attract any more attention. Not with fucking Pete or someone like him in the building next to me. I sat there in the alley, forearms on my knees, closed my eyes, and breathed in and out, repeatedly until the urge to rid the planet of the Rottweiler subsided.

I wasn't getting anywhere just sitting on my now sore ass. Pushing myself up, I glanced over at the transmission shop, then jogged around to the back of the pawn shop where an alleyway separated the strip of businesses from a row of houses. Down the alley, I found another crack in the metal fence behind the pawn shop.

Ignoring the snarling Rottweiler, I eased closer to get a better view. Scanning one side of the yard to the other, I could just make out part of the old gray Ford pickup.

Yes!

I'd done it! Well, with help from Thomas. Together, we'd found Mr. Gerard and hopefully the casket as well. I made fists with both hands and shook them a couple times, silently celebrating my victory over the forces of dumb-fuckedness opposing me.

There was a side door to the storage building. Could the casket be in that building? Of course, it was. At least, I hoped. Was I going to pull this thing off after all? Would it be so easy as just getting in the building and out with the casket?

There was a video camera mounted on the eave closer to the pawn shop so I ducked away from the opening. Did Mr. Gerard also have eyes in the alley? I looked all around me, but no security cams glared down at me. At least none that I could see. Was there like, a tiny one somewhere, like a spy cam or something?

Vic used to say haste is the sister of regret. Acting without thinking wouldn't get me what I wanted. I had no reason to feel confident in my skills as a thief. I mean, I'd been easily caught by a chain-smoking, cancer-ridden mortician the last time. Still, that didn't stop me thinking I could do it this time if I had a good plan. At least I wasn't dealing with hunger clouding my vision. Of course, as soon as I had that thought, my stomach growled.

The alley behind the pawn shop led

straight back to the Fiesta parking lot. I headed back to the hearse. My phone buzzed, an alert telling me my battery was at nine percent and was in power save mode. *Shit!* I'd forgotten to charge the thing up while I was back at the funeral home all those hours.

Stupid. The word echoed through my head repeating until finally it lost its meaning. Thomas had looked that phenomenon up, repeating a word until it lost its meaning. Semantic satiation he'd called it. I tried the same tactic with the word idiot, which was also running through my mind, but that word for some reason had more staying power.

I added the low battery to the growing list of reasons why recovering the casket was probably impossible. Short of pole vaulting over the sheet metal and razor wire or parachuting into the yard where an eating machine awaited my tender skin and muscle, I couldn't think of any way to get inside the storage building. As much as I wanted to do it on my own, I had to admit I could use some help.

The sun reddened as it disappeared behind a cloud of dust and smoke from wildfires way out west of the city. The growing darkness just heightened my urgency. The skin over most of my body tingled.

The sky turned from orange to blue and, under the lights in the parking lot, back to orange again. Dark places formed in the alley behind the pawnshop, and in my mind where worries and doubts grew like mold on the walls of our old apartment.

I leaned back in the seat, my hands slipping from the steering wheel into my lap. The whole quest suddenly seemed futile, ridiculous even. I was putting myself and my brother and sister at risk by trying to get the casket back. If I got caught and arrested, that would be it. Thomas and Jess would be off to foster care and I'd end up sitting in a cell in juvenile detention. Or worse, adult jail.

So why was I still trying?

Locked in the Pharoah's Machine

I talked myself through it again. If the cancer hadn't gone to Vic's brain and he wasn't crazy and was telling the truth, finding the casket might be my only hope of both seeing him again and having a place for all of us to live together. For us to be a family.

Was that what I wanted? A family? Hell, yes! Who wouldn't want a place to call home, a place to belong and always return to if life didn't work out. People I could see every day if I wanted, and didn't have to work to remember what they looked like. Thomas and Jess, Vic, Pastor Priest, even creeping Lucy. My insides quivered with a longing for all of them. Just to be at home, sitting around hearing them all talking, moving around, doing things, living life, all of us together.

Could the old casket restore Vic's life? Was there a chance we could be a family for a long time. The flickering pilot light of hope burst into flame again. *That* was why I was still out there in the Fiesta parking lot about to do something effing crazy. Or, something unlikely to succeed. Yeah, that was more specific, more eloquent.

There were four of us now, including Pastor Priest. Four *complices* working to accomplish what Vic had asked. But when it came down to bringing the casket back, I was on my own. A year ago, I would never have trusted anyone except myself. I had no idea what a *complice* even was back then. I mean, the whole concept was foreign. I was on my own and trusted no one else to help. Now, I both needed and wanted someone to help. But I was on my own.

Five hours, ten minutes, twenty-two seconds.

The pawn shop closed at eight and it was already twenty minutes till. Maybe at closing time Mr. Gerard would go out for a beer with some buddies and I wouldn't have to worry about getting caught. Then again, did Mr. Gerard seem like the kind of guy who had any friends? Yeah, probably not. He was definitely too … paranoid for that. I resisted adding a certain effing modifier to that phrase.

I had a feeling Mr. Gerard lived at the pawn shop just like Vic lived at the funeral home. Not sure why I thought that, though. Maybe because he seemed to have no life other than buying and selling and making a profit. I left the hearse, bringing the tools with me, and strolled down the alley trying not to look like I was on some mission. Looking like you were trying to accomplish something was a sure way to attract assholes. If anyone asked what I was up to, I'd just say I was just taking the tools to the pawnshop. You know, to sell. Then again, what I was doing was no one's fucking business but my own. Couldn't resist that little modifier there.

Concealed by one of those big heavy metal trash bins in the alley, I tossed the crowbar over the fence into the yard where the Rottweiler lurked. She didn't erupt in a fury, just made one of those sounds dogs make when they're confronted with something weird. The one that seemed to ask "what the hell?"

One of the gaps in the fence had been covered with pieces of wood. The chain link had been either cut or torn. Had the Rottweiler escaped the yard before? A plan, if you could call it that, formed in my head. If I could get the dog out of the yard and find a way into the yard, I could cover the hole where she'd escaped.

The more I looked at the tree trimmers, the less they looked like they were meant to be used on trees. I mean, there was no sap or anything on the blades. I wondered if they were sharp and strong enough to cut through metal.

In the alley next to the heavy trash dumpster, I knelt in front of the fence. I had barely touched the chain link with the trimmers when the Rottweiler bellowed so loud my whole body convulsed and I had to drop to one knee to keep from falling over. The insane dog couldn't get past a piece of sheet metal propped against the other side of the fence. The cutters bit through the metal fencing like they were made to do just that. Then it occurred to me that was exactly what they were for. They were chain cutters not tree trimmers. Why would a mortician have a set of chain cutters in an old shed? Did Vic use them somehow to extract corpses from precarious places?

I kept cutting until I'd made a slit big enough for me to get in and, if I was successful, the casket to get out. But my problem remained. The deranged dog was still in the damn yard. The fence closer to the transmission shop rattled. I was about to peer into the yard again when the Rottweiler roared again, this time from the end of the alley.

Fuck!

Terror seized me like a pair of cold hands grabbing me from behind. The Rottweiler had somehow escaped the yard and I had maybe two seconds to react before the sharp teeth racing toward me penetrated whatever part of my body was left on that side of the fence.

As I launched myself into the gap, my leg got stuck on something. I yanked on it a couple of times, and eventually tore it loose, ripping my jeans and my skin in the process. Inches away, the Rottweiler bellowed as I frantically moved the sheet metal back in place.

The fence rattled and swayed from the force of the dog trying to get back into the yard. I got to my feet, ran over to the other gap in the fence. The dog's paws and claws clicking along the concrete racing me to the same spot. I tripped over the metal spike in the ground where the Rottweiler had been chained landing on my elbows in front of the chain link. Pushing myself up, I crawled over and covered the opening with the slats of wood that had been knocked out of the way as the dog escaped the yard.

I waited for the Rottweiler to attack the wood I'd stuck in front of the opening, but nothing happened. I turned to see if it had run over to the other opening, the one I'd covered with the sheet metal. Nothing. No growling, snarling, barking. Just silence. Had the Hound of Hell gotten a task of freedom and just run off?

Liquid oozed down my leg into my shoe. I lifted my pant leg and saw dark red streak along one ankle. Ignoring my injuries, I turned to face the storage building, staring up at the camera mounted on the eave. It wasn't exactly pointed straight at the yard. Could Mr. Gerard see me yet? Was the thing even on?

I hustled over and picked up the crowbar I'd tossed into the yard. Standing in Mr. Gerard's backyard, taking back the casket had become real and not just some vague idea. Vic once said, "Do not open a door you cannot close." Once I'd pried open the door, there was no closing it. I had to finish what I started.

I reminded myself it wasn't actually a crime, what I was doing. It was a recovery project, righting a wrong, turning the tables on an *actual* criminal. Anyway, that's what I kept telling myself as I shoved the crowbar into the gap between the door and the frame.

I was in the right, but the cops wouldn't see it that way. If I failed and got caught, I'd have only my own sorry ass to keep me company. At least until I turned eighteen. Would I be out of jail by then? Would Thomas and Jess even want to be around jailbird me?

I had the door open in a matter of seconds. Placing the crowbar on the ground, I pulled the door shut to keep everything looking mostly normal, at least on the outside.

There was just enough light inside the dusty, musty storage building to create silhouettes of the contents. The thick air rubbed against me like smooth sandpaper scraping my skin.

I groped around in near darkness looking for the old casket. Cardboard boxes stacked four or five high formed a sort of maze. I ran my hands over box after box, cardboard, wood, plastic, and metal. All that seemed to be in there was a bunch of effing boxes. Was the casket even in there?

Heat rose up my neck to my face as frustration sucked the thoughts from my head. My head felt like it was about to explode. Then I felt it. Power, energy of some kind. I moved around trying to find where the feeling was strongest. My foot hooked on something on the floor, and I stumbled forward. My hands came to rest on a hard, oily surface, a buzz running up my arms into my shoulders.

There you are motherfucker. I'd found the casket, or maybe it had found me. The device had power of some kind. That much I believed with the certainty of my next heartbeat. I still wasn't sure, though, what that power could do.

I'd pushed the casket maybe two feet toward the exit when door closest to the pawn shop rattled then opened. A wedge of pale light pierced through the dark and the specter of Mr. Gerard appeared holding a phone to his ear.

I tried to duck, but mainly fell, down behind a stack of boxes. It took me back to a time in the old apartment when I barricaded the bedroom door with our dresser while Mom and some random guy had loud sex in her bed next door.

A set of fluorescent lights flickered and buzzed overhead. Hunched over and shaking with terror, I sort of waddled over to the casket and took hold of the lid. My butt pocket buzzed loud enough I thought anyone within a block of the pawn shop could hear it. It had to be Tina. I yanked my phone out, fumbled with it, pushing buttons trying to get the thing to shut up.

Mr. Gerard stopped his conversation and

looked around the storage room. His Adam's apple bobbed up and down once, and he started talking again.

Desperate for a place to hide, I grabbed the lid of the casket. A familiar buzz of electricity ran from the ancient wood through my fingers. That power was my hope. The lid made a groaning sound when I shoved it back. I froze.

Mr. Gerard was still talking and maybe didn't hear the lid slide. He wandered toward the back of the room, uttering things like "excellent investment," "appropriate financial commitment," and finally "first come, first served."

I moved the lid a little more each time he spoke, the wood groaning and grinding across the top of the casket. Eventually there was enough room for me to slide inside. Lying down in the old box, I used both my legs and arms to move the heavy wooden cover over me as quietly as possible. Mr. Gerard ended his conversation so there was nothing to hide the sound of what I was doing. It would have been perfect timing for Tina to text back at that very moment.

"Why settle for a mere pittance," Mr. Gerard said, apparently to himself. "When I can have it all."

Those were the last words I heard the man utter as the last bit of light disappeared from the gap between casket and lid. A moment later, there was a click and a clonk, kind of like someone locking a heavy door. Something rattled as if a machine was starting up. The box vibrated underneath and all around me, almost as hard as one of those massage chairs they have in some shopping malls.

Through the thick wood, Mr. Gerard's voice sounded mostly like mumbling. Then the mumbling stopped. I lay still as a corpse, but I worried my pounding heart would betray me. Was it loud enough someone outside the casket could actually hear it?

My nose twitched and I felt a sneeze coming fast. My arms were pinned close to my sides, so I couldn't pinch my nose. I scrunched up my face as much as I could, but the sneeze still came.

There was silence a moment, then it sounded like someone scratching the outside of the casket. Was he trying to get the lid off? Could he? I prepared to be exposed, wondering if I could put the past month or so of weight training at school to good use and kick the guy in the head and knock him out. After a few seconds, all was quiet.

He grunted something. Then, nothing. I tried pushing with my legs against the lid, but it would not budge. Was I, in fact, locked inside? Was that what the clonking sound was from before?

If there was a locking mechanism, there had to be a key or some way to unlock it. The box, apparently some Pharoah's machine, had been Vic's hope for a future. He'd need a way to get out. Unless, of course, he had help from someone else. But he didn't say anything about needing help getting out. Only help getting in. Neither of us anticipated me getting into the device.

I felt around the best I could, mainly along the sides around my thighs. I managed to get my elbows to bend enough to touch the inside of the lid. My fingers felt only the smooth curve of the wood above me, no switch or handle that might open the box.

How do you get out of here, Vic?

Caskets had no need for an oxygen supply, no air holes for any living thing trapped inside. How much air did I have left? Was I going to suffocate? Was it now *my* casket permanently? What if it worked on me without being burned? Since I was alive, would it have the opposite effect? Would it make me some kind of zombie? Or just ... dead.

Shit!

A weight settled on my chest. I had the strange feeling my body was being pushed and pulled into the wood, like sinking beneath the surface of water. I sucked in air, a wheezing sound in my throat. I couldn't get a deep breath. Panicked, my movements became jerky and desperate. I felt dizzy, my eyes wanting to close.

Then came the whispering. Like someone hissing words I couldn't quite ...

Time is short, the end is near ...

Jesus, no fucking kidding. Was I hallucinating? Again?

All will be well, do not fear.

When you heard voices, did they always speak in verse?

Your hope is new, once in the light ...
Freedom awaits, but you must fight.

Fight. The word echoed through my numb brain. Hallucination or not, I felt a surge of energy. Frantically, my fingers slid over the inside of the casket until, as if guided by some invisible force, they found a rough spot in the center of the lid. It had a circular shape to it almost like a large button.

Gathering my fingers together, I pressed as hard as I could. There was a clonk and a click, and I could see a tiny bit of light, just a light gray color really. It was enough to know there was a crack between the lid and the casket.

I pushed up with my knees and hands and moved the lid a little bit. I was able to move the cover enough to make an opening big enough to get my head through. I sucked in the cool air as it rushed in, my chest heaving until breathing returned to normal. Twisting and turning, legs pumping, I half-crawled, half-fell out onto the concrete floor.

"Fuck you, Amenhotep!"

Once free of my wooden tomb, I found the room mostly dark again. I looked around for Mr. Gerard, but he'd probably gone back to the pawn shop. I pushed the lid back in place and started to move the casket. I stopped to shove stacks of boxes out of the way, clearing a path to the side door.

I noticed the set of candelabras sticking out of a box and tossed them inside the casket along with a couple silver plates and a golden cross. If nothing else, we might need a way to pay for food at some point. I'd seen places that bought silver and gold, including the pawn shop I was in the process of robbing.

I pushed the old box as far as the side door, all the time wishing Mr. Gerard didn't wander back in there. I hoped some customer had gone in the pawn shop looking to buy or sell something. If not, I could always hope Mr. Gerard had to take a lengthy shit and was in the bathroom long enough for me to make my escape.

Had the Rottweiler returned? Was Mr. Gerard waiting out in the yard? I took a deep breath and pushed open the side door ready to climb up on something should the Rottweiler be waiting for me. But there was no sign of the dog who was apparently out terrorizing the neighborhood.

I considered tossing some more of Vic's treasures into the casket, but decided the old box was already heavy enough and pushed the casket into dim, dusty light of early evening.

Your hope is new, once in the light.

What was that voice? Had Pastor Priest sent me a spell or prayer or something? Was it the ritual thing we'd done with the Carnelian and the herbs? Or, maybe it had been my own personal Death Angel giving me encouragement. Was the Grim Reaper a poet? Did they even bother with encouragement to live? Didn't they specialize in encouraging people to get on with it and die?

I'd worked up a sweat, and a slight breeze and cool fall air chilled my skin. Mr. Gerard was right about one thing. First come, first served. I grinned at the thought. It was only a few feet to the gap in the fence, but moving the casket along the uneven dirt was harder than over smooth concrete. After just two or three feet I was breathing as hard as I would after running laps around the cemetery.

"What, may I ask, do ya think yer doing?"

The force of Mr. Gerard's words hit me from behind hard enough I lost my balance and staggered off to one side. I turned around to see him standing about twenty feet away, hands on hips. His revolver was still in its holster. He didn't seem eager to gun me down.

"You know," I said, my voice quivering enough to make me angry with myself for being scared. Again.

All will be well, do not fear.

"I'm afraid I cannot allow that. The box is too valuable to waste in such an endeavor."

"Vic needs it."

One side of his mouth twisted up in a half-Grinch smirk. "My former employer is deceased and no longer needs anything. I, on the other hand, am alive and could use the money."

I had no words left. I was tired of talking. I didn't do talking that well anyway.

Freedom awaits, but you must fight.

Everything hinged on what would happen in the next few seconds. My family was depending on me. Taking a deep breath, I took a couple of steps toward him, trying to seem casual, but also looking around for anything I could use as a weapon. He glanced around the yard.

"What has become of Executioner?" He tilted his head. "Have you harmed her?"

"Who?"

"My dog," he said.

I shook my head. "She musta got out."

He looked skyward and sighed. He seemed about to say something else, but I rushed at him. Taking him by surprise, I hit him head-on, knocking him to the ground.

My biggest worry was the gun, so I went for it. I had no idea what I was doing. Keep it in the holster or get it out. Mr. Gerard was a wiry little guy and quickly twisted out from under me.

We rolled around in the dirt, both of our hands wrestling for the still-holstered gun. Thrashing, fumbling, neither of us were able to do much. He could only get one hand on the weapon while I got both my hands on the handle. One of my fingers slid alongside the trigger.

Two loud cracks split the cool evening air.

The Lonely Rottweiler

I struggled to my feet and stumbled backward, my legs wobbly as warm cheese sticks. I stared down at Mr. Gerard, his hands quivering over his chest like the little flappers of some sea animal.

I suddenly realized I was holding the pearl-handled revolver. I stared at the thin trail of smoke vapor rising from the barrel. I was literally holding the smoking gun. For some reason, I laughed out loud.

"Shootin' me would be a serious error in judgment," Mr. Gerard said.

"Goddammit, I'm not trying to shoot anybody," I yelled. "Jesus, did it hit you?"

He felt around on his leg. "Apparently, I am uninjured."

I wasn't a murderer, not yet at least. I held the gun in front of me, the barrel resting in my left palm. The guy was right about shooting him. Beating someone up was one thing, shooting them was a whole other matter.

He started to get up. I raised the gun, gripping the handle with both hands, and pointed it at him. My hands were shaking enough he could probably see how scared I was. He sat back down, his legs crossed, his hands on his knees.

"If ya shoot me, you'll go to prison," he said. "Maybe for the rest of yer life. Yer brother and sister will go to foster care. Ya might never see 'em again."

No fucking kidding. Mr. Gerard leaned back on his hands, extending his legs. The silver revolver felt heavy, enough that my shoulder ached holding it up. I lowered the gun slowly until it was dangling from one hand next to my right thigh. The guy was a thief and kind of an asshole, but I decided my motto for that situation was I didn't have to shoot an asshole just because I had a gun in my hand.

Mr. Gerard sighed not once but twice.

"I don't need any more dead adults in my life." Other than every part of my body buzzing like my finger got stuck in an electric socket, nothing hurt. No gunshot wounds oozing or gushing blood.

"Ya can't sell that thing without me," Mr. Gerard said. "I'd be willing to partner with ya, say seventy-thirty split. On all those valuables, if ya want."

"I only want the casket for one thing: To bring Vic back to life."

"Oh, so he's infected your brain with that nonsense."

Part of me wondered if the guy was right. Was it all nonsense? Mr. Gerard acted like he was going to stand up.

"Don't make me shoot you," I said, waving the gun around a little. "I might hit something important, like an artery or major organ."

Mr. Gerard pulled his legs up and hugged his knees. "If I may say so," he said, "you're welcome to leave anytime, no questions asked."

"You know I can't do that," I said to him. "He needs the casket."

"Ya already know my position on that."

"If speech be of silver, silence is gold," I said.

"I was simply offerin' ya an alternative."

"Damn, would you just shut the fuck up." Sometimes eloquence just doesn't get the job done.

"One I see is unacceptable."

A single siren whelp sent an electric shock through my chest to my backbone.

Shit.

Red and blue lights flashed out in the alley, not thirty feet from where Mr. Gerard sat at gunpoint. He opened his mouth to speak. I lifted the gun a little but didn't aim it directly at him. I placed my pointer finger to my lips. Voices came from out in the alley. It sounded like a man and a woman. After what had to be a full minute, doors slammed and the police cruiser pulled away.

Realizing the cops had gone, Mr. Gerard spoke: "There's some rope and some tape just inside the door ya come out of. If you'd like to tie me up er somethin', we can conclude our business."

"Our business won't be concluded until you return all Vic's stuff." I moved closer, still pointing the revolver in Mr. Gerard's general direction but not right at him. The guy's Adam's apple bobbed up and down.

"I've helped yer family in the past. I hope you'll remember that." I half grinned. "Lord, have mercy," he mumbled, looking off across the dirt yard.

"Write kindnesses in marble," I said. "Injuries in the sand."

"That from the Bible?"

"Nope," I said. "Your employer. You can thank him later for that bit of wisdom." He just frowned at that. Then I remembered how scared he'd been of Lucy. "I wonder what Lucy would think of what you've done." I should have invoked her name earlier because it was like I'd kicked him in the stomach.

"Dear Lord," he said. "Please, please don't tell that woman, that thing, what I ..."

His mouth kept moving but no words came out. A little mental torture, I decided, was acceptable under the circumstances. Okay, it was goddamn fun and might even help. "You should bring back all Vic's stuff. Or, I swear I'll fucking tell Lucy where you live."

He leaned his head back and closed his eyes. I didn't think he knew exactly what Lucy was, but I did. She had no interest in him. He had his own personal Collector to deal with. I wondered, if I pointed the gun straight at him, would he see some unnaturally dark shadow form in the corner of the backyard?

I made Mr. Gerard crawl into the storage building. I had no idea how to tie knots with a rope, so I got him to tape his feet together then rolled him over and taped his wrists together behind his back. I turned him over to tape his mouth. He looked up at me, eyes pleading. "If ya happen to come across Executioner, might ya consider returning her to me."

"You named her Executioner?" I asked. "That's, that's major fucked up."

"She may seem a monster to ya, but she's my friend." He looked straight ahead and for a moment I thought he was going to cry. "My *only* friend."

I had no intention of going anywhere near that dog if I had the misfortune of seeing her. But some part of me felt sorry for the guy. Having no friends was like walking up a set of stairs everywhere you went.

He smiled vaguely, then nodded. I slapped a strip of tape over his mouth. He made some unintelligible sounds while looking up at the fluorescent lights.

"You want me to leave the lights on?" I asked.

He nodded. I thought about leaving him

in the dark, but decided I'd tortured him enough with the threat of a visit from the Angel of Death.

Kindness is not in vain.

Looking the revolver over, I set it down on one of the boxes. I considered taking the gun, but it felt so heavy in my hand. I could have stuck it under the waist of my jeans, but with my luck I'd have accidentally shot myself in the ass. Freed of the responsibility of holding a weapon of mass destruction, my whole body felt lighter.

Outside, I nudged the casket up to the fence. I used the cutters to create a slit about four feet long in the chain link, then shoved the casket into the gap. Scrapping all attempts at eloquence and uttering a continuous string of curse words, I managed to get the heavy box through the sharp edges of the metal.

Once free of the yard, I bumped the casket along, grinding and inching down the alley past the rear entrances to a dry cleaner, a *carniceria*, and a thrift shop.

The orange lights in the Fiesta parking lot lay ahead. I stopped just short of the street, my heart pounding from the exertion. There was no way I could just push-pull the casket across the street all the way to the hearse. I'd end up blocking traffic on the side street and nosey people would ask what I was doing. I needed to go get the hearse.

From the end of the alley, I looked across Old Home Road where there was a medium-size Catholic church. Out front stood a life-size statue of the Virgin Mary, her arms extended in an apparent welcome. Or perhaps exasperation, as if asking, "What the *hell* are you people doing?"

I jogged into the street toward the Fiesta parking lot and stepped right in front of a police patrol car speeding down the side street, no siren but lights flashing. The cop driving slammed on the brakes and two police got out, drew their guns, and pointed them directly at me.

The urge to run was mind-numbing. I ended up backing up a few steps as if into the arms of the exasperated Virgin.

"Freeze!" one of the cops, a woman, screamed.

"Hands in the air," the other one, a young guy, shouted.

"Down on the ground," the female officer barked at the same time.

I wasn't sure what they wanted me to do, so I sat down cross-legged on the warm asphalt with my hands in the air. I glanced back at the casket still sitting in the alley. I'd come so close to getting it done.

Blackbirds gathered on the electric lines along the road and on the eaves of the Fiesta. Hundreds of them cawing back and forth to each other. They were probably making fun of me again. Sitting in the middle of the street, I was an easy target for them. Plus, there was that damn grudge they had against me apparently for just existing.

The cops approached, still aiming their guns somewhere between my neck and belly button. How heavy did those weapons feel in *their* hands? I was glad I hadn't taken Mr. Gerard's revolver. No telling what the cops would have done if I'd been armed. I'd probably have been lying in the road, blood streaming from multiple unnatural openings in my body.

People in the Fiesta parking lot, some pushing carts, others holding bags, all had stopped to stare at me sitting in the street. Some people had their cell phones out videoing the whole thing, including a tall, heavy-set guy with long dark hair and a beard.

"Hey, I know her," Fat Jesus shouted.

Yeah, you changed the locks on our apartment.

"She's unarmed," he continued. "Why you pointin' your guns at her?" Was he trying to help us now?

"Stay back, sir," the guy cop said. He holstered his weapon and moved toward me while his partner stood maybe ten feet away with her gun still leveled at me.

"Turn over on your stomach," he said.

"Hands behind your back."

I did exactly what the guy said and was handcuffed, still face down in the street staring at the alley, thinking of Vic rotting in the storage drawer instead of rising from the dead the way we all needed him to. I was a total fucking failure. I gathered myself together enough to speak. *Eloquence.*

"Um, can I ask what's happening? Why am I handcuffed?" I knew full well why I was handcuffed. I'd just robbed a pawn shop, and maybe deserved to be in handcuffs.

"I know her," Fat Jesus said. "She's a good kid."

"Just sit tight," the cop said to me. "Suspect in custody," he said, obviously not to me.

I angled my head to see the other cop, gun still drawn but pointed up in the air, moving into the alley.

"Wait for back up," the guy said.

"I'm just seeing what I can see," the woman said.

"Why you running?" the guy asked me.

"I was just going to the Fiesta for something. Some idiot's Rottweiler got loose and I was trying to get away before I got chewed up or killed."

"Hey," the guy yelled at his partner. "She says there's a Rottweiler down there."

"Don't see anything," she hollered back.

A familiar clicking of nails on concrete came from further down the alley and sent my skin crawling. "Dog!" the male cop shouted, drawing his gun again.

The woman cop backed out of the alley, her gun aimed at what I presumed was a barking, snarling Executioner. I wondered why the dog hadn't just attacked, then I noticed she was limping a little.

"Hey," I said. "Take these cuffs off and I'll handle the dog."

"Are you nuts, honey? That thing'll tear the face right off your skull."

"I know her," I said. "We've done business before."

"I can vouch for her, officer," Fat Jesus said. "She used to live in my apartments. She's a good kid … just had a tough life."

Eviction or not, I was beginning to appreciate that guy. The cop looked over at Fat Jesus, then down at me like I was crazy. After a moment, his expression softened. He holstered his gun, leaned down, and undid the handcuffs. Some of the blackbirds lifted off from the eaves of the Fiesta and flew off across the street. Chicken shit little trolls.

"Look, I don't know what's going on here, but if you can get that thing back to its yard that'd be excellent."

I got to my feet rubbing my wrists, then stepped toward the alley. The female officer backed past me into the street, gun still drawn, aiming at the Rottweiler or me. Probably both.

Executioner barked and snarled. But she had less energy. It was almost like she was just going through the motions. It occurred to me Executioner had endured my worst nightmare. She'd been separated from her home, such as it was. She had siblings at one point. There in the alley, she was alone, sad, and probably scared. Same as me.

All will be well, do not fear.

I neared the Rottweiler, hands at my sides, looking at her but not directly into her eyes. I inched forward, moving under a streetlight. I moved a little closer, until I stood next to her. Executioner growled but did not bark or lunge at me.

"Hey," I whispered. "You trying to get home?"

She looked off to the side as if to say, "Can't you see I'm lost." Breathing slow and regular, I bent down and extended my hand until I could feel Executioner's warm breath. She sniffed at it then looked at me, her black eyes reflecting the strange orange light from the Fiesta parking lot.

"Come on," I said. "Let's go home."

I rose slowly and dragged my fingers over the back of her neck. Together, we walked back down the alley toward the pawn shop. Some of Pastor Priest's magic must have worn off on me because damn if Executioner didn't follow along. I forgot about the cops. It was just me and a tired, sad Rottweiler in that alley.

We walked past the dark casket, completely out of place on the concrete behind the *carneceria*. Executioner stopped and growled when we were almost to the pawn shop.

"Come on," I whispered. "You're almost there." Once at the spot where the chain link was ripped open, I squatted down and held the two sides of the metal fence apart enough she could squeeze through.

I stared back down the alley toward the Fiesta. The cops looking at me seemed to shrink, as if they were farther away than they actually were. I could have run. Hell, I could have just walked around the corner and disappeared into the neighborhood.

But I had to finish what I started. I had to bring the casket home for Vic. For my family. So I walked back toward the cops still standing around by their patrol car at the end of the alley. They must have been too distracted by Executioner or their own guns to notice an ancient casket partially blocking the alley. At least they'd holstered their guns, though the woman cop kept a hand on hers.

As I approached, another patrol car drove up. By the time I was strolling past the casket, there were six cops all standing around talking in the middle of the street like it was a family gathering or something.

I got to the end of the alley and damn if two of them didn't pull their weapons and aim them right at me. I just shook my head and raised my hands. I had no weapon, yet there I was staring down a firing squad.

Funeral Procession

One of the original two cops, the guy, motioned at his apparently trigger-happy friends. They lowered their weapons but didn't immediately holster them. I moved a little closer to the guy who seemed more interested in talking than shooting.

"What happened with the Rottweiler?" he asked.

"I got her home," I said. "I think she was just tired and afraid."

"I think there's a lot of that going around," he said.

Jesus, do ya think? We stood there a moment. "You can put your hands down." I didn't realize I still had them in the air.

"So, what was all that about?" I asked, gesturing at the street where a few minutes ago I lay face down and handcuffed.

"We got a call about possible gunshots in the area."

I nodded. "Yeah, I heard something like that. Thought it was firecrackers or something."

"You got any ID? I just need to get your name and address in case we need to ask you anything."

"Sure," I said. "I don't have a license or anything."

I didn't even have my high school ID and

obviously didn't have a driver's license. So I gave him a fake name and our old apartment address, and we were done. I just had to make sure the guy didn't see me get in the hearse and start driving.

As I went on across the street toward the Fiesta, the rest of the blackbirds took off from the electric lines and flew away. For them, the show was over. For me, it was just act two. Get the casket back to the funeral home.

Back in the hearse, I thought about the situation. The hard part was done, but I couldn't just drive into the alley and load up the casket. The cops were still gathered there in the middle of the street. How long were they going to stay? I looked at the timer on my phone.

Two hours, twenty minutes, ten seconds.

I had the length of a superhero movie to get it all done. How much time would it take to get back to the funeral home, load Vic's corpse in the hearse, drive to some remote location, unload Vic into the casket, and ... set it on fire?

The cops must have taken a dinner break of something because it was an hour before they left on some other call, lights flashing, sirens wailing. Trying to stay calm, I drove the hearse over to the alley and parked a little further down from where the casket sat so it wasn't directly under a streetlight. From there I opened the back, then started pushing the casket that direction. It made a loud grating sound dragging over the rough surface. Would anyone notice and call the cops again? Was Mr. Gerard still tied up? How long would it be until he worked his way free?

I squatted down and crammed my fingers under the front edge of the casket, scraping the skin from my knuckles in the process. Cringing through pain, I rocked it back and forth until I was able to get both my hands under it and could try lifting it.

Wrist to shoulders, down my back and through my legs, my muscles strained. I eventually got the casket off the ground enough to let it set on my thighs as I sat on the back end of the hearse. Something large blotted out the streetlight. I looked up to see Fat Jesus looming over me.

"Can I lend ya a hand?"

Together we got the casket off me and propped up on the bumper. "Do I want to know what you're doin' here?"

"Nope."

Moving around to the back end of the casket, we each got a grip on it with both hands.

"Ready," Fat Jesus said. "One ... two ... three."

Together we lifted it up and pushed with everything we had. It wouldn't slide smoothly into the back, so we ended up banging into it first with our shoulders then our butts, moving it inch-by-inch until it was fully inside the hearse. I sat on the bumper, breathing hard, sweating in the thick night air.

"Whaddaya got in this thing? Your gold?"

I grinned. "As a matter of fact ..."

I pushed the lid of the casket aside enough to get my arm inside. Feeling around I found the stuff I'd thrown in there and grabbed the crucifix.

Fat Jesus stared at it. "Jesus," he said. "You did have your gold in there. Is this shit for real?"

"As far as I know," I said. "It's heavy so it must be, right?" He continued to admire the crucifix and all the jewels embedded in the shiny gold. "You can have it."

"You shittin' me?"

"No shitting. You could maybe get out of the apartment business. I got no way to sell it anyway. The only one who does is, uh ... Well, he probably wouldn't do me any favors."

He nodded. "I got a buddy who might help with that."

We looked at each other for a moment. He scratched his neck, then spoke. "Francis," he said. "Francis Cappelli."

"Callie," I said.

We shook hands.

He sniffed, took a deep breath, and let it out. "I'm gonna get out of here," he said. "You be okay?" I nodded. He saluted using the crucifix, then bounced down the alley toward the Fiesta.

I had to get my ass in gear. I jumped into the driver's seat of the hearse and fired up the engine. My gas gauge was touching the empty mark, my phone battery was down to three percent.

Fifty-three minutes, forty-four seconds.

Driving through dark neighborhoods and past the even darker Evergreen Cemetery, it took me ten minutes to get to the funeral home. Every now and then I'd glance in the rearview mirror admiring my work. I had actually done it. Stolen the casket back from Mr. Gerard. I'd gone from thief to, well, thief but on a higher, more noble level. I'd managed not to shoot anyone or get shot. And my family was still intact, even if one of them was in cold storage.

Thomas and Jess tumbled out onto the back porch as soon as I pulled in the driveway. They must have been watching for me.

"Did you get it?" Thomas asked. I raised my arms in the air a moment to celebrate completing the hardest part of Project Resurrection. "So, we just have to get Vic in it and ... "

"Set it on fire. Yeah, that's all."

Pastor Priest came out to join my brother and sister. The pastor smiled gently. "I thought your brother and sister could use some company."

"Thanks," I said. I started to add 'for the babysitting,' but didn't want to offend Thomas or Jess either one.

There was no damn way I was going through the process of getting the casket out of the hearse onto the driveway, toss Vic into it, and load it up again. It was hard enough to get the casket in the back of the hearse without the extra hundred-some-odd pounds of dead weight.

Back in the funeral home, I opened the cold storage drawer. The others gathered around. The gurney was still parked where I'd left it the night before. Thomas and I got hold of Vic's stiff body by the shoulders while Pastor Priest grabbed his feet, and we lifted him up and onto the gurney.

"Rigor mortis," Thomas said once we had Vic secured. "The cold prolongs it."

I had no idea how watching us handle a dead person would affect my little sister, or Thomas for that matter, later in life. I also did not have time to worry about it.

Vic's stiffness made it easier to get him onto the gurney but was a problem once we'd wheeled him out to the hearse. "So how do we do this?" Thomas asked. "There's not enough room for him in back with the casket."

I thought for a moment, hands on hips,

my body quivering from hunger or my fight with Mr. Gerard or the run in with the cops. Probably all three. The dream I'd had the night before. Me driving the hearse, Vic in the passenger seat next to me, both of us traveling through the universe together.

"Okay, let's just put him in the front," I said.

Me, the pastor, and Thomas managed to get Vic shoved in longways across the front seat with his head next to the steering wheel and bare feet sticking out the door at the other end. I got around to the driver's side, pushed Vic upper body so I could get my knee under him. Using my knee as a fulcrum, I folded him up at the waist enough to prop him against the steering wheel. Meanwhile, Thomas managed to bend Vic's knees until his legs were fully inside the hearse. Together, Thomas and I got Vic twisted around facing forward. I squeezed between the dashboard and Vic's body, then sat on him just below the hips, pushing against the dashboard until he fit upright in the seat like a regular living person.

By the time we were done, I was breathing hard and my skin glistened with sweat. Thomas got in next to me, and Jess sat on his lap. If there was any decomposition, my nose couldn't detect it. Even in death Vic still smelled mostly of cinnamon.

"Makes me think about those families on

YouTube," Thomas said.

"The ones that keep their dead family members around for days or weeks or months before burying them?" I asked.

"It's like they never really died," he said.

"Yeah," I said. "They just got really ugly."

Pastor Priest went to her car. I went to start the hearse, but all it did was crank over and over. The gas gauge was a little below the empty mark.

"What's wrong?" Thomas asked.

"I think it's out of gas again," I said.

"Again?" he asked.

"Yeah, I'll tell you about it sometime."

We'd accomplished the hard part in finding the casket. If we absolutely had to, we could always unload it, put Vic inside, and light the thing on fire right there in the driveway. But, as Vic said, it would be better to set the fire somewhere no one was watching.

I stared across the backyard at the barely visible silhouettes of the bean vine lattices in the dead garden. My eyes shifted to the dark silhouette of the storage shed off in the corner of the yard.

I threw open the door and jogged across the yard, opened the shed, and found an old rusty gas can. It was probably half full, meaning we might have enough to both get the hearse started and set fire to the casket.

"What's happening?" the pastor asked from her rolled-down window.

"Just have to fuel up," I said. "Unless you got a spell that might help."

She shook her head. "Though the fossil fuel industry has been after me for years, I lack such technical skills."

Like the tow truck driver showed me just that morning, I put a little gas directly into the carburetor. Pretty soon everything would be back to normal. Actually, it would be better than ever. Vic would be back alive, and he wouldn't be smoking any weed. In fact, if he started smoking anything, even with that fancy *hookah-shisha* thing, I'd kill him. Gummies, maybe.

By the time I'd gotten the hearse started, it was after eleven-thirty. We had plenty of time but that little bit of gas I'd put in the tank meant there couldn't be any detours.

I turned on the car radio mainly for distraction. It was tuned to a pop station I'd listened to searching for the casket earlier, but I turned the dial to Vic's favorite oldies station. It seemed appropriate. Some people liked hymns at their funerals, but I thought Vic would be more than happy with his "accessible" oldies rock.

"Where are we going?" Thomas asked.

Earlier that day I'd passed a public park that, according to the map app on my phone, backed right up to the Trinity River and had an actual parking lot. That's where we were headed.

We came to an intersection with a red light. The gas gauge was touching the empty mark again. An image of the Visa logo floated through my mind. Damn, if I'd have thought to grab the card there'd be no worries about running out of gas. I rolled my eyes but wasn't going back to get the card.

I looked both ways, and gently ran the light. Hopefully, hearses were granted the same privilege as emergency vehicles. Our situation was definitely an emergency as far as I was concerned. Pastor Priest waited at the light, but I drove slow enough she could catch back up. Together, we began our own private funeral procession down to the Trinity River.

I thought about the song Vic played for me that one day in his bedroom. "And When I Die," it was called. As the opening notes played in my head, that song came on the radio.

Vic's head tilted forward a little and his jaw opened slightly as if in amazement at the timing of the song. I was fairly sure he was just thawing out some from his day in cold storage. Probably.

"Does it creep you guys out?" I asked. "Sitting this close to a dead person?"

"I guess I just don't think of him that way," Thomas said.

"It's just Vic," Jess said.

"Okay," I said. "But if you start dressing like a Goth, with black fingernails and lipstick, and put up a bunch of death shit all over your room someday, I'm going to go shoot myself."

"What's a Goth?" Jess asked.

"Never mind," I said.

"Actually," Thomas said, keeping it going, "black would be an appropriate reflection of the ambiance of our lives, don't you think."

"I kind of like black too," Jess added.

God, I should have just kept my mouth shut. I looked at the timer on my phone. Twenty-two minutes, seven seconds.

It only took eight minutes to get to the park next to the river, but we found a gate blocking the way to the parking lot with a sign attached saying the park closed at sundown. I stopped the hearse, got out, and saw nothing holding the gate in place so I just pushed it open.

Pastor Priest hung back on the street, and I wondered what she was up to. We'd only driven a few feet into the parking lot when a vehicle pulled in beside me, blue and red lights flashing. For fuck's sake! The cops were nowhere to be found the first sixteen years of my life. Now they wouldn't leave us alone.

There was only one of them and he didn't get out, which I thought was a good sign.

He rolled down his window and shined the brightest light I have ever seen right in my face.

"This park closed at sunset," he said. "Any particular reason you opened the gate and parked here illegally."

Uh, yes, officer. My brother and sister and I need to put our friend here in a casket and set it on fire. "Just looking for a place to chill," I managed to say.

Could the cop tell Vic was dead? I twisted around so most of my upper body blocked his view of Thomas, Jess, and Vic's corpse.

"Look elsewhere," the cop said.

"Yes sir," I said, deciding to pull as much respect out of my ass as possible. "We'll just go then." The cop nodded.

Twelve minutes, thirty-eight seconds.

We drove around for exactly three minutes, until a tight ball formed in my belly. We drove back to the same park. Not seeing any cops, I drove completely through the parking lot, over a curb and down an embankment toward a grove of trees that I hoped stood at the edge of the Trinity River. Pastor Priest didn't follow us down there. Because of the cop, I wasn't even certain she was coming at all.

I'd turned off the headlights so we wouldn't be seen by the cops or anyone else. Not wanting to drive into the river, I turned the lights back on.

A black chasm loomed not ten feet in front of us.

Strange Fire

Slamming on the brakes, the casket impacted the back of the passenger seat. I caught Jess with my arm and Thomas braced his arms against the dashboard. Vic's body didn't fall forward as much as it rose up, his head hitting the top of the hearse bending it to one side.

"You okay, guys?"

"More or less," Thomas said, examining one of his hands.

The moon hadn't risen, and it was as dark outside as the hallway inside our old apartment. Keeping just the orange parking lights on, I got out and stared at the black water flowing past, silent and surreal. The sounds of the night creatures, mostly insects and frogs, provided the soundtrack for the final act of our private family horror movie.

I opened the back of the hearse and yanked a few times on the casket while Thomas pushed from the inside until it teetered on the back edge of the hearse. "Come out here and help me."

I motioned Thomas to one side and told him to push it toward me. Jess moved around to help him. As the heavy box slid off the bumper, I let it rest on my thighs. Together, the three of us settled the wooden box onto the damp riverbank with a thud.

We pushed and pulled the casket, heavy

as a concrete block, across slick grass and damp clay over to the passenger side of the hearse where Jess had opened the door for us. We slid the lid off and Thomas and I pulled Vic out any way we could. Banging his head, legs, and arms against the side of the casket, he eventually fell inside. If we injured him, I took comfort in the fact the casket was about to heal him head to toe. Or so I hoped.

What little light there was glinted off something inside the casket and I remembered the candelabras I'd tossed in there back at Mr. Gerard's. Feeling around, I found them down near Vic's feet and set them inside the hearse.

Thomas and I covered Vic with the lid, resulting in the same click and clonk I'd heard before when I'd hidden in the old box at the pawn shop. Magic or not, there was definitely some mechanical thing inside Amenhotep's contraption.

"What was that?" Thomas asked.

"I think it like locks the person inside," I said.

"Do I want to know how you know that?"

"Nope."

I stared at the casket, amazed we'd gotten that far. But, my sense of success didn't take root. There were things yet to do.

The casket seemed to double in weight with Vic inside. I mean, it felt like moving a refrigerator that had the little wheels missing from the bottom. The best we could do was bump and bang it inch by inch along the wet grass. It seemed to take forever to get it even close to the river itself. I wasn't sure what to do from there. Thomas and I both stood up, breathing hard, and looked around.

Heavy mist had formed over the surface of the black water. River creatures croaked and cicadas wailed funeral hymns. The black birds had gone to bed or whatever the hell they did at night. No heckling or trolling from them.

"I don't think we can build a funeral pyre," I said.

"It would have been pretty cool, though," Thomas said. He looked past me, squinting his eyes. "Hey," he said, pointing. "What's that?"

I turned my head that way and saw an old wooden dock that stuck out maybe ten feet into the slow-moving water. We walked over and found an old, rusted metal rowboat tied up there.

I said to Thomas, "If we can get the casket into the boat, we can set it on fire and shove it out into the water."

"Like the Vikings," he said, his face threatening his patented huge grin.

"Wouldn't be his first time doing that."

I went to get the gas can from the hearse. For a few seconds, I thought I might burst into tears. I have no idea where all the emotion came from right at that moment. I mean, why then? I shoved it back down some dark alley of my mind.

Up toward the parking lot, car headlights shone across the grass and high into the grove of trees. Was it the cop again? Surely the guy had something better to do.

We were far enough down the embankment I didn't think we'd been seen so I got the gas can from the floorboard of the hearse. I heard a familiar voice singing, turned, and saw a dark figure headed down the embankment. Pastor Priest, our family witch, had arrived.

"We don't have much time so if you're gonna do the prayer, you might get started."

The pastor had dressed for the occasion wearing a black, hooded robe Walking over to where the casket sat on the riverbank, she pulled out her glasses and a little book from somewhere inside the black robe. Thumbing through the book, she slipped on her glasses and started reading.

"You have lived and now have come to the end of your journey ..."

I let the pastor talk while Thomas and I discussed what to do next. "Maybe we should just set the casket on fire here on the riverbank," I said.

"Why?" Thomas asked.

"Don't you remember that story Vic told about the Vikings and how he ended up in the casket out in the North Sea alive again but without anything to drink?"

He nodded. "But there's something poetic about him floating off. It would be like sending him down the River Styx toward the afterlife."

Pastor Priest had mentioned the River Jordan in her sermons before, as a symbol of both living and dying. Rivers were apparently important in religion. Resurrections as well, it turned out.

The pastor continued: "May this transition be swift and easy, may this gateway bring you peace ..."

Then I realized something. We had no way to start a fire. No matches, no lighter, nothing.

Shit! I'd spent the entire day dealing with helpful tow truck drivers, and cops, so many cops, Mr. Gerard, a sad Rottweiler and I was going to fail because I didn't have a goddamn lighter.

I set the gas can down. The only place I could possibly find a lighter fast enough might be some convenience store. I'd have to steal it though as I didn't have any money left. I put my hands on my hips a moment, then marched up the embankment.

"Hey," Thomas shouted. "Where are you

going?"

"Shhh," I whispered as loud as possible. "I need to get a lighter."

"Callie," Thomas yelled. I turned to see what looked like a blue-green flame floating in thin air in front of the pastor. What the hell?

I slid and slipped down to where Pastor Priest held in her hand a small ball of flame. "I may have mentioned I am a practicing witch."

"That is so cool," Jess said.

Pastor Priest apparently had some actual magic. I checked my phone. My heart sank into my stomach. It was three after midnight. I showed Thomas my phone.

"You put him in cold storage for a reason," he said. "Come on, let's do this."

Then I remembered I'd set my phone timer ahead a little just to be sure we had enough time. Plus, maybe he wasn't, like, completely dead right at midnight. Maybe it took a few minutes to complete the process or something. Truth was, I didn't know how long it had been since Vic had died.

I undid the little boat, pulled it through the water to where the casket sat, then dragged it a few feet onto the riverbank until it was steady. Thomas and I tugged the casket up close and got one end of it onto the back of the little boat. The front end of the boat lifted out of the water, the rear sinking a couple inches into the mud.

Jess came over and tried to force the rowboat down into the water but slipped and fell into the mud. "Sorry, guys" she said. "Can't help much."

Shoving, bumping and banging, Thomas and I barely moved the casket.

"You guys hold the boat still," I said.

The pastor extinguished the fire in her hand and took hold of one side of the casket. Thomas grabbed the other side, the two of them struggling to keep the boat from getting pushed further into the river while I nudged the casket into place.

Working together, the three of us were able to slide the boat into the river. The whole thing wobbled a little but remained upright once in the dark, misty water.

I opened the gas can and emptied it on top of the casket. "Y'all stand back."

Pastor Priest extended her hand, a blue flame appearing as if she'd turned on a gas stovetop burner. The pastor, conjurer of flame in the heart, mind and hand.

She reached down and the ancient casket erupted in flames. The pastor was able to deflect the fire away from her face with her free hand. I wasn't so lucky. Positioning my feet like I was about to take off running, which I was, I'd slipped in the mud and ended up with the tips of my hair glowing and my face feeling hot like a bad sunburn. Rolling away through the mud,

I stared at the flames, heat flowing against my face like a Texas summer wind.

We'd done it. Vic's casket was on fire with him in it. I stood, shoving my emotions away again, pushing them down somewhere. I couldn't hold them back forever, though.

Pastor Priest continued: "We cannot go with you on this journey, but we can help you begin."

My eyes clouded, but the flames dried my tears before they could wander down my face for all to see. Relief set in. There was nothing more I had to do.

I'd been a good *complice*.

The rowboat turned around completely one time before getting caught up in the current. The flaming casket moved slowly along the Trinity hissing like some chemical reaction was taking place.

"We hold the gate open," the pastor proclaimed. "With love and grief, we watch you go through."

The fire, unlike anything I'd ever seen, turned the milky mist hovering over the surface of the Trinity River a rainbow of colors. The casket itself turned bright orange like lava or molten metal.

Pastor Priest went on: "Lead us from the unreal to the real, from the darkness to the light. Lead us from death to immortality. Peace be, peace be. *Shanti*."

Shadows bobbed up and down and side to side along both shorelines like demons dancing. The strange fire lit up the faces of my brother and sister.

"The flames of hope," Thomas said.

My eyes welled up at my brother's words. The casket glowed deep red, and blue sparks shot out from it and across the water as if an invisible welder were at work. The trees along the shore rustled, a wind swirling through them. Above, the dark sky seemed to split, revealing stars and planets, galaxies. It was like the universe was present to witness what was happening. It also reminded me of one of Lucy's dresses. Was she still with him?

"I read that hope improves your immune system and can lengthen your lifespan," Thomas said. "That's ... the fact of ..." He trailed off. His face contorted, tears glistening in eyes reflecting the colors of the fire.

"Should we say something?" Jess asked.

Thomas sniffled. "The universe is a really big place." I looked at him, thinking he'd retreated into some fantasy world again. I managed to keep my mouth shut, though. "Carl Sagan said the vastness of space is only bearable through love. Vic gave us that, he made our universe more bearable, even good."

Someday I'd learn not to doubt my brother. He'd pretty much summed up everything about Vic and our family in a couple of sentences. I couldn't think of anything else to add.

"We love you, Vic," Jess said.

Except that. Why didn't I think of that? Wasn't that the obvious thing to say?

Jess buried her head in my side, her tears soaking through my shirt onto my skin. We stood there in silence a few moments. The casket moved down the lazy river, sparks flying off it like it was the Fourth of July. A dark cloud hovered over the casket, smoke from the flames I thought.

"Hail the traveler," the pastor called out. "Farewell."

I should have had something to say, but the words just weren't there. The tears, however, came freely. I used to hate it when I cried. Staring at the casket, I welcomed the tears. Not the wet heat of anger, but warm streams of grief.

From somewhere deep inside me came a sound. It was just a moan at first, then I let it all out. Loud, sobbing, shaking uncontrolled. I didn't care who heard. I wanted it out there for all creation to hear, the universe to witness.

Jess and Thomas grabbed onto me from either side as if I were about to fall off a cliff. I cried for my mom, for the happy person she once was and could never be again. I cried for my dad who meant to come home, who wanted to come home, but never made it. I cried for my brother and sister and everything they'd ever lost or just never had. For the shit they'd seen instead. For the lives we could have had but didn't, and all the family photo albums we never made.

I cried for me. Stupid me. Couldn't save my mom or convince Vic to get help. Unable to change a damn thing. The list of my failures was long as my memory would allow. The only thing I'd managed to do was get Vic in his casket. At least I'd done that. I sucked in a breath of wet night air until it caught in my throat. I let it out, steam rising up and away from my mouth like a spirit. One of hot rage and cold grief.

The three of us turned and trudged up the embankment toward the hearse. I took a couple steps then stopped, a heaviness lodging itself in my chest. I stared back at the blazing casket slowly disappearing into the darkness.

"Thank you," I rasped.

After I'd driven the hearse back up to the parking lot, we stood around next to the pastor's car. None of us knew what to do. The pastor broke the silence. "Seldom do opportunities to help others in this manner present themselves."

She took me by the shoulders, smiled gently, then pulled me into a hug. She released me after a moment and got in her car. She looked at me from her car window.

"Hey," I said. "Did you, like, send me a spell or something earlier?"

"Perhaps. Why do you ask?"

"I was in kind of a sticky situation and I heard this whispering, like a poem or something."

A smile stretched across her face. "Whatever that was must have come from within you."

I scoffed at that. I was no poet, unless I was swearing. She started up the engine and the little yellow Fiat drove out of the parking lot.

Thomas and Jess had already gotten into the hearse, and I was about to join them when I felt a vague unease. I gazed back down the embankment toward the riverbank where an unnaturally dark splotch seemed to hover.

In an instant Lucy appeared not six feet away and forcing me back a step. Black vapor flowed off her like a waterfall, only the shape of her head clearly visible. She drew near enough for me to see her expressionless facial features. A single tear leaked from one eye and trailed down her cheek. She cocked her head to one side, then her form dissipated into the cool breeze.

What did that mean?

Shockingly, we had enough gas to get back to the funeral home. Once inside, Thomas and Jess trudged upstairs, tired from their second late night in a row dealing with death. I stopped on the back porch and stared at the wicker chairs. The tin can next to one chair still held the ashes of Vic's last few cigarettes. The insects gathered around the yellow porch light like they had the first night we'd spent in the funeral home just a few months earlier.

Vic moved around the funeral home in a certain way, his steps and movement creating a sound all their own. I could easily pretend I heard him banging around in the kitchen, his chair squeaking down in the office, walking down the staircase. Standing in the kitchen, I thought I could pick out the scent of every delicious thing he'd ever made for us. I waited for the tears to return, but the only thing I felt was an ache from the vacant lot that was my heart.

In the hallway outside the Visitation Room, I could still smell the floral tributes to the customers whose final goodbyes had been in that chapel. How many people had I seen in those shiny metal caskets? I'd gotten so used to seeing the dead, they'd become more like furniture, just part of the funeral home décor.

The grandfather clock sounded a single chime sending a wave of electricity over my shoulders and down my spine. I eased down the hall to stand in front of the tall clock. Its long pendulum swished silently, some internal mechanism quickly ticking. Were there more things in heaven and on earth? God, I hoped so.

Walking up the stairs to the second floor, each step provoked a memory. Crawling up to my room after I'd gotten sick, coming downstairs to go to church that first Sunday, listening to "And When I Die" on the record player in Vic's bedroom, him trying to play the tune on his harmonica.

Thomas had already gone to bed in his little closet room. I found Jess sound asleep in our bed. I went over and opened her dresser drawer. Only my sister's clothes laid inside. No food. I guess at some point, she'd decided she didn't have to do that anymore.

I pulled off my T-shirt and wadded it up. Putting it to my face, I savored the strange chemical smell of the smoke from the flaming casket. The smell of hope. Hope that filled the empty funeral home as well as my head and heart.

It was November 2nd. Dia del los Muertos. The Day of the Dead. I imagined Vic showing up back at the funeral home someday, his arms open wide. Would he? At that moment, I decided he most definitely would.

I tugged off my jeans and slipped on another shirt and an old pair of gym shorts. I crawled into bed next to Jess, pulled up the covers, and sank into the darkness.

Life Goes On ... and On

I checked Vic's bedroom the morning after watching his burning casket float off down the Trinity River. I'd found it exactly as I'd left it the day before. The kitchen, the office, even the Preparation Room were just as unchanged. No sign of life.

Vic never said how long it would take the old casket to resurrect him. I'd thought maybe a day. Jesus was in the tomb three days before he supposedly showed up again. Three days later: No Vic. Still, maybe he'd have had to find a ride back to Dallas after crawling out of the casket. That would take some time. Unless he called me to come pick him up in the hearse. But he didn't have a phone and would have to borrow one. I checked my texts and voice mails, like, every minute or so for some days.

After a month, I started to doubt. After two months, I was able to see our efforts trying to get him in the casket for what they were. Childish at best, crazy maybe. I'd been ridiculous to put my faith in some old wooden box or in Delamorte's strange beliefs. He'd been losing his mind to cancer or just lost in fantasyland. Hoping for something that wasn't ever going to happen. That could *never* happen. He was probably still floating down the Trinity River somewhere on his way to the Gulf of Mexico.

And he wasn't coming back.

Like my mom and dad weren't ever coming back. The old casket was just that. Something you buried a person in when they were dead. Not a magical object. Its mechanical sound, just an elaborate lock.

The words inscribed on the casket, "What has been, will be again," turned out not to be true as far as Vic was concerned. In his case, the truer words were "what's done is done" and "water that has passed shall not return." And neither would Vic.

There was one thing, though, that nagged me like a whining mosquito. I had no explanation for why there'd be a button on the *inside* to unlock the casket. Maybe just in case someone got put in the casket that wasn't quite dead yet?

Lucy remained a total mystery. Had she been some kind of magician? An illusionist? She'd convinced me she was the actual Grim Reaper. Was what I'd seen the night Vic died just some show she put on for our sake? I had no effing clue as to why.

No matter what Lucy was or wasn't, it got me thinking. It was true death had followed us around. I mean, look at all the dead adults in our wake. As for me personally though, I'd met Death a bunch of times and never known it. I'd lived to tell the tale each time never realizing how close I'd come to spending the rest of eternity in some metal box in a graveyard. So, yeah. One of my beliefs about the world had been totally wrong. Turned out, Death and I were like old friends.

My grief, so intense the night Vic floated out of our lives, had eased some. But when I'd finally let the realization sink in that he wasn't coming back it became a physical sensation that burned in every joint of my body before cooling to a dull ache. Vic had been the closest thing I'd had to a dad, at least since my own dad went away. In some ways, it was like I'd lost two dads. In Vic's case, though, there was a fresh sting that lingered.

I'd cried a few times since that night at the Trinity River. Just a few normal tears, not the blubbering, ugly version. Pastor Priest helped me accept crying as a necessary part of life like breathing. Letting out my grief was just something I needed to do every now and then. Something normal, not something to feel embarrassed about. Something everybody did.

But, it wasn't just grief I felt. I was also grateful. Like the Phoenix, I'd risen from the ashes. All three of us had. And it was mostly thanks to Vic. His kindness was not in vain. It had given us a new life.

It seemed to me that no matter how old a person was, it was possible to live many different lives in that span of time. That wasn't some quantum reality or parallel universe thing. It was just a fact. Looking back, I'd had several lives — two or three, maybe more — in my seventeen years. I'd been wrong about having just the one. I'd already had a few do-overs, used more than one extra life and, most recently, started the game over. I guessed that was probably true for a lot of people if they chose to see it that way.

* * *

I'd worried no one would find Mr. Gerard tied up in his garage and he'd die of dehydration or terror thinking of Lucy lurking somewhere in the corners of the storage building. Thanks to the internet images Thomas had shown me, I could visualize Mr. Gerard's decomposing body liquifying over the concrete floor.

Someone needed to feed and water the Executioner. So, the day after launching Vic down the Trinity River, I did her a favor and left an anonymous tip on the city Crime Stoppers line suggesting they might want to investigate the building behind Mr. Gerard's pawn shop. If he told anyone how he got there, I'd have my own story to tell about him stealing the artifacts. Of course, there'd be questions about Vic's body that I wouldn't have an answer for.

* * *

I'd crapped out in volleyball, couldn't handle a

basketball, and soccer was never going to happen. Turned out I wasn't good at anything except running. So, I ran. And kept running. And running. I'd always known I was fast. Eventually, I started winning races. People started noticing.

Vic died in in the fall of my junior year in high school, and by the spring I was good enough to compete for my school in the District Championships.

It was a beautiful Saturday morning in early April. Thin, silver-white clouds passed in front of the morning sun, and there was a little bit of a breeze. That could mean a tail wind or head wind, depending on how they laid out the race.

I searched the stands for Jess and Thomas, but there were like hundreds of people in the stadium. Trying to find anyone was like looking for a speck of dirt in the funeral home carpet. I had to shake off a sense of being completely alone, abandoned. My new family was still out there. I just couldn't see them.

Up in the press box were the coaches, the sports writers, and, according to my coach, college recruiters. He said I might get a scholarship offer if I did well. Honestly, I didn't feel any pressure as college was still kind of a foreign concept.

It felt like I'd come a long way the past year. For one thing, I wasn't afraid of people like I used to be. I'd met some people who'd given enough of a shit to not let us be someone else's problem. Meeting just one person like that can change your outlook on life. I started keeping my eyes open for others like them. They were out there somewhere.

My new asshole motto was simple: Not everyone was an asshole. I could at least give people the benefit of the doubt and let them prove themselves one way or the other. It turned out there were other ways to deal with people — and Rottweilers. Knowing that, I felt somehow older.

The sun pierced through the clouds and burned into my skin. It was warm and the air felt thick and heavy. Sweat formed on my face, neck, and arms.

"Callie!"

I heard Jess's little voice and turned in that direction. She stood waving at the railing down close to the track. I jogged over.

"Hey," I said. "Where is everybody?"

Hearing myself say the word reminded me that not everybody was there. Someone important to me wasn't going to see me run. Actually, several someones. Vic wouldn't have missed it for anything. Presumably neither would my dad, or so I chose to believe. As far as I knew, Mom hadn't been into sports, but I still wanted her to be there. Were they all there in spirit? Of the three, I could only picture one:

Vic. In my mind, my dad had faded to a brown and green blob, like a watercolor painting smeared by rain. The mental image of Mom's innocent smile I'd once held onto so tightly now often morphed into that of Pastor Priest. My mom from another timeline. One who'd had shit happen to her but had made different decisions.

It was true that life goes on without the people we loved. It wasn't fair, but that's how it was. But, when most people died it left a hole in the lives of everyone that knew them. That empty place itself was like a memorial. It was the unwritten epitaph, good, bad or indifferent, burned on a person's heart when you lost someone you loved.

The same would be true when I left this world permanently. I'd be remembered in the same way I remembered Mom and Dad. Thomas and Jess, the pastor ... they'd each remember me. Vic would have, too, if he'd stuck around. I also decided that thinking about if and how I'd be remembered wasn't something I wanted to spend a lot of time doing. I'd rather just ... live. And let my epitaph, in hearts or stone, take care of itself when my life ended.

"We had to sit up high," Jess said.

I gazed into the stands. Thomas had brought a book in case, God forbid, he got bored. He managed to look up and give me a little wave. Pastor Priest stood up and waved, sun glinting off her orange-red hair. She lifted both arms waving her hands and looked like she was saying something. She brought her hand to her mouth and acted like she was blowing something in my direction. Maybe a blessing. I pretended like something hit me and she smiled. Yeah, my life was cursed, but blessing had still managed to come my way. Sometimes by means of sheer dumb luck, but also through Vic and the pastor. Even Lucy in her own strange way had been a blessing.

"Are you alright?" Jess asked. "You don't ..." She trailed off. I could only imagine what she saw. My little sister would make an awesome fortune teller. She could see some tiny little change in my face that revealed everything going on in my head.

I could see the shadow of grief within and around her deep blue eyes. They weren't as bright as they once were. Most of it was disappointment, but part seemed to be anger. Like she'd been lied to or something. I hoped it was temporary; I feared it was permanent. She'd always been a believer in everything, but not so much anymore. Since Delamorte died, she'd questioned more and more things. I knew part of that was normal. She was getting older. Still, I mourned the loss of the little kid part of her. I just wished that one of us still believed in magic.

"I gotta go," I said.

"Good luck," she said.

I turned and headed for the starting blocks. A single blackbird cawed. Fuck them and their damn grudge. I was alive. They could get over it. Same with everyone else.

"Take your mark," a track official called.

I tried out my feet in the blocks, then adjusted them a little and got back in position.

Time to meet my fate. The runners silently moved into their staggered positions along the curve of the track. Everyone tried to keep moving as long as possible to not get too tight. No one wanted to pull a muscle right out of the blocks. All of us faced forward.

It was the only direction to go.

The stadium grew strangely quiet. As if some cosmic event was about to unfold. A breeze picked up carrying with it the vague sound of a harmonica. I strained to listen to what I recognized was a familiar tune. It was the opening notes from the Blood, Sweat & Tears song Vic showed me so many months ago. The one written by Laura Nyro when she was my age.

Then I saw him. Leaning against the railing near one of the exits. A tall, dark-skinned man with short black hair and a full black beard. The guy seemed so familiar, but I couldn't think of any reason I would know him.

I'd seen my dad at times or thought I

had. At a track meet, on a street corner, at the funeral home. I'd seen my mom at the graveyard the night I was trying to get Vic into cold storage. I wasn't even sure she was dead. Either way, both my parents had always vanished into the mist or the crowd or thin air.

A silver-haired woman in a long purple dress sidled up next to the man at the railing who then grinned. I stared at them. The woman tilted her head to one side, studying me with icy blue eyes.

I didn't have time to wonder about anything or anyone in the stands, real or imagined. I concentrated on pressing my feet into the starting blocks.

The light wind brought the scent of something that sent goosebumps up my back.

Cinnamon.

"Set!"

The judge's last words were still echoing around the stadium when the starting gun fired and I exploded out of the blocks. My body sliced through the warm, wet air, the white lines of my lane led me through the curve into the straightaway. My strides long and powerful, I streaked toward the finish line alone.

Everything else was a blur.

Acknowledgments

This story was more than a decade in the making. The names of all who made subtle contributions would constitute a long list. At the top of that list would be Carmen Goldthwaite, storyteller and teacher. Most of what I learned about writing is the result of my experiences with Carmen. More recently, Suzanne Potts, my developmental editor, and Jeff Braucher, my detail and mindless error fixer, helped me put the finishing touches on my story. Before that, Sara Kocek at Yellow Bird Editors set me on the right track. Special thanks to my own kids, some of whom, or parts thereof, were the inspiration for my characters.

On average, over 1500 children are taken into foster care daily in the U.S, most due to neglect. Much of that neglect is secondary to parent or caregiver drug use. All have experienced some type of trauma, some acute, most chronic and lifelong. There is a shortage of caregivers and professionals to help the children of trauma. The National Foster Parent Association offers information for those interested in becoming foster caregivers. Court Appointed Special Advocate (CASA) programs exist in many states, offering opportunities to get involved without becoming a foster parent.

About the Author

Eric Van Allen has been a psychologist for thirty years, working primarily with children and teens in the foster care system. When not working, he enjoys writing in coffee shops throughout the Pacific Northwest. He also enjoys photography, exploring, sometimes cooking, and wondering what he is going to be when he grows up. He currently lives in or near Seattle, Washington with his cat.